PLAYING
WITH FIRE

D0685665

Also by Deborah Fletcher Mello

Just Desserts series

The Sweetest Thing

Craving Temptation

All I Want Is You
(with Kayla Perrin)

PLAYING WITH FIRE

Deborah Fletcher Mello

Kensington Publishing Corp.

http://www.kensingtonbooks.com

DAFINA BOOKS are published by

Kensington Publishing Corp.
119 West 40th Street
New York, NY 10018

All Kensington Titles, Imprints, and Distributed Lines are available at special quantity discounts for bulk purchases for sales promotions, premiums, fund-raising, and educational or institutional use. Special book excerpts or customized printings can also be created to fit specific needs. For details, write or phone the office of the Kensington special sales manager: Kensington Publishing Corp., 119 West 40th Street, New York, NY 10018, attn: Special Sales Department, Phone: 1-800-221-2647.

Dafina and the Dafina logo Reg. U.S. Pat. & TM Off.

ISBN-13: 978-1-61773-776-3
ISBN-10: 1-61773-776-3
First Kensington Mass Market Edition: March 2015

eISBN-13: 978-1-61773-777-0
eISBN-10: 1-61773-777-1
First Kensington Electronic Edition: March 2015

10 9 8 7 6 5 4 3 2 1

Printed in the United States of America

Prologue

"You know I love only two things in this whole world," James Burdett said, the rich bass of his voice low and seductive. "My piano, and you, sweetness." He paused, allowing the whisper of his words to tease the delicate line of her ear. Everything in the room was pleading, begging, along with the man who'd dropped to his knees in want of her full attention. The small expanse of space was clouded by his pleas, the intensity of his yearnings tinting the coat of pale blue paint against the four walls a deep shade of desperate. "Please, baby, come with me," he implored, the ebony of his eyes appealing to her frailty.

James pursed his full lips as if blowing her a kiss, and the sensual motion made her shudder. He smiled, flashing her a row of pearl white teeth that illuminated his deep, dark complexion. He repeated himself, this time wrapping his arms around her thin waist as he pulled her close against him, pressing his cheek to her abdomen. "Come with me, Irene. Pack a bag and let's go. Leave with me tonight. Come on, baby," he continued to plead, pulling at her with those eyes. "Please!"

Irene Marshall shook her head, rolling her gaze

toward the ceiling as she diverted her eyes from his. "James, I'm not going anywhere. This is crazy. How you gon' go off to New York like this? How you plan on living?"

"It don't matter. We'll just figure it out as we go. I'll play with the band and we can see the world together, just you and me. Say yes, Irene. Say you'll come."

Pressing her hands to his shoulders, Irene pushed him away. As he came to his feet her gaze flew up and down his lean figure, inhaling his image. James was dressed in a white dress shirt opened just low enough to expose a faint brush of silky hair against his chest. Black knit pants fit him nicely, accentuating his thin build and high rear end. His Nat King Cole haircut was flattering to his narrow face, his dark eyes and high cheekbones complementing the chiseled lines of his sculptured features. The faint hint of a mustache and the beginnings of a goatee gave him an air of maturity, Irene thought to herself, noting how his confidence spilled past his smile. He was a pretty man with his deep sienna complexion. Too pretty, and his fans, both male and female, frequently let him know it. He wore their compliments well when he played piano for the small jazz and blues band he claimed would be his ticket to the big time, swearing they would make him millions. He wore them like an abundance of priceless jewels wrapped around his shoulders. Irene shook her head.

James clasped his eyes shut, closing them tightly as he searched his heart for all the right words that would convince her to leave with him. When he opened them again, Irene had turned her back on him, her arms crossed over her chest, her stance tense. He moved against her, wrapping his arms and body around the lush curves that girdled her frame. He kissed the back of her neck as he inhaled the floral scent of her perfume. She smelled like heaven, he thought, brushing his lips against her butterscotch complexion. He'd loved her since forever, the woman having filled every crevice of his large heart. Now he struggled between a rock and a hard place, unable to fathom being away from her again, but still wanting to follow the dreams he'd had since he was six years old.

"Then say you'll think about it, Irene. You don't have to give me an answer right now. We can leave tomorrow and catch up with the band in New York. But I have to go, baby. I have to go do this and I want you to go with me."

Irene turned back around to face him. "Do what you have to do, James. But I can't go with you," she said, resignation painting her soft face with stern determination.

"Why not?"

"Because I can't. I don't want to live my life on the road. I can't do it. I *won't* do it."

"Don't you love me?"

Her eyes widened and a wave of ire flooded her expression. The woman lifted a finger in his direction, pointing at him angrily. Her response was terse, embodied with emotion that reached out to slap him with the back of its hand. "If this had anything to do with love, you'd want to stay. You'd want to build a life for us together. Here. You would want us to have some stability and a place we can call home. So don't you dare talk to me about love, James Burdett. Don't you dare question what I feel when you don't know what you feel your *damn* self." The woman blew a harsh gush of warm air out with her last words. Her jaw tightened, her teeth clenched tightly together as her gaze narrowed, her eyes drawn into thin slits.

James took a deep breath. He turned his attention toward the other woman, who'd been listening quietly throughout the entire conversation. She sat like a fly on the wall, observing them, her presence almost ignored if one didn't make an effort to search her out. James met her intense stare and smiled, the expression warm enough to melt a glacier. "Aleta? Can't you talk some sense into her?"

Aleta Bowen shrugged her narrow shoulders, shaking her head from side to side. Her shoulder-length flip bounced with the movement. She glanced from one face to the other, and back again, then dropped her gaze to the floor. Her silence told them both that she had no intention of getting in the middle of their battle.

James nodded his understanding, then turned back toward Irene. "I'll wait until tomorrow. I'll be at the bus stop by two o'clock. I hope you'll be there," he said, pulling the woman into one last embrace as he kissed her lips, pressing his mouth tightly to hers. "Two o'clock," he repeated, whispering it with warm breath past her lips.

A tear rolled out of Irene's eye. She wiped at it quickly, willing the others that wanted to follow not to fall. "I won't be there, James," she said. "I'm sorry, but I won't, so don't you bother to wait for me."

With his hand on the doorknob, he stood staring at her one last time. "I love you, Irene," he said, waving his head in her direction. "I'll always love you."

As he turned toward the door, his gaze met Aleta's and he smiled again. "Take care, Miss Aleta. I'll catch you on the go round, girl," he said as he tossed her a quick wink.

The other woman smiled sweetly, giving him a quick wave of her hand. "Stay safe, James Burdett. You stay safe," she said as she watched him exit out the door.

As the clock slowly ticked time, the two women sat quietly, neither of them saying a word. The finality of James's departure was slowly seeping into the room, filling the space with melancholy.

"You should go, Irene," Aleta finally said, her eyes meeting her best friend's. "You know you want to."

"No. It's not about me anymore. I have to think about this baby."

"You need to tell him. He has a right to know he's about to be a daddy."

Irene rested a hand against her stomach, the faint flutter of new life tucked warmly beneath her palm. She shook her head, the tears finally falling to the floor. "Never. If James stays, he'll stay because he wants to. Not because he thinks he has to for this baby, or for me."

Aleta shook her head. "Are you ever going to tell him?"

Her friend stared at her briefly. She waved her head from side to side. "If he loved me as much as he loved that damn piano, he would have stayed because I stayed. He doesn't. James will make his own way in this world, and me and my child will make ours. James doesn't need us and we won't need him. I'll see to it."

Aleta rose to wrap her arms around her friend in a warm embrace. The two women held on to each other as Irene's tears finally escaped, dripping with ease down her cheeks. Aleta shook her head with her last pronouncement. "You're wrong, Irene. Everybody needs someone."

One

The line into the Playground Jazz and Blues Club extended past the bolted doors and barred windows of Lem Young's Chinese Cleaners and Harper's Florist, which neighbored the old brick building. Except for the patient souls waiting to get inside, the street was bare. A crisp breeze blew teasingly under tight-fitting skirts, while firm bodies, suited to the nines, paced anxiously, examining the evening's offerings.

Once inside, having paid the ten-dollar cover charge, the privileged few permitted admittance walked a dimly lit corridor, past a mirrored wall reflecting a kaleidoscope of characters. Romeo Marshall, the club's owner, stood in the entranceway, greeting each of them personally, many by name, as he pointed them to the few remaining tables and the stools at the bar.

Within the inner sanctum of the club, a pale blue light cast an eerie glow over laughing, crying, flirting faces. On the dance floor, couples clutched each other tightly. Shuffling in small circles, their bodies melted one into the other. The heavy aroma of strong perfumes and stale tobacco filled the air, and vision was dulled by swirls of thick smoke that clouded the room. It was

Saturday night and the room was filling to capacity as scented, powdered bodies swayed eagerly inside. The audience pushed toward the stage, rollicking to the music, bodies bumping shoulders to shoulders, hips to hips, barely enough room remaining for a swallow of air to pass between them all.

Heads bobbed in time to the music. Bodies swayed to the beat. The music was hot, the room was hot, and the heat was rising with each new body that entered the room. The sounds were low and husky, the guttural strains pressing at skin moist with perspiration. The vibration of the music could be felt deep down inside, creeping from the pit of liquor-filled stomachs, up into haze-filled minds, spreading its infectious spirit copiously throughout relaxed muscles, down into tingling limbs.

Along the rear wall, bodies were pressed tightly against the salmon-colored stucco. At many an occupied seat, creeping hands could be caught pressing along trembling thighs, groping anxiously at knees pressed tightly together. You could smell the passion, a heavy, musky aroma of wanton lust, its dampness glistening like stardust against sun-blessed skin drenched in salted sweat.

Romeo guided his staff with lingering looks, slight nods, and every so often a slight gesture of his hand. His body spoke for him, his eyes mouthing his words. He stood imposingly, his six feet, six and one-half-inch stature long and lean. Taut muscle massed his solid frame, his smooth, sable complexion complementing the vibrancy of his blue black eyes. He had a penetrating stare, piercing through the chaos of the crowded room. His eyes missed nothing, catlike in his observations, and observe he did. The Crayola cast that paraded about from night to night fascinated him.

The Playground was his personal concourse, nurturing the childlike qualities hidden within his soul. Moving passively from table to table, he'd instigate the games and establish the rules. His massive hands would tease, the long chocolate fingers stroking a bare back or resting lightly atop a crossed knee. Laughter danced on his thick lips, curling past snow white teeth lined perfectly in a row. His laugh was deep and rich, echoing in the hollows of his dimpled cheeks.

Born Lawrence Alexander Marshall, he'd been called Romeo since he'd been four years old. His mother's best friend had blessed him with the nickname, proclaiming the moniker his as he'd batted his long, ebony eyelashes at the old women in the Laundromat for a small piece of candy or an extra sugar cookie.

"He's going to be a Romeo," she'd remarked, pinching his dimpled cheeks and planting kisses on his curly head. "Going to romance all them pretty girls, he will."

For him, it had always been a game. A game he could play better than most, and now he only played whenever it suited him. Music had always fascinated him, but he had no particular talents in that direction and his mother had insisted he focus his attentions elsewhere. He had excelled athletically, baseball and track being his fortes. An athletic scholarship, betrayed by a knee injury his sophomore year, had opened the doors for a degree in engineering. After graduation and two years of starched white collars and navy blue suits, he'd realized the corporate boardroom was definitely not his calling.

Taking a yearlong hiatus, he'd traveled across the United States, settling for brief periods in the bars of New Orleans, New York, St. Louis, and Chicago. He'd spent his nights studying people who wandered as aimlessly as he did, searching for something that belonged only to him. Then one day, shortly after returning home to North Carolina, he'd found the Playground. It had been a deserted shell, inhabited by a dark infestation tainted with dirt and grime. Together with his fraternity brother Malcolm Cobb, they'd nursed it to health with the help of their savings, a small bank loan, much back-breaking labor, and their own salted sweat. Everything else had fallen into step with the music.

No night at the Playground was ever the same. The mood of the evening moved with the flow of the crowd, influenced by the voracity of the music. The tones would be sweet and rich one night, wicked and sultry the next. Romeo liked it that way. He'd spend his days ordering booze, balancing ledgers, paying bills, and counting cash. The daily routine was the same, never changing, but his nights were always varied. He'd successfully recreated a gin joint comparable to any of the hottest clubs that had rocked well before his time. Relishing the satisfaction of his accomplishments, he welcomed the onset of evening and all of its uncertainty.

The Playground was now the place to be and Romeo and Malcolm the men to know. The success of the Playground had propelled both right into the spotlight. Although Romeo was still driven by the desire to do and be more, he could bask silently in the warmth of already having attained a level of contentment and accomplishment others would never know. He found great satisfaction in that fact.

Warm air suddenly blew eerily against Romeo's neck as long arms snaked seductively around his chest. Soft lips, painted a vibrant red, brushed gently along his neck, teeth nipping lightly at his flesh. As pink polished nails were clasped firmly across his midriff, a familiar voice whispered hot against his ear.

"You still feel too good, lover."

Romeo laughed, turning to encircle his sturdy arms around a lithe body draped in a fluid, black silk pantsuit. Brushing his lips against the woman's, Romeo savored the taste of wintergreen and mint. Allowing his hands to glide down her lean back, he rested his palms lightly at the rise of her buttocks.

"Not as good as you do, Roberta. How are you, darling?"

"Better. Now."

Romeo laughed again. "So where have you been hiding yourself, lady?" he asked, the scent of her perfume suddenly too familiar.

Roberta shrugged, pressing herself closer to Romeo. "I wasn't hiding, honey. I just found a man who would *marry* me. I got tired of waiting for your good-looking behind."

Romeo squeezed her gently. "So, you're happy?"

"Would have been happier if you'd married me, but I'm not complaining." Roberta goosed him gently, resting her hand warmly on his backside.

"Woman, you know I am not a marrying man," Romeo exclaimed. "I would have never made you happy."

The woman chuckled. "True, but you sure knew how to make me feel good," she said, kissing him again.

Romeo laughed with her, shaking his head from side to side. "So, where's this new husband of yours?" he asked.

"Home with the baby. It's ladies' night tonight."

"A baby too!" Romeo exclaimed. "Damn, girl, you work fast!"

Roberta laughed again, a warm rise of noise that filled what little space there was between them. "So how about you? Who's got your heart?"

Romeo grinned. "You know that's a game I don't play, girl. I'm too busy trying to keep myself afloat to be in a serious relationship."

Roberta nodded. "But business is good, right? I mean, the place is bumping! And everyone's talking about it."

Romeo gestured toward the crowd, releasing his hold on the woman. "I can't complain. This place definitely keeps me on my toes."

"I'm really happy for you, Romeo. You really deserve all your success," Roberta said with a nod, her shoulder-length bob swaying from side to side.

He smiled, the lift to his mouth warm and seductive. "Thank you. I really appreciate that."

Roberta smiled back. "Well, I need to get back to my friends. I know they're peeing in their pants with envy," she said, pointing to a table of women staring intently in their direction.

Romeo nodded, pulling her back tightly against him. "Mmmm," he hummed. "Too bad you have a husband now."

"Liar," Roberta said with a slight giggle as she punched him playfully in the chest. "Stop by the table and say hello," she said. "I'd love to introduce you to my girls."

"I'll do that. And you take care of yourself," Romeo said, placing his lips lightly atop hers, savoring the quivering lips one last time. He moved to kiss her gently against the cheek, whispering in her ear. "Got to give your girls something to talk about," he said with a soft chuckle.

"Damn," Roberta said, shaking in her six-inch heels. Squeezing his hands between her own, she paused briefly as a chill swept down her spine. "We could have been so good together, Romeo. Too bad you messed up."

Romeo smiled broadly as he watched Roberta walk away, the familiar scent of her perfume fading with her departure, then lifted his hand to wave at the other women who still sat staring at him.

"You need to stop!" Odetta Brown, the head waitress, said with a deep laugh as she brushed past him.

"What?" Romeo asked. "I'm not doing a thing."

"Uh-huh," Odetta said, shaking her head. "Just keep it up and see if you don't get yourself in trouble."

Romeo laughed with her. "I just can't help myself, Odetta. Some of my clients require a bit more attention from me than others."

As Roberta sat back down her best friends began talking over themselves, each one eager to comment on what they'd just witnessed.

"I cannot believe you kissed that man!" Taryn Williams exclaimed, her tone scolding. "Did you forget you had a husband?" She narrowed her gaze on her associate.

Roberta giggled. "What I remembered was that my husband's not here right now and how that man could make me feel back in the day," she replied. She took a big gulp of her vodka tonic, fanning herself rapidly as she swallowed. A wide grin spread across her face.

Taryn shook her head. She tossed Romeo Marshall a quick look, the man knee deep in conversation with another woman at another table. She rolled her eyes skyward. Everything about his demeanor told her he was no good for any woman looking for a relationship worth more than an ounce of salt.

"Please, tell me you did not date that man for long," she said, giving the other woman a questioning look.

Their friend Marsha chimed in. "They didn't date. All they did was—" she started.

Roberta interrupted. "What we did was enjoy a mutually satisfying adult relationship. Don't hate," she said.

Marsha laughed. "Like I started to say. What they did never took them out of bed. I doubt she even got a meal out of the deal."

"Oh, I ate," Roberta said with a laugh. "I ate very well, thank you very much! And he did too. In fact—"

Taryn held up her hand, stalling the crude comment she knew was coming from her friend's mouth. "Please, spare us the nasty details."

Laughter rang around the table.

"Actually," Roberta said after downing the last of the beverage in her glass, "Romeo is a really great guy and one day he's going to make the right woman an incredible husband. I just wasn't the right woman and we both knew it. But we knew how to have really great sex!"

Marsha shook her head. "I sure wouldn't mind riding him," she said with a woeful sigh. "Just one time."

Roberta laughed, her head waving from side to side. "He's not your type," she said matter-of-factly. "I was thinking he'd actually be a great catch for you, Taryn." She tossed her friend a raised eyebrow.

"Girl, please! That man's a dog. Pure hound," Taryn answered as she rolled her eyes skyward. She tossed Romeo another quick look. "No, he's too much of a player for me," Taryn added.

Roberta shrugged. "Girl, he is not that bad! I wouldn't count him out if I were you. He's one of the good guys and there aren't too many of them left. Trust me when I tell you!"

Taryn's gaze moved back across the room, eyeing Romeo curiously. As if he sensed her staring, his gaze suddenly turned in her direction, meeting the look she was giving him. Their eyes locked and held and then he smiled, a sly, seductive bend to his mouth that illuminated his dark face. She felt her breath catch in her chest as she tore her gaze from his, suddenly dropping her eyes to the table and the empty wineglass she twisted nervously in her hands. She took a deep breath and then a second.

Roberta bumped her shoulder. "If I were you I definitely wouldn't count that man out just yet."

Two

He had made a sizeable profit off other people's addictions. As Romeo Marshall twirled a bottle of vodka in the palms of his hands, the thought tripped a heavy path across his mind. Upon hearing the ornately carved wooden door open and then close, he looked up from the glass he was filling. A damp breeze preceded the emaciated black man who'd found his way inside out of the evening rain. The old man's hollow eyes scanned the perimeter of the room. Exhaustion wove an intricate pattern of crimson lace against the white of his cornea. The gaunt figure, nourished by too meager a diet and too much alcohol, stared openly at Romeo, then nodded his gray head hello. Brushing the raw drops of moisture from his shoulders, he eased the heaviness in his limbs toward a small table in the back and sat down.

Romeo placed the vodka-filled glass on the counter just as his head waitress swept by to pick up her order. "See what the old guy wants," he said, nodding his head toward the man at the rear table.

"Uh-huh," Odetta replied. Chewing heavily on a

stale piece of bubble gum, she rolled her eyes as if annoyed when Romeo winked at her, flashing her a full smile.

Romeo propped his elbows on top of the long cherry bar, the solid wood supporting the weight of his well-built frame. He watched with amusement as Odetta crossed the room, the strut of her wide hips swaying to the beat of the music. The woman shuffled her way to the man's side, spoke to him briefly, and then pulled a seat up to the table to sit down beside the stranger. Watching their interaction closely, Romeo found himself focusing his full attention on the old man. He looked familiar, Romeo thought to himself, the man's aged features reminding him of an acquaintance he might know, but couldn't quite place. Then, as Odetta threw back her head, laughing briskly, he didn't think he looked familiar at all. Romeo felt his body relax. He found the sensation awkward since he wasn't quite sure why he'd become tense in the first place.

Romeo glanced down to the small black clock perched on the counter below the bar top. The digital numbers glowed in the dim light. It was half past eight. He sighed, knowing that business would soon pick up in spite of the rain. Folks would never let a few rain-drops keep them away from a good time, and Romeo worked hard to ensure his patrons always had a good time. As he busied himself in preparation, Odetta's sudden return pulled him away from his thoughts.

"Looks like you made a new friend," Romeo said teasingly.

Odetta laughed, the warmth of it helping to brighten the room. "He's actually kind of sweet. I like him."

"You like all old black men," Romeo said. He leaned his body against the bar, staring down at her.

"That's not true," she said, her smile widening. "I like old men, period. I don't discriminate." She chuckled warmly. "Anyways, the man said he doesn't want anything but a glass of ice water," she said, still chomping heavily on the gum in her mouth. There was a mild glimmer in her eyes, as if the duo had shared a secret no one else had been privy to.

Romeo raised his eyebrows ever so slightly.

"Told him this won't no homeless shelter," she said, heaving her thick body onto a bar stool in front of him. She paused, taking a deep inhale before finishing her comments. "Then he said good 'cause he preferred sleeping on the park bench. He's just an old fool," she said, a loud huff of air blowing out her last words. "He's sweet though, and too fresh," she concluded, chuckling under her breath ever so softly. "That's one fresh old man. He actually had me blushing and you know that takes some doing!"

Romeo looked toward the man, who was himself staring in Romeo's direction. They studied each other momentarily, then the elderly man's dark, sunken eyes dropped down toward the table, looking as if he'd been caught doing something he had no business doing. Reaching to the counter behind him for a clean glass, Romeo filled it with chipped ice and cold water, and handed it to Odetta. "Here, take this to him. Tell him this one's on the house."

"You need to throw the old fool out with his fresh self," Odetta muttered as she took the glass from his hand, pulling herself up off her seat. "Shoot. If the water's free I guess I can't be expecting no tip."

Romeo laughed. "Be nice, Ms. Brown. You know good and well that I'll take care of you."

"Hmph," Odetta grunted, turning to deliver the cold drink to the stranger.

Romeo watched as the old guy nodded in his direction, then lifted the glass in a gesture of appreciation before pulling it toward his lips.

Romeo shook his head, eyeing the stranger, who was still stealing glances in his direction. After drinking his fill of the icy fluid, the old man rose from where he sat and moved slowly toward the bar, the two men still locked eye to eye.

The small club was comfortable, the senior citizen thought to himself, his stare moving from the young man behind the bar and skating around the expanse of tables and the drunks who filled the seats. Music hummed from the speakers and his head bobbed slowly as he inhaled each slow note. They were playing an eclectic mix of blues, fitting for the cold rain that fell outside. At that moment Etta James was singing a duet with Sugar Pie DeSanto. Keb' Mo' had played before her, and before him one of the youngsters too new to the game to really know what it was to feel the blues ripping through his soul. The music felt good though, filling his insides with a wanting that was both bitter and sweet in the same breath.

As he finally reached Romeo's side, he extended his massive hand in the younger man's direction. "Thank you," he said softly, his thick voice barely a loud whisper. "Thank you much."

Romeo nodded, his own large paw lost within the worn flesh. "No problem."

"I don't take no charity, so do you think I can work off what I owe you?" he asked, staring questioningly at Romeo.

Romeo chuckled. "It was only a glass of water. Don't worry about it."

The man shook his head. "No. I owe you and I'm willing to work."

Romeo hesitated, briefly turning his attention toward a couple who sat across the way. A tall woman with large brown eyes, a cocoa-colored complexion, and a short, Halle Berry haircut had wrapped her arm lazily about her companion's shoulder just as he was gesturing toward Odetta for a refill.

"What can you do?" Romeo asked, turning back to the conversation.

"I can play that piano over there," the old man responded, pointing toward the large black instrument perched on the stage.

Romeo's eyes followed the line of the man's crinkled finger, his gaze resting upon the instrument and its highly polished wood. He nodded, then lifted his hand toward the dais. "Be my guest, and we'll call it even."

Strolling the length of the bar, the newcomer dropped his seedy, wool jacket onto a bar stool, then sat his aged body comfortably on the piano bench and began to play, replacing the recorded music that Romeo had turned off. Blues suddenly spilled forth from the man's long fingers like a flood of tears, the mournful strains indicative of a heavy heart.

It was a symphony of one that filled the space with an intoxicating, consuming blend of musical notes. Notes that were teasing and tormenting, unfolding a story that probably should have been left untold. The music girdled them, the undulation of the piano dancing in time to the rain beating against the window outside. In no time at all, the piano player had captured everyone's heart and was pulling at their spirits like St. Gabriel and Satan going head to head for possession of their souls.

Romeo fixed a third round of drinks for the tall

woman and her friend. When he was certain that no
glass was empty and the clientele was content, he
moved from behind the bar. Crossing the room, he took
a seat at the same table the elderly man had occupied
just minutes before. Like everyone else in the room, his
eyes were fixed on the piano player.

Romeo studied the man intently. Tar-black flesh
clung hungrily to thick bones. His dark complexion
complemented the snowcapped crown of thinning curls
on top of his head. A full forehead, narrow nose, and
thick lips blended into the heavy age lines etched in his
flesh. There was an uneasy sadness in his eyes and
Romeo sensed that whatever had locked such emptiness away in his heart would one day cradle the old
man in his grave.

Glancing about the room, Romeo took note of the
tapping feet and swaying shoulders of the men and
women who sat listening. They were as enthralled as he
was, the music carrying them toward forgotten times
and distant places. They were each lost in another
realm, intoxicated, as if the music combined with the
drink had taken full control of their sensibilities. The
old man had been right about his being able to play that
piano.

The door opened again, ushering in Romeo's best
friend and business partner. Malcolm Cobb waved in
Romeo's direction, then stopped short, staring toward
the stage. Shaking his head in disbelief, he turned and
gave his friend a thumbs-up, grinning broadly. Romeo
lifted the length of his body from the seat, strolling
slowly across the hardwood floors to join the man
behind the bar.

"Hey, what's up?" he said softly, the volume of his
voice just a step away from being a whisper.

Malcolm pulled a small apron around his waist.

"Hey, Rome! Where did Piano Man roll in from?" he asked, nodding toward the entertainment. "It's been a long time since I last heard him play."

"You know him?"

"Most folks from around here know Piano Man. At least the older ones do. Man, my mother had a serious crush on that old dude! Burdett something or other is his real name. He was playing the chitlin' circuit years ago, then he up and disappeared. He pops up every so often and if you're a true blues aficionado, then hearing him play is like winning the lottery. My man can play that piano now!"

Romeo nodded his head in agreement, his gaze resting yet again on the old man behind them. "Do you have the bar?" he finally asked.

Malcolm bobbed his head up and down. "I'm on the clock," he responded.

Returning to his seat, Romeo watched as the room began to fill, a mélange of chocolate and vanilla confections filing through the front door. Odetta and Sharon, the new waitress, bounced from table to table filling orders. Up on stage the piano player continued to play.

An hour or so later Romeo was tired for him, but the man's fingers continued to glide easily across the keys, seeming to move on their own accord. They were oblivious to the exhaustion that had to be consuming the rest of the man's body. From the expression on the old guy's face, Romeo sensed that he was completely lost somewhere in the music.

Romeo tossed another look around the room, in awe of how attentive the audience was. Across the room the piano man was still playing as if his life depended on it. Romeo blew a deep sigh.

Rising from his seat, he passed by the bar for a

refill of his beverage, then moved toward the stage. Romeo placed a warm hand on top of the old man's narrow shoulder and smiled. "Take a bow, and come talk with me a minute," he said, his tone polite, but commanding.

Piano Man nodded, bringing the song to its end. Rising from the piano bench, he clasped his hands in front of him and smiled as loud applause rang through the space. Waving a hand toward the audience, he followed Romeo back to the rear table. On the other side of the room, Malcolm switched on the sound system, flooding the interior with the heavy wail of B. B. King.

"It's an honor to have such a distinguished musician perform here at the Playground," Romeo said as he sat down.

Piano Man shrugged as he took his own seat. "I ain't 'stinguished. I just play the piano is all."

Romeo extended his hand. "My name's Lawrence— Lawrence Marshall—but everyone calls me Romeo."

Piano Man grasped his hand in a firm shake, pumping it up and down lightly. "Pleasure. They calls me Piano Man."

Romeo nodded. "So, what do you drink besides water?"

Piano Man grinned, a wide display of teeth and gums filling his face. "Well, I ain't never been one to turn down a glass of good scotch."

Gesturing for Odetta, Romeo sent her to bring them two shots of Black Label and a second glass of water. "How long have you been playing like that?" he asked, turning his attention back to the man who sat across from him.

Piano Man shrugged his shoulders. "Most of my

life. Started playing when I was a baby and ain't never stopped."

Romeo nodded just as Odetta placed the glasses down in front of them, his eyes briefly meeting her inquisitive stare. As she walked away, he and Piano Man both paused, following the woman with their eyes, appreciation flowing like water over the lush curves of her frame.

"You come from these parts?" Romeo asked, gazing back at the old man as he fingered the shot glass between his hands.

Piano Man leaned back in his seat. "Come from a lotta places. Just happen to be here now." Pulling his own glass to his chapped lips, he quickly downed the bitter contents.

"How long is *now* going to last?" Romeo asked.

The man shrugged, his thin shoulders jutting upward. Romeo stared at him curiously; the man's dark eyes were haunting, their deep intensity drawing the breath from him. Inhaling deeply, Romeo slowly blew the air out past his lips. Reaching into the pocket of his linen slacks, he pulled out a roll of hundred-dollar bills and quickly counted off five, laying them on the table in front of Piano Man.

"If you're interested, I could use a regular piano player. I'll pay cash, and I'll pay in advance."

Piano Man fingered the crisp currency, lightly caressing the paper with his fingertips. He pulled his hand back into his lap, leaving the money where the other man had placed it. "I can't make no promises 'bout how long I'll be staying."

Romeo nodded. "No problem. Work off what you owe me. If you decide to stay on after that, you let me know, and I'll give you another advance."

"How you know I won't just take this money and go 'bout my business? I could just disappear and not come back."

Romeo rose to his feet, adjusting the waistband of his slacks. The two locked eyes, each gazing intently at the other. "You could," Romeo finally answered, "but I'd like to think that I can trust a man who doesn't take charity and will work to pay for a glass of water."

Piano Man came to his feet. "I was working off the ice and the clean glass. The pretty lady said the water was free."

Romeo smiled, his head bobbing slowly against his thick neck. "You got somewhere to stay?"

Piano Man nodded, raising a cash-filled fist to his heart. "I does now. A room at the Madison is forty dollars a night. Cheaper if you pays by the week."

"Tell you what—let me make a call. I know a woman who owns a boardinghouse not far from here. I can probably swing you a better room for half the price, and she's been known to throw in a few meals if you talk sweet to her," Romeo said, giving his new employee a slight wink.

Piano Man grinned. "Well, I do believes I can expect to be eating well then," he responded, the lines of his face drawing back as he smiled.

Romeo laughed. "I thought you'd like that," he said, turning around. He paused, then looked back over his shoulder. "I'm sorry. I forgot to ask. What's your full name?"

Piano Man hesitated, twisting the cash between his palms. "My daddy named me James. James Burdett."

Romeo nodded, shaking the man's hand one last time. "Welcome to the Playground, Mr. Burdett."

Piano Man stared after him as Romeo headed toward his office at the rear of the club. As the younger man closed the door behind himself, one could almost see the sadness creep back into Piano Man's eyes. Pushing the green bills deep into his front pocket, he sauntered back to the stage and let his fingers cry against the piano keys.

Three

Piano Man was not alone. The band had stopped by and was playing sweetly beside the old man—Randy "Too-Smooth" Biggs on saxophone, Billy "Blues" Tyler on bass, and Little John Clark on the horn. It had taken less than a week for Piano Man's friends and admirers to search him out in order to amuse themselves with the music. They now came every night to play and they would play until they were bored with one another, or the crowd, whichever came first.

There was a brief pause as the band rose to take a break. Malcolm quickly switched on the sound system. The low drone of Muddy Waters filled the room. Across the way Romeo watched Piano Man as he took a quick drag from a cigarette he had palmed off Odetta and followed it with two shots of Black Label. Gliding over to the stage, Romeo tapped the old man lightly on the shoulder.

"Don't start," Piano Man said emphatically. "I ain't in no mood to hear it."

"Tough," Romeo responded, taking the nonfiltered tobacco stick from the man's hand and crushing it out in the ashtray Piano Man had laid on top of the piano.

Piano Man cussed. "Boy, you a pain in my ass. Man can't do a damn thing with you around."

"That's right. Do what you want as long as you don't do it around me. Now you know if you work for me you don't drink on the job. Drink on your time, not mine. You losing your mind?"

"I don't need no caretaker, boy," Piano Man grunted, rising from his seat. "I'm a free agent."

"You don't have a caretaker. I'm only protecting my investment. I paid in advance, remember?"

Piano Man grunted again as he lifted his body from the bench and stepped down off the stage.

"Where are you going, now?" Romeo asked, eyeing him suspiciously.

"Going to kiss them pretty girls over there. That one in the red sweater came up to pinch my cheek before and I promised her I'd let her buy me a drink. Is that okay with you*?*" he asked sarcastically.

"No, it's not okay, but I don't have the time to sit here and mother you right now. You just keep yourself out of trouble and make sure there's nothing in that drink stronger than ginger ale."

Piano Man muttered under his breath. "You need to go kiss that girl you been staring at all night and not be minding my business."

Romeo bristled. "What girl? What are you talking about?"

Piano man laughed. He shifted his gaze toward a side table and the woman who sat alone, her eyes dancing around the space. "You know what woman," he said as he gave him a half salute, then turned on his heels.

Romeo blew a soft sigh as he watched him ease his way over to sit with three overdressed senior citizens who sat blowing kisses in the old man's direction. The three women immediately made a space for him, each clamoring for his attention. Romeo laughed, shaking his head from side to side, then turned his attention back to his duties.

"He's right, you know," Malcolm said, moving to his side.

"About what?" Romeo asked, eyeing his friend curiously.

"That girl."

Romeo laughed. "Did I miss something?"

His friend laughed with him. "You might have, but we didn't," Malcolm said. "And you know nothing gets past Odetta's eagle eyes!"

"That's right!" the woman exclaimed as she suddenly joined them. "I saw how you were staring at that woman."

Romeo shook his head. "I don't know what y'all are talking about. I stare at all the women!"

Odetta chuckled, her head waving from side to side. "Well, her name's Taryn. Taryn Williams. She and your girl Roberta work at the same company."

Romeo tossed a quick look toward the table. A man had joined the beautiful woman and she was laughing warmly. The tall stranger was built like an NFL linebacker, wearing a wool suit made for a steeplechase jockey. Tight and small, it was busting at the seams. Romeo watched as she politely refused the man's advances, sending him on his way. Romeo knew it wouldn't be long before another single male took his place, eager for her attention. She was a woman alone, and the raging testosterone in the room considered her desperate or easy. But they were quickly discovering she was anything but as she'd had them dropping like flies since she arrived.

His friends were right. He had been staring for most

of the evening, the intensity of his attraction catching him off guard more than once. Now he was embarrassed that he'd been so obvious about it.

Taryn Williams was a regal beauty, her splendor wholeheartedly natural. Her composure was serene and majestic as she sat listening to the music. Her complexion was flawless, skin the color of red clay, a dark caramel with rich red undertones. Her eyes were large and round and a deep blue black that shone brightly, penetrating straight into the core of his being when she deigned to look back at him. Dark chestnut brown hair in a shoulder-length cut flattered her curvaceous body, and she looked exceptionally young. He fathomed her healthy countenance belied her true age.

A form-fitting black lace dress clung to her voluptuous body. She had curves in all the right places, her attire complementing each dip and rise. With her full cheeks and sensuous lips, he was reminded of wet, sweet mangoes, waiting to be tasted. He suddenly imagined her mouth had been made for long, slow kisses and sweet promises blowing in his ear. A wave of heat shot through his southern quadrant, moving him to shift from one leg to the other to stall the sensation.

He shook the feeling, his eyes blinking rapidly. "I am not interested in that woman," he said aloud.

Odetta laughed heartily. "Yes, you are."

Romeo rolled his eyes skyward as Malcolm joined Odetta in laughter.

The conversation was suddenly interrupted by a commotion coming from the other side of the room. Hearing her name being called, Odetta turned toward a thirsty patron, flipping her hand in his direction. "Hold your horses, Henry James. You see I'm busy," she quipped loudly, racing toward the table. "You ol' bald-headed fool! Why you got to be causing all this ruckus calling me!"

The two men were both still laughing as the robust woman rushed across the room. Malcolm tapped his friend against his back. "At least go introduce yourself," he said. "What can it hurt?"

Romeo shrugged his broad shoulders as he blew a heavy sigh. "Brother, you know better than anyone else that I don't need another woman who requires a lot of attention. That woman looks very high maintenance."

Malcolm shrugged as he headed back toward the bar. "Just say hello and see what happens. You never know."

Romeo eyed his friend. He needed to refocus—too many distractions throwing him off track. He blew another deep sigh, his gaze quickly scanning the room. Catching Piano Man's eye, he pointed first toward his watch, then the piano, then he lifted his palms toward the ceiling.

Pointing back at him with his own wrinkled appendage, Piano Man rose from his seat. After kissing each of the three women in turn, he called to the others, then headed back to the stage. On cue, Malcolm switched off the music, Koko Taylor's "Beer Bottle Boogie" fading into the distance. Taking his place on the bench, Piano Man's hands raced across the keys. The room was soon coated with a rich, deep tune that rushed forward like a storm wind ready to do battle.

Romeo continued to make his rounds. Women leaned up against him, eagerly pressing kisses against his cheeks. The men met his outstretched hand in firm handshakes while slapping him across the back. He occasionally sat to catch up on an old acquaintance's activities or the escapades of a former lover, his calculated responses and exclamations smooth and endearing. He was in his element and he was happy.

Boosted by his good mood, he turned in the direction of the woman named Taryn, hopeful that her suitor for the moment had moved on. Disappointment suddenly painted his expression. The woman named Taryn was gone.

Taryn couldn't begin to reason why she had gone out to the club at all. Knowing she had to be at the office early in the morning should have been enough to keep her at home. But listening to her friend Roberta had been her downfall. Roberta had begged her to come out for a drink, claiming she needed to talk. Taryn had sat there for over an hour waiting for the woman when she'd finally gotten a text message that she'd been stood up, Roberta needing to get home to her husband and baby.

And there she'd been, stranded at the Playground by herself, and so Taryn had stayed, enjoying the music and most of the attention that had been lavished on her. Now she was second-guessing her decision. She hated to admit it, but she'd secretly gotten caught up in Roberta's enthusiasm and was curious to know more about the owner of the Playground. However the owner hadn't been the least bit curious about her.

She made one last check of her front door, insuring the alarm was engaged. Moving through her North Hills home, she stripped out of her clothes as she made her way up the stairs to the second floor.

For the first time she found the home's quiet almost unnerving. The hum of the refrigerator, the ticking of the grandfather clock in the hallway, and the creaking of the floorboards beneath her feet were the only sounds echoing through the space. She didn't own a pet, having neither the time nor the inclination to be bothered, but she couldn't help but wonder if maybe coming home to a cat or a small dog might feel less lonely.

Taryn heaved a deep sigh, appalled that such a thought had gone through her mind. She wasn't lonely. Not really. In fact, she'd always been quite content with her life. She loved her job. As the president of sales and marketing for a national design chain, Taryn spent a fair amount of time traveling around the world, searching out product to boost her company's bottom line. The intensity of her schedule and the pressures of her responsibilities had never been conducive to a long-term relationship with any man and so she had never really given one any consideration. She had never needed a man in her life and had yet to meet one she wanted for longer than a quick moment.

Thoughts of Romeo Marshall suddenly flashed through her head. Something about that man intrigued her and she hated to admit that she was curious to know exactly what that was. She hadn't given him much thought that first night when he hadn't bothered to make his way to where she and her friends had been sitting, and although Roberta had been dismissive, continuing to extoll his many virtues, Taryn hadn't been convinced. Tonight she'd been disappointed; he had not made the small effort to stop by her table to ask if she was having a good time.

Taryn shook her head, frustrated that she even cared. She already knew that Romeo Marshall, with his less than stellar reputation, wasn't the kind of man she wanted to invest any energy in. Besides, the prospect of being with a man who had once sexed her friend felt all sorts of wrong, despite Roberta's assurances that Taryn was being way too sensitive about the whole thing. "I'm not kidding," the woman had extolled, "even if it doesn't turn into anything permanent, you'll still thank me. That man is God-sent!"

Taryn blew another deep breath as she rinsed her mouth and swiped a warm bath cloth over her face and eyes. Easing into her bedroom, she drew back the covers and slipped beneath them. *God-sent.* She should only be so lucky, she thought as she reached for the television remote and began to surf the stations.

The tinkling of breaking glass and the loud curses of a gin-splattered patron caught Romeo's attention. Excusing himself from a conversation, he rose from his seat, sauntering over to his customer's side just as the onslaught of tears rose to his waitress's eyes.

"Sharon, please bring Mr. Jenkins's table a round of drinks on the house," he said quietly, gently squeezing her shoulder.

"Yes, sir, Mr. Marshall, sir," the young woman responded, gratefully fleeing the discerning eyes upon her.

Gesturing for a busboy to bring a broom, Romeo smiled his warmest smile. "My apologies, Sam. Just send me a bill for the suit and the Playground will take care of it."

"Ain't no big thing," Samuel Jenkins slurred, the whiskey punctuating his speech. Briskly wiping at the moistened jacket and wrinkled pin-striped shirt, he chortled loudly, the sound vulgar and harsh. "Was just trying to work a little of my mojo," he said, cackling harshly. "These young girls today don't know how to take a little joke."

"Sam, they have no problems with the jokes, man. It's when you tell your jokes with your hand on their asses that they have a problem."

The man snorted, breaking into a semitoothless grin. "Ain't no big thing." The other two men seated at the table with him grinned back, nodding their heads.

"Just keep your hands off my girls, Sam. It's hard enough getting a good night's work out of them without you being a distraction."

"Ain't me, Romeo. It's the beast in my pants," he stammered, laughing heartily.

Romeo smiled slightly, shaking his head. Slapping the man on the back of his shoulders as he swept by, Romeo reiterated, "Just don't give my girls a rough time, please."

Making his way to the bar, he stopped to console the young woman struggling to regain her composure. "Are you okay, Sharon?" he asked, concern sparkling in his dark eyes.

"I'm so sorry, Mr. Marshall," she whispered, "but he grabbed my behind, and was reaching for my chest, and . . ."

"It's okay. Sometimes they can get out of hand. Let Malcolm bring the drinks over, and after this round, I'm going to cut the three of them off. You just stay away from them for a while." Looking around, he gestured for Odetta to join them. The robust woman smiled in their direction.

Romeo smiled back as she shimmied over, the white of her teeth gleaming under the lights in the room. Odetta had worked for him since he'd opened six years ago. She was a gregarious, big-boned, voluptuous woman with a chocolate-kissed complexion. Short jet black hair framed a full face resplendent with large nut-brown eyes and a full pout. Brusque in her manners, she was loudly expressive and the customers loved her.

Most times Romeo found her unencumbered style and curt mannerisms refreshing.

"What's up, sweetheart?" she asked, popping her signature piece of chewing gum in his face. "Sam being his usual pain in the ass?"

"I need you to take over table six for me, Odetta. Mr. Jenkins is giving poor Sharon here a rough time. She'll take over table twelve."

"No problem, sweetie. I'll put old Sam in his place. Thinks he can cop a feel whenever he wants. Break them fingers one by one if he don't sit down and behave his self."

Romeo laughed. "I knew I could depend on you, Miss Brown."

Odetta smiled her biggest smile. She adored Romeo, her affection for him bordering on hero worship. Many women did. All he had to do was smile that dimpled smile of his, and fix his gaze with just a hint of seduction, and the female sex would melt in the palms of his hands. Sharon also stared up at him, adoration upon her face. Romeo had learned early in life how to work his good looks, and although he'd profess not be vain, he readily admitted that his chiseled features were more of an asset than they had ever been a hindrance. It also hadn't hurt that he had a heart of gold and the spirit of an angel in training.

"All right, ladies, let's make these alcoholics happy," he said, sending them back to work. He moved behind the bar, helping Malcolm to deliver the promised drinks.

He and Malcolm Cobb had been friends since pledging Alpha Phi Alpha. They'd been line brothers, their bond irrefutable. After college both had gone in different directions, his friend building a successful architectural design business in the Maryland area, which was his ex-wife's hometown. They'd maintained contact and after his divorce Malcolm had come back home to Raleigh, North Carolina.

They'd been working the bar together almost since Romeo had gotten the bright idea to throw caution to the wind and step out on faith. Initially Romeo hadn't wanted a partner, but he had afforded Malcolm the opportunity when the coal black man had cued him to the thieving actions of the club's first bartender.

A loyal customer from day one, Malcolm had occupied the third stool on a regular basis, never nursing anything stronger than a glass of tonic with a twist of lime. His passion had been for the atmosphere, not the alcohol.

One day he'd pulled Romeo aside and whispered in his ear. "Lose Pete," he said. "Every fourth drink is a no sale for you, cash in the pocket for him."

Afterward Romeo had watched Pete in action. His routines had run the gamut from palming the cash from every other diluted sale, to overcharging the number of drinks served to a large group running up a tab. Pete had skimmed a sizable fortune from Romeo before he'd been caught. The same day Romeo had kicked Pete's butt out Malcolm had agreed to be Romeo's cohort in crime. Going against the grain of everything else they both knew, neither could fathom any reason why running a juke joint together wouldn't work for them. And once it had, the association afforded them both something they'd been missing.

Sharon was relatively new to their little family. She had much to learn, but she worked hard and Romeo liked her. She was a small young woman standing just over five feet tall. Copper-colored hair pulled tightly back into a full bun set off her peach-toned skin, and dark freckles danced lightly across her pug nose.

Malcolm had brought her in one day and had implored Romeo to give her a chance. He had found her singing in a small, storefront Baptist church one crisp Sunday afternoon. According to Malcolm, she had called out to him with the voice of an angel sent from heaven above. He had sat in the rear pew of that old church every Sunday for over a month. It had taken two weeks before he'd discovered her name. By the third week, he knew that the closest thing to home for her was the West Creedmoor Women's Shelter and that she had no family and no job to speak of. At the end of the month, he'd taken her under his wing and into his heart and was hell-bent on delivering her from her miseries.

Last week, when the crowd was sparse, Sharon had leaned across the piano and sung. The melodic tones had been indicative of too many good times as she caressed the audience with the clear, lyrical strokes of her deep voice. She and Piano Man had fed upon one another, the melodies stirring their insatiable appetites, and whetting their need for the music. Theirs had been a sensual, spirited passion devoured by the hungry eyes and lustful ears of those fortunate to be present. Tonight, when the crowd thinned out, Romeo had promised he would allow her to sing again. For now though, he needed her to wait tables.

Romeo tossed his friend a quick look. "Hey, did you see when she took off?"

"Who?"

"Taryn. The woman who was sitting over there by herself."

Malcolm nodded. "I told you to go say hello."

Romeo rolled his eyes skyward. "I was trying. By

the time I found a quick moment she was gone. She left early!"

"She'll be back."

"How do you know?"

"She told Odetta that she planned to bring some friends with her so they can hear Piano Man play."

Nodding his head, Romeo fell into thought, quietly kicking himself for not getting the woman's number before she left. He hoped she would come back but he wasn't willing to place any bets on it. People came and went all the time, sometimes returning, sometimes not. There'd be other women, he thought, trying to shake thoughts of *that* woman from his mind.

He watched as Malcolm placed a round of drinks down on the table in front of Jenkins and his cronies, enlisting a hearty round of laughter with one of his racy jokes. The old boys were in high spirits and Romeo knew cutting off their flow would not be an easy feat to accomplish. The three were on a binge and would settle for no less than going home as shitfaced, cock-eyed drunk as they could. They would crawl home reeking of stale swill, vomit, and tobacco, waking obese wives from their sound sleep just so they could proclaim promises they'd not remember when sobriety once again reclaimed their bodies. He knew Odetta would keep them entertained for a period, but he'd have to send them packing sooner than they were prepared to leave. He sighed, lightly shrugging his shoulders.

The room had filled quickly. The nights were always too busy, but that came with the territory. Across the way, Sharon had finally stopped shaking. She was busy taking orders from a party of six women who had not long ago entered. Romeo recognized four of them and made a mental note to swing by the table to say hello. He would kiss their rubescent cheeks, squeeze a strapless shoulder, and flirt teasingly. They'd swoon under the attention as Romeo would revel in the beauty, a part of the territory he enjoyed most.

Glancing at his watch, he rose from his seat. It was past time for him to continue his rounds and be host at the door. He nodded at Odetta, who was perched coyly on Jenkins's knee, and smiled.

Four

Racing to the ladies room, Odetta pushed her way into a vacant stall. "Damn, I'm tired," she said to no one, and to everyone.

"Romeo working you too hard, Odetta?" a familiar voice responded.

"Hey, Sarah. How you doing, sweetheart?" Odetta called back.

"Doing real good, girlfriend. Real good."

"Wish I could say the same," a second voice piped in. "I got me the three no's."

"The three no's?" Sarah questioned.

"Yes, girl. No man, no money, and no ride."

"Oh, I hear that," Sarah said, laughing.

Flushing the commode, Odetta exited the small cubicle, lit a cigarette, and then leaned against the sink. "You ladies having a good time tonight?" she asked, taking a long slow drag off the cigarette.

Sarah nodded, brushing the hair from her brow. "Be better if I could get me some Romeo tonight," she said, primping in front of the mirror, adjusting the length of her skirt.

"You and everyone else," a long-legged, brown-skinned girl said, a tight yellow dress clinging to her narrow hips.

"Yes, Lord!" Sarah chimed in. "Romeo is one fine brother."

Odetta laughed, nodding her head in agreement. "My Romeo's special too, but he's not looking at the moment."

"The best ones never are," Sarah's friend chimed in as she inspected a small run threatening to creep eagerly up her thick leg.

"Odetta, how's your friend Carol?" Sarah interjected, lighting a cigarette of her own, blowing small smoke rings past tangerine glossed lips.

"Pitiful girl. Still chasing that piece a trash she got pregnant for."

"When she get pregnant?"

"Honey, girlfriend had a baby boy last year. Ugly child, too. Nothing but head and ears. Took right after his daddy!"

"Damn shame," Sarah said, flicking the ashes into the sink. "'Cause she sure 'nuff had herself a good man. This girl used to go with Big Ben. Then she messed up. Got caught with this no account brother," Sarah said, addressing her tall friend, who had carefully painted a thin coat of bright red nail polish across a chipped nail.

"Ben White? Big Ben White?" the other woman sputtered, blowing warm air across her wet fingertips.

"Yes, girl." Odetta nodded. "He treated her real good too, but she kept complaining that she needed a man who could do the nasty without sweating all over her."

"As big as Ben is, brother can't do nothing but sweat," Sarah said. "But as long as he's helping to pay the bills, who cares? Just give the man a towel!"

The women around her laughed.

"Brothers are all dogs. All of 'em," Sarah's friend stated matter-of-factly.

"She just got dumped," Sarah said to the others. "Her man moved back in with some tramp he used to go out with before he met her. And she ain't nothing but a high yella' bitch with a two-dollar weave down her back. That ho's young enough to be his grand-daughter!"

"Bitch, just tell all my business!"

"Girlfriend, I ain't telling all your business. Shoot! Ain't telling nothing people don't see with their own eyes. It's etched so deep in them bloodshot eyes of yours, it plays out like a big screen movie."

The girl rolled her eyes, fighting back tears. "Son of a bitch. He'll get his. Didn't know what he had, but bet you when that tramp start working some stank root on his tired ass he'll find out."

The women in the room nodded their heads sympathetically. A pregnant pause filled the space as each fell into the memories of their own lost relationships.

"Still could use me some Romeo though," Sarah repeated wistfully.

"Y'all see that fine thing sitting at the bar?" a short, heavy-chested woman in a red silk top questioned, changing the subject. "The tall brother, reddish hair, in that Brooks Brothers suit?"

"See him? Did him, baby," a tall, rusty girl chimed in. "Trust me though, brother may dress sharp and he can smooth-talk a nun into his pants, but he ain't packing nothing another eight inches wouldn't help. Brother . . . ain't . . . got . . . no . . . dick," she said, punctuating each word slowly.

Odetta slapped her hand against her thigh, laughing. "Whoa, girl, you a mess!" she said. Taking the last drag off her cigarette butt, she tossed it into the commode and flushed. "Well, I've got to go," Odetta said, running her soaped up hands under a warm stream of water. "Romeo's gonna kick my butt if I don't get back to work."

"Ask him if he got any openings," the unemployed woman, with too much makeup and a too-tight dress, called after her. Then to the women in the room, "Better yet, tell him I need a good man with some money."

As the ladies room door closed slowly behind her, laughter spilled out into the hallway. Grabbing a clean towel and a tray from the bar, Odetta returned to her station, brushing against Romeo's back as she went by. "The ladies is happy tonight, Romeo," she called over her shoulder.

Romeo nodded, a smile tugging gingerly at the side of his mouth. "Then so am I, Odetta girl. So am I."

Walking through the crowd, Romeo continued kissing upturned cheeks and shaking outstretched hands. As he made his way back to the bar Malcolm greeted him with a cup of rich coffee, the dark aroma pungently sweet. Taking a cautious sip from the hot liquid, he savored the deep flavor cradled in a bath of warm cream. "This is good, Malcolm. Real good," he said, nodding his head slightly.

"You look like you needed it," Malcolm said, passing a gin and tonic and a glass of white wine to a couple perched at the other end of the bar. Picking up the money passed to him in exchange, Malcolm rang up the sale. When he had finished, he strolled back over to where Romeo stood. "Good crowd tonight. The register's filling up nicely."

"Can't complain then, can we?" Romeo said, taking

another sip from his coffee. "How are my three friends holding up?" he asked, nodding in the direction of Jenkins's table.

"Nothing to worry about. I've gotten a cup of coffee into each of them already. The big guy with them was starting to look a little green around the edges. I think he was kind of glad to be cut off. Meant he didn't have to try to keep up with Jenkins and that other boozer they're with. Besides, he's been rubbing on Odetta for the last hour. That's kept him occupied. I think she's just about ready to send him home to his wife."

Romeo nodded. Turning his back to the bar, he looked out over the crowd. Most were focused intently on the band, a few dancing cheek to cheek, some shimmying at their tables. Others huddled close in conversation and all looked happy to be where they were. Turning back to Malcolm and his cup of coffee, he sat himself on a bar stool, content. "Can't get any better than this, Malcolm," he said, nodding his head into the ivory cup.

A wave of quiet passed between them as both sat in deep contemplation, absorbing the sounds and sights around them. Romeo was grateful for the moment, taking a quick second to give thanks for the blessings. Malcolm met his gaze and nodded as if reading the man's mind.

"So, how are your girls, Malcolm?" Romeo asked his friend. "You haven't brought them by in a while," he said, referring to Malcolm's twelve-year-old twins.

"They're good, I guess. My ex-wife has visitation this week and she took them to Maryland to visit with their grandmother. They're supposed to come back next week."

Romeo nodded his head. "Things any better between you and Shanelle?"

Malcolm shrugged, drying rings of water from some freshly washed glasses. "No better, no worse. She doesn't have any time for me and I've got even less for her," he said, his tone dry.

Understanding that Malcolm's relationship with his ex-wife was a source of consternation to him, Romeo changed the subject. "I heard Odetta say you had a date the other night. How'd that go?"

Breaking into a wide grin, Malcolm danced a slight two-step behind the bar. "I had a good time. A really good time. I don't know if you remember the cute little redhead who's been here hanging at the bar every Tuesday? Her name's Vanessa. She's actually very sweet," he said, grinning even wider.

"I hear she's a church-going girl, too," Sharon piped in, having joined them. "Who knows, maybe she can even get you to go more often."

Malcolm raised his eyebrows, his lips still stretched across his teeth. "Stranger things have been known to happen," he said with a shrug. "What do you need, darling?"

"One whiskey sour, a double shot of tequila, and two black Russians," she said, rolling off her order. "Nice crowd tonight, huh, Mr. Marshall?" She turned her attention to Romeo.

"How are you doing now, sweetheart?"

"I'm doing much better, and thank you again for before."

"That's what I'm here for, Sharon," he said, patting her lightly on the shoulder.

As Sharon stood waiting for Malcolm to finish mixing the drinks, she pressed anxiously at Romeo's elbow. He could sense that she, like the crowd, was in the mood for something more. "Okay, Sharon, what's up?" he asked, finally prompting her to ask whatever it was that had her so antsy.

"Do you think I might be able to sing now, Mr. Marshall? I know it's still kind of early, but Odetta said she'd cover for me and I promise I'll make sure all my tables are served before I start," she whispered timidly, searching his face for approval.

Pausing, Romeo smiled, studying Sharon closely. She was a pretty girl, but still very much a girl. Although Romeo knew she was twenty-four, about most things she had the innocence and the naïveté of a child half her age. Not wanting to disappoint her, and longing to hear her sing himself, he finally nodded his head yes.

"Just keep the crowd happy, Sharon," he answered, brushing his fingers lightly along the length of her blushing face.

"Thank you," Sharon gushed, jumping up and down. "I promise I'll do good."

Turning to Malcolm, Romeo laughed. "I think Piano Man has created a monster," he said, both men shaking their heads in unison as the young woman raced from their side.

"What do you think about him?" Romeo asked, shifting in his seat.

Malcolm glanced toward the stage. "Nice old guy. Bullheaded though."

Romeo nodded his head. "He's definitely stubborn."

"I don't get the impression he's very well either, do you?"

Romeo shrugged. "His age is definitely catching up with him, there's no doubt about that." He nodded pensively.

Malcolm stared where Romeo stared, the two men watching Piano Man in action.

"That old bird has got to be well over seventy by now. He's probably pushing eighty, if I'm not mistaken. I imagine at that age something's bound to catch up with you sooner or later."

Romeo smiled as he turned back to meet the other's man's gaze. "Do me a favor and just keep an eye on him. Let me know if you see anything unusual," he said.

"Anything in particular?"

"No. Just anything, and no more booze while he's playing. He can have what he wants after we close, but not while he's on stage. If he asks, tell him to come see me. Make sure Odetta and Sharon know also."

"Sure. What is it about him that's eating at you?"

Romeo looked toward the stage, shrugging his shoulders. "Can't put my finger on it. There's just something about him."

Malcolm smiled. "I understand. You see someone like that, and they remind you of something or someone else, and you know you have to give them a hand or you just don't feel right about yourself." Malcolm's head bobbed up and down as he passed a damp cloth across the bar top. "Yes, sir, I know exactly how you feel," he finished.

Romeo spun about in his seat to scan the room just as Sharon brushed past him grinning from ear to ear. After rushing to deliver her last round of drinks, she passed her apron to Malcolm, then approached the stage, eagerly taking the microphone Piano Man handed to her. She beamed out into the crowd, her self-assurance blossoming beneath the spotlights.

The crowd leaned toward the stage, enthusiastically waiting for the first note to roll off her tongue and glide past her lips. A quiet lull fell over the room, teasing the sounds from the piano. A low throaty trill rose from the depths of Sharon's insides and surged out into the room. As Sharon kissed the patrons with a fierce, passionate embrace of lyrics and music, a chill crept up Romeo's spine. *". . . If you want my lovin', if you really do . . . don't be afraid, baby, just ask me. . . ."* Not since Aretha Franklin had Romeo heard that song sung with so much energy and passion.

"Damn, that girl can sing," he said out loud, agreement echoing across everyone else's face. *I'm going to have to make her a featured performer and hire a new waitress,* he thought to himself, the business potential racing through his mind.

As if reading his thoughts, Malcolm spoke the words aloud. "We need to rethink her position," he said, meeting his friend's stare. "That girl's a gold mine!"

Fingers tapped easily along tabletops, as toes rapped across the floor. The music felt good, bringing people to their feet to swing wide hips, gyrate pelvises, and snap their fingers to the beat. Romeo scanned the smiling faces, heads bopping from side to side, then nodded in Sharon's direction. From where she stood on stage, she could see that he and Malcolm were pleased and so she sang for them both, a wide grin spreading across her face. *". . . I love you, I love you, I love you, baby, I love you. . . ."*

A love song was playing on the radio, the lyrics chanted over and over as Justin or Chris or whoever was singing was trying to drive home the point that the woman he was singing to, or about, had his heart. Taryn rolled her eyes skyward, a gasp of exasperation blowing past her lips.

It had been a long day and she was exhausted and in

less than six hours she had to be on an airplane headed to Paris. She was trying to run down the list of everything she had to do in her head, but she was distracted, her thoughts on something and someone else. She blew another sigh.

Roberta had worked her last nerve, the woman suddenly obsessed with hooking her up with Romeo Marshall. Every other sentence out of her friend's mouth had been about the man until Taryn had had enough. She thought back to the conversation.

"Is that why you left me stranded at the club with your boyfriend?" Taryn had asked.

Roberta sneered. "He's not my boyfriend. Never was. And I didn't leave you stranded! I really had to go home!" she'd exclaimed.

"But you were hoping I'd hook up with him?"

Roberta had shrugged. "Would that have been a bad thing?"

"I don't think it would be a good thing."

"Why not? Romeo's a great guy. I consider you both friends and I think you'd be a great couple. I want to see my friends happy."

"Well, your boyfriend didn't even bother to look in my direction," Taryn said matter-of-factly. "He was too busy looking in every other woman's direction."

Shaking her head, Taryn could only listen as Roberta extolled Romeo's merits one more time. Once the conversation was over, Taryn couldn't get the man out of her head, and it was really starting to irritate her because she had more important things to be thinking about. And on the radio some crooner was singing about how much he loved his woman.

Taryn turned off Duraleigh Road and pulled her Mercedes into the parking lot of the Harris Teeter shopping center. Shutting down the engine, she heaved one last sigh, determined to get her head back on track. She took a quick glance down to her watch. It was late but she hoped they hadn't yet taken down the salad bar. There wasn't an ounce of food in her refrigerator at home and she wanted something to eat that didn't have to do with her ordering at the drive-through window at McDonald's.

Once inside, Taryn wasn't surprised to discover she was hours too late. The late night produce clerk, a long, lean drink of chocolate with dreads down to his shoulders, apologized profusely, but he eagerly made suggestions, sharing a host of his quick and easy favorite recipes. His enthusiasm made her smile as he flirted shamelessly.

"I could come cook for you when I get off," the young man said, his eyes narrowed as he studied her intently. "I'm a great cook."

Taryn laughed, the gesture easing the stress she'd been feeling. "I appreciate the offer, but I don't think that's a good idea."

"Why not, ma?"

She shook her head. "How old are you?"

"Age ain't nothin' but a number, beautiful. In fact, I'm writing a book about relationships between older women and younger men. How it's all about the physical and emotional connection and nothing at all to do with the age difference between them."

Taryn laughed out loud. "Sounds intriguing, but the answer is still no. Besides," she said, with a flip of her hand, "I'm not *that* much older than you are."

The young man laughed as well, tossing her a quick wink. "Well, if you change your mind you know where to find me," he said as he proceeded to unpack a box of fresh spinach, loading it onto the cold shelf.

Nodding her appreciation, Taryn headed in the opposite direction and the frozen food section. Clearly, dinner was going to be gourmet microwave in a box. As she stood in front of the freezer door debating between the meat loaf and the chicken tetrazzini, she didn't see the man who'd turned into the aisle from the other direction. But Romeo Marshall saw her.

Romeo had left the club earlier than normal. It had been a slow night, affording him the opportunity to head home for some much needed sleep. Also in need of a loaf of bread and a bag of potato chips, he had headed to the late night supermarket.

He stood eyeing her rear view. She was dressed in a form-fitting gold-toned silk suit. The designer jacket was fitted, cinching slightly at the waist, and the pants tapered to a flattering length at her ankles. She stood on five-inch, red-bottomed heels. Her hair was pulled up into a loose chignon atop her head, and for the first time he noted the small tattoo that decorated the back of her neck. She suddenly pulled open the freezer door and bent forward, leaning inside as she reached for something on the bottom shelf. Her lush backside reminded him of two nicely sized melons filling her slacks. A smile pulled wide and full across his face.

As she stood back up, reading the back of a food container, he moved to her side, clearing his throat to announce his presence. Taryn jumped, suddenly startled as she turned toward him. As she met his gaze he licked his lips ever so slightly, the gesture salacious and teasing without any effort on his part. She gasped, her eyes widening in surprise.

"Well, hello," Romeo said, his deep tone a loud whisper.

"Hi," Taryn answered, her gaze dancing swiftly over the space he filled.

He extended his hand toward her. "Romeo Marshall. I don't know if you remember me or not, but we met the other night when you were at the club with my friend Roberta."

She nodded. "Actually, we didn't meet. Not officially. But I know who you are."

Romeo nodded slightly as he acknowledged her comment. He took a deep breath, holding it for a brief moment. "You're right, we weren't properly introduced, which is why I wanted to say hello and introduce myself," he said, still waiting for her to shake his hand.

Taryn finally eased her fingers against his, watching as they disappeared beneath his firm touch. A wave of heat suddenly coursed up her spine and she felt the air catch in her chest. "Taryn. Taryn Williams," she muttered, fighting to catch her breath.

Romeo smiled, light shimmering in his dark eyes. "It's nice to meet you, Taryn Williams. Officially, this time."

There was an awkward pause as the two stood staring at each other. It was unusually quiet, the store practically empty in the late night hour. The hum of the cooler units behind them was a low, dull drone that seemed to amplify the uncomfortable silence wafting between them.

Taryn took another deep breath, finally speaking first. "Well, I need to be going. It was nice meeting you too, Mr. Marshall."

Romeo smiled. "I hope we run into each other again. Or maybe you'll stop by the Playground sometime soon?"

She nodded. "Maybe," she said, her soft voice an easy lull in the space. "I'm sure I will."

Romeo nodded. "Good. I look forward to seeing you again. Well, have a good night," he said as he eased past her and moved down the aisle. He tossed her one last look over his shoulder, his smile still brightening his face.

As he disappeared from sight Taryn released the breath she'd been holding. She leaned back against the freezer doors, her knees suddenly quivering with excitement. She felt like a teenager facing her high school crush for the first time. The sensation surprised and unnerved her. She took a deep breath and then a second to stall the emotion sweeping over her. When her nerves were calmed she headed toward the register.

Romeo stood in the parking lot, pacing back and forth behind his car. The space was dark save the faint light emanating out of the store and the three light poles spaced sparsely apart in the lot. He glanced down to the Rolex on his wrist. It was after eleven and he should have just headed home, but something about the encounter with Taryn was holding him hostage. He leaned back against the trunk of his car, folding his hands in front of himself.

The woman was stunning, and truth be told he was slightly intimidated. He was used to women fawning over him, their not-so-subtle messages allowing him full control of his romantic situations. Taryn hadn't fawned. In fact, she'd seemed almost indifferent, and that had thrown him off his game. He felt like he'd fumbled their first meeting despite trying to appear calm, cool, and collected.

Just as he was replaying the encounter over again in his head, Taryn exited the building. Romeo drew his body upright. He adjusted his suit jacket, buttoning it around his torso as he stepped toward her. As he approached, the beautiful woman came to a sudden stop, surprised to still find him there. She tossed a look over her shoulder and around the parking lot, seeming to collect her bearings, in case she needed to make a quick exit. The gesture made him chuckle ever so softly. He called her name, the hint of a question punctuating each syllable.

"Mr. Marshall, hello again," she said, curiosity sweeping between them. "Is something wrong?"

He shook his head. "No, nothing's wrong. I was just wondering if you might be interested in getting a drink with me. Unless you have a husband or boyfriend you need to get home to?" He shifted his weight from side to side.

Taryn eyed him curiously, then swept her gaze across the parking lot behind him as she pondered his question. She shifted her eyes back to his. "I appreciate the invitation but unfortunately I can't. I'm sorry."

He nodded. "Maybe we can get together for coffee tomorrow? Or I'd love to buy you lunch. Or dinner."

She shook her head. "No. I don't think so. . . ." she started.

Romeo's head continued to bob up and down. "Hey, don't worry about it," he said abruptly, cutting her off. "I just thought I'd ask. You don't know me and I didn't mean to make you uncomfortable." He paused, taking a deep breath before finishing. "Have a good night, Ms. Williams." He turned, spinning around in his black leather shoes.

He'd made it back to his car when Taryn called his name, moving behind him.

"Yes?"

"I leave for Paris on business in a few hours and I'm not even packed yet. Otherwise, I would have loved to go get a drink with you. And I won't be returning until Saturday, so there's no way I can plan to see you tomorrow. But if you're still interested I'd love to get a cup of coffee with you when I get back," she said.

Romeo felt himself grinning broadly. "Oh. Okay. Great. It's a date."

Taryn smiled, the wealth of it shimmering in her eyes. "No, it's just coffee," she said, a low chuckle easing past her lips.

Romeo's smile widened. "Just call me at the club when you get back, if that works for you. We can firm up our plans then."

She nodded. "That works. And please, call me Taryn. Ms. Williams was my mother."

"As long as you call me Romeo."

Spinning on her high heels, Taryn eased her way to her own vehicle. She tossed her grocery bag into the passenger seat and eased inside. As she pulled out of the parking lot, Romeo was still staring after her.

Five

As Malcolm wiped down the bar, one couple sat huddled in the corner, their long limbs entwined together. Piano Man and Sharon had just finished the last set together and now sat at the end of the bar entertained by Odetta and the tale of one of her last escapades. The crowd had dwindled down to just a few. As tired bodies made their way out of the club, the rest of the band packed up their instruments to go search for an after-hours joint to play until sunrise.

Turning up the lights, Romeo knocked gently on the small wooden table, disrupting the young couple from their embrace. "Time to take it home, people. Bar's closed."

The young woman looked up, only slightly embarrassed, then smiled when she recognized Romeo "Can't fault a girl for having a good time now, can you, Mr. Romeo?" she slurred sloppily, clearly intoxicated.

"Not at all, Miss Carmen. But it's time you go have your good time at home."

The young man rose to his feet, grinning. Two gold-capped teeth gleamed under the bright lights, casting an eerie glow across his lips. Extending his hand, he clasped Romeo's in a weak handshake. "Sorry about that, partner. But you know how it be sometimes." He chuckled, holding his suit jacket over his shoulder and the girl under his arm.

"Let's go, Lloyd," the girl whined. "I wanna go home. I'se got something I wanna show you!"

"Who's driving?" Romeo asked.

"I am. Don't you worry," the man named Lloyd responded, tugging at the twisting of braids that graced the girl's head. "I'll make sure my baby gets home safe and sound."

Romeo nodded, escorting them both to the door. Giving the restrooms one last check, Romeo locked the door behind them, then twisted the kink out of his neck, turning his head back and forth. A slight yawn passed over his lips as he stretched his arms up toward the ceiling. "I'm getting too damn old for this," he muttered.

"Never too old for a good time," Odetta responded. "You either gets better at doing it or you just gets better at pretending to do it."

"From what I hear," Piano Man said, "Romeo ain't got no problems doing it. It's working so hard that's kicking his butt."

Romeo laughed. "And who have you been listening to, old man?"

"Young gals today don't do nothing but talk. All you got to do is sit where I sit every night and watch them pretty little things whispering after you every time you moves."

"Yes, sir," Odetta agreed. "Women do love them some Romeo," she said, a hint of sarcasm in her tone.

Shaking his head, Romeo ignored them, visibly embarrassed. Malcolm had closed out the cash register and was passing the money bag to Romeo. Romeo pushed the contents back into the man's hands. "Yo, brother, do me a favor and you drop it off in the night depository on your way home, please?"

"No problem, Romeo," he responded, placing the bag and his jacket on top of the bar. Pouring himself a glass of tonic, he leaned across the polished wood.

"This was some night tonight. You were on the money, Sharon," Malcolm said.

"Thank you," she responded, a rush of color rising in her cheeks. "And thank you, Mr. Marshall, for covering some of my tables for me. I didn't mean to sing so long."

"Sharon, it was my pleasure," Romeo said. "In fact, I think you and I need to sit down and talk about you singing full-time. You're wasting your gift and I guess I can't allow that to happen."

Sharon looked from Romeo to Piano Man and back. Each was smiling at her brightly, delighted by her reaction.

"I just couldn't," she sputtered, tears forming in her eyes.

"Well, it pays more money, but if you're not interested I'll understand," Romeo said, laughing.

"No, no," Sharon gasped. "I do, but . . ." she stammered, looking toward Odetta.

"Romeo, I don't know what we're going to do with this child. She's enough to drive you crazy." Odetta giggled, hugging Sharon warmly. "Honey, you better go on and say yes. Romeo won't ask twice, and between you and me, you're a hell of a lot better at singing than you are at waiting tables. Besides, when you sing, I get bigger tips. You get these folks happy and they start pulling money out of their pockets like crazy!"

Hugging both of them, Sharon shook her head yes,

her expression glowing as a faint trickle of a tear dripped onto her cheek.

"Good. I'll need you to come over tomorrow, say around one o'clock, and we'll hammer out the details. Okay?"

"Yes, sir," Sharon responded.

"And, Odetta, I guess you better come too so that we can talk about hiring another waitress, maybe even two."

"One's enough. You start cutting into my extra spending money when you start hiring too many waitresses around here."

Romeo nodded. "In fact, Piano Man, I'd appreciate it if you came by also. I know it's Sunday, but I'd like to get some promotional photos done if we can. That would probably be a good time to get all of our staff business done and out of the way."

Piano Man shrugged. "Yeah, I guess."

"You people have worn me out," Malcolm said, pulling on his coat. "Sharon, do you need a ride home?"

"Thanks, Malcolm. I'd really appreciate it," she answered.

"What about you, Odetta?" he asked.

"Thanks, sweetie. Do you mind dropping me off at Keith's place? He said he was going to wait up for me." Rolling her large hips and winking an eye, Odetta purred, "I promised him a late night snack."

"You keep feeding that man all your sweet stuff, Odetta, and he gon' drop dead from suga'," Piano Man said with a laugh.

"Just never you mind," she said. She kissed Piano Man lightly on the cheek. "This woman knows how to take good care of her man. Would take care of you too if you weren't so old."

Piano Man laughed some more, squeezing Odetta

close. "Don't let my being old fool you, woman. I still knows how to do the doing when it needs to be done now."

Shaking her head, she swatted her hand at him. "Ohhhh. You too fresh!"

The two women followed Malcolm out the door. "Good night, everybody," Sharon called out over her shoulder.

"See you tomorrow," Malcolm and Odetta echoed.

"Good night," Romeo and Piano Man called after them.

Romeo bolted the heavy wooden door, then pushed in the last empty chair.

"So, old man. How's that advance holding out?" he asked. It had been a few weeks since he'd first placed some money in the man's hands.

Piano Man grunted, pulling his hands through the wool of his hair. "I ain't decided whether or not I'm staying yet."

"You got somewhere else to go?"

"Maybe. Ain't decided. Been a long time since I was in N'Orleans. Might go to N'Orleans. It ain't too hot yet."

Romeo laughed softly. "It's been a long time since I was in New Orleans myself."

Piano Man came to his feet. "I'll let you know when you owes me mo' money."

Romeo smiled, nodding his head. "Do you need a ride home?"

"Ain't goin' home. The boys going over to Amber House to play. I told 'em I'd catch up to 'em when I was finished here." He paused, inhaling deeply. His gaze flickered over Romeo's face, then settled on a spot behind the younger man's shoulders. Piano Man fidgeted with nervous energy, his mouth opening and closing as he debated whether or not to speak. Romeo eyed him curiously as the man finally continued. "You wanna come with me? The liquor is cheap and the music gon' be good. Or does you got a woman expecting you home?"

Romeo looked down at the watch on his wrist. For some reason he found himself thinking of Taryn Williams again. He had half expected to hear from her, but the Saturday had come and gone with nothing from her at all. "No," he finally said. "There's no one home waiting for me."

Piano Man headed for the door. "Come on then. They should be warming up right 'bouts now."

Romeo stared after the old man just briefly before nodding his assent. He took one last look back over his shoulder to make sure all the lights were off. Following Piano Man out the rear entrance, he closed and locked the door behind them.

It had been some time since Romeo had last set foot in Amber House. The small after-hours club boasted a regular clientele of party lovers who needed to explore the dangerous side of midnight and find themselves perched on a bar stool when the sun rose. Booze flowed freely, there was always a band storming, the patrons were soaked with sweat, and the dance floor was jammed tight with one body too many.

Draping his coat across the back of an old wooden chair, he blew a kiss in the direction of Aleta Bowen, the club's owner. A long time friend of his mother's, Aleta had welcomed his return home with open arms. She'd been as supportive of his endeavors as his mother would have been, and had welcomed the opportunity to teach him what she knew about the business. Aleta had always regarded him as her own and would often mother him when he needed it the most. Romeo had the highest respect for her.

The petite woman, who looked barely half her age, smiled at him warmly, making her way over to his side. "Hey, baby boy! Where have you been? Long time since I last saw you," she exclaimed, grasping his hands firmly between her own as she placed a wet kiss against his cheek.

"I had to come check out the competition, Aunt Aleta," he said, smiling back at her.

She laughed, her umber-toned complexion rippling under a fine layer of makeup that attempted to hide the few lines of age that graced her face. "Didn't know my place was in your league. From what I hear, the Playground has gone big time."

Romeo laughed with her. "Don't believe everything you hear!"

"What can I bring you, darling?"

Romeo sat down in the chair behind him. "Scotch. Please."

Aleta nodded, racing to get him an unopened bottle of Chivas Regal and an empty glass. Returning, she set it on the table before him. "It's on the house tonight. I owe you."

Romeo raised his eyebrows, rising to pull out a chair for the older woman to sit down on.

"What could you possibly owe me for, Aunt Aleta?"

She nodded toward the front of the club where Piano Man and his associates had gathered with their instruments. "Piano Man's back in circulation. Word on the street is that you brought him back," she said as she took her seat.

Romeo shrugged. "I can't take credit for that."

Aleta filled his glass. "Well, my business always picks up when he plays and he's not played for a real long time. It's nice to have him back no matter who had a hand in it."

"Do you know him well?"

Aleta grinned. "I know him real well. I thought about marrying him once."

Romeo looked up, mildly stunned, as Aleta smiled warmly in Piano Man's direction.

"Don't look so shocked. I used to be a real looker, and Piano Man was a good catch for a woman back in the day."

"I don't doubt that. And you're still a good-looking woman."

Aleta laughed, brushing her palm against the back of his hand. "Your mama sure raised you right, boy."

"So what happened? Why didn't you marry him?"

A wistful look crossed her face as she responded. "His heart was somewhere else and we both knew it." She smiled, changing the subject. "So, what's going on with you? Are you still chasing after some no good woman?"

Romeo paused for a moment. Women had never been a problem for him. They fell into his path the way the leaves fell from the trees during the autumn, and Romeo, true to his name, had played like most boys who find a pile of leaves at their feet. But things were changing. Romeo no longer had any interest in the one-night relationships that once fueled his spirit. But if pressed, he didn't know if he could tell anyone what it was he did want.

Romeo suddenly thought again about the woman whose phone call he had spent half the day hoping for. He hadn't bothered to ask for her number, just in case, and he was still kicking himself. He'd thought about calling Roberta for the information but had changed his mind, not wanting his old friend in his business like that. But the prospect of knowing more about Taryn Williams intrigued him. As he pondered the possibilities, the longings of loneliness pulled at the muscles in his chest. He inhaled deeply, then smiled as a little white lie fell past his full lips. "No, ma'am. I'm not chasing after any woman. I don't have the time or the energy."

Aleta gave him a long look, studying him intently. There was no missing the expression that crossed his face. "It's your lie, baby, tell it anyway you want," she said with a soft chuckle.

Romeo shook his head from side to side, his grin wide and full. "Honest, Aunt Aleta. I've changed my wanton ways!"

Aleta nodded. "Then whoever she is, she must be very special."

Romeo's gaze locked with hers and held. He blew a heavy breath as he shrugged. He didn't bother to respond.

Aleta rose from her seat, one of her staff calling for her attention. "Well, you enjoy yourself and I'll catch up with you before you leave."

Romeo rose to his feet, leaning to kiss her cheek one last time. "Yes, ma'am. I know I'll have a good time. This is my second home, remember?"

They both chuckled. "Well, come see me more often then," Aleta said as she sauntered away, adding, "I've missed you."

Romeo finally gave in to the music and the drink. It had been a long day and he was exhausted, his body worn. He watched as Piano Man pushed his own over-tired bones past the point of no return. The man's fingers had been parading up and down the ivory steps for hours, and Romeo marveled at his ability to still be able to play as brilliantly as he did.

When the band finally rested, packing up their instruments one last time, Romeo was relieved for them, knowing that Piano Man needed the break whether he wanted to admit it or not. He watched as Piano Man strolled over to Aleta's side, wrapping his arms around her in a large bear hug. They whispered together only briefly before she filled a tall glass with ice and water, pressing it into his hands.

Sitting up straight as the elderly figure made his way to the table, Romeo said, "Nice set. You guys play well together."

Piano Man nodded his gray head. "Thank you." He lifted the tall glass to his lips and drank, draining the glass dry. "Ahhh . . . playing makes me thirsty."

"I'm surprised you're not drinking scotch."

Piano Man nodded in Aleta's direction. "She won't let me drink here. Says I'm an alcoholic. Says she won't be contributing to my disease."

"Are you an alcoholic?"

"Aren't you?"

Romeo paused, not sure if he should respond. When no words fell from his mouth, he figured it best not to answer at all. They sat in silence, taking in the motion of all the people around them. The moment was awkward as Romeo rolled his nearly empty glass between the palms of his hands.

Piano Man finally broke the silence. "So how long you been knowing Aleta?"

"Since I was in diapers. She and my mother were best friends and we've always been close. After my mother died, she sort of filled in that empty spot."

Piano Man wiped at his mouth with the back of his hand, then reached for the bottle of scotch on the table, filling his glass half full. He glanced quickly over his right shoulder before pulling the glass to his chapped lips. Romeo drained the last of his own drink, the two men swallowing in unison.

"She's a fine woman. Tried to get her to marry me once, but she wouldn't have none of it. She gave me my walking papers, put my black behind on a bus, and changed her phone number." Piano Man chuckled. "Couldn't blame her none though."

"Have you ever been married?"

"Once."

"Any kids?"

Piano Man paused, filling his glass again. "Not by my wife. My wife couldn't have no babies. It's a good thing too, 'cause Beulah was sure 'nuff ugly." He chuckled softly. "And she was mean as spit. Ugly and mean ain't a good combination for nobody's mama."

Romeo laughed. "Why did you marry her?" he asked.

"Beulah had a good heart when she wanted to and she could cook up a storm. Made the best biscuits and red-eyed gravy I ever tasted. And she never once give me no lip 'bout my comings and goings. Lord knows I did that woman wrong more times than not, and she never once said a word. Besides, a man don't like going lonely all the time. It was nice to wake up to a warm body in my bed."

Romeo nodded his head knowingly. "So, what happened to Beulah?"

"She left me for a man who told her she was pretty. Just packed her bags one day and disappeared. No good-bye, no nothing."

"Sounds like you deserved it though."

"Yeah, I had it coming. Can't expect no woman to put up with but so much garbage. I don't care what you think you got going for you, if you don't show a woman how you feel about her, she gonna pack her bags one day and leave." Piano Man bobbed his graying head up and down as he continued. "They also get a bit testy when you cheating on 'em too. Women can be sensitive about the damnedest things."

Romeo laughed. "Don't I know that!"

"Now, I know you ain't rocking no more than one bedpost, is you? You ain't that stupid, boy."

"Not at the moment, but I was known to juggle more than one woman a long, long time ago, when sex was safe and love was free. At least until I got caught, that is."

"Yeah, that getting caught can be a bitch." Piano Man swallowed the last of the bitter fluid in his glass. Wiping his mouth one last time, he rose to his feet, pulling at the oversized slacks falling about his lean hips.

"I needs me some sleep if I'm gonna get anything done today."

Romeo came to his feet also, pushing his chair up to the table. "I'll give you a ride."

Piano Man shook his head no. "I needs to walk. Need me some fresh air. Sleeps better that way. Thank you anyway."

Romeo nodded. "Well, I'm out of here then. I will see you later." Stopping to hug Aleta one last time, Romeo pulled his overcoat about his body and headed out the door.

As the large wooden door closed behind both of them, Piano Man stared off into the distance. After buttoning his jacket, he pushed his hands deep into his pockets, lowered his head, and strolled slowly down the unlit, empty street. Behind him, a full moon peeked out shyly from the veil of a billowy gray cloud, the gossamer formation gliding across the dark sky.

Six

It was a short ride from Amber House to Romeo's Olde Raleigh home. Romeo pulled his black Jaguar F-Type coupe past the gated entrance into the complex of designer houses. A quick ride toward the northern cul-de-sac placed him at his front door.

He smiled slightly; he always smiled when he came home. It had taken a number of years for him to be able to afford the luxury property with its intricate blend of simplicity and strength. Romeo had been drawn to the house's powerful architecture the moment the real estate agent had pulled up out front. Closing the front door behind him, he quickly punched in the six-digit code canceling the security system.

He hurt. His firm body wept for sleep. Pressing the palm of his hand over his mouth to suppress a yawn, he pulled his long limbs up the flight of steps to his bedroom. After carefully hanging his clothes in the walk-in closet, he threw his brief-clad body across the length of the king-size bed, settling himself into the folds of cotton sheets and cashmere blankets. Despite the fatigue that permeated his person, sleep eluded him.

Tossing from side to side, his dark eyes danced with the shadows cavorting along the ceiling and walls.

He suddenly wondered what it might be like to have a woman like Taryn there to ease the loneliness coating his brow. He found himself fantasizing about them falling to the living room floor, tearing the clothes away from each other's body. Moving to the melodious tunes of Anthony Hamilton, he pressed himself into her, molding her softness around his own chiseled frame. Taryn's rich caramel would coat his taste buds, its sweetness sliding easily down his throat. He imagined it would be better than good and now his loins throbbed as he dreamt about what he might be missing. He sighed heavily.

Rising, he switched on the light by the nightstand, flooding the room with cool white rays. Reaching into the nightstand, he pulled a small leather flask from the back corner and brought it to his lips. The bitter liquid fell into his dry mouth, coating the back of his throat. Thoughts of Piano Man knocked at the door of his mind, rudely pushing their way inside.

The old man had asked him if he was an alcoholic. He grimaced slightly, twisting the cap of the flask tightly. He suddenly wondered why no answer had fallen from his lips as easily as the warm liquor now slid down his throat. He didn't believe himself to be an alcoholic, although he knew there were times when he'd abuse the drink to ease a long day or to erase an emotion threatening to possess his spirit. He didn't thrive on booze though, nor did he need it to get him through his daily routines. "No," he thought aloud, emphatically shaking his head. "I am not an alcoholic. I just drink too much."

Making his way to the other side of the room, he settled himself down in the oversized easy chair, lifting his long, dark legs up on the matching ottoman. He had worked closely with an interior designer to weave the luminescent mesh of celery, cactus, and eucalyptus, which adorned each room. The colors, complemented by a hint of eggplant, a dash of ivory, and a touch of muted golds, were surreal and soft, reminding him of the California shore at low tide under a setting sun. He stared about the space. He was most comfortable in this room. He thrived on how it invited him to simply lounge and sprawl lazily about.

Stretching his body upward, Romeo lifted his arms above his head, pulling his torso toward the ceiling. He yawned, expelling warm breath outward. "Damn," he said aloud, "why can't I sleep?"

On the mantel above the fireplace a picture of his mother, looking warmly toward a camera, smiled down at him. Romeo missed his mother. He had been a true mama's boy, everything about his life intent on pleasing her. Her death had come quickly, the dark angel sneaking in like a common criminal to steal her away. His mother had been an intense woman who'd been devoured by her own loneliness. As dementia usurped her mind, the dark spirits of a bitter past had paraded brazenly in, consuming her. No amount of effort on Romeo's part could pull her above and beyond it.

As a young boy, he had watched her struggle alone on a daily basis to ensure that not only were his basic needs met, but that the man he grew to be was one she could be proud of. There had been no limits to her love or the swift slaps across his rear end to keep him in line when like most boys he would test the waters and push the boundaries set for him. There had been no woman in all his thirty-five years who had inspired him the way his mother had. And no woman whom he'd been willing to let into his heart, allowing himself to feel any emotion like the emotion he'd felt for his mother.

He sighed, turning his body slightly in the chair. He hoped to hear from Taryn soon, he thought to himself, the promises between them abundant if he allowed them to be.

Reflecting on his long day, his thoughts turned back to the aged black man. Romeo found his reflections about the old man nagging, sweeping through his spirit like an unwanted virus. Rising again, he turned off the light and lay back across the massive bed. Minutes later he imagined the tinkling of piano keys stroking the tightness across his temples and he breathed easier, the warm darkness comforting as sleep finally possessed him, an easy exhale of blues wafting through his dreams.

On the other side of town, Piano Man took the length of steps one at a time, his left leg dragging heavily behind his right. At the entrance of his room, he eased himself slowly inside, noisily closing the heavy wooden door behind him. The one light on the corner table was brightly lit. The bed was turned down invitingly. He grinned, chortling lightly to himself.

Miss Hazel, the woman who owned the boardinghouse, was going out of her way to make him feel at home. He chuckled again. He liked Miss Hazel. She was a round, busty woman, warm and soft like freshly mixed biscuit dough ready for kneading. As he'd gotten older, Piano Man found himself drawn to robust women with healthy chests to cradle his head against. Miss Hazel's only flaw, as far as Piano Man was concerned, was the ugly black poodle that followed her about from room to room. The animal reeked of dog smell, a rancid mixture of wet fur, urine, and garden dirt. Whenever Miss Hazel wasn't looking and the stench came within kicking distance, Piano Man would give it a swift shove with his foot.

Kicking the black loafers from his feet, he sat himself easily on the edge of the bed. "Should take my clothes off," he thought out loud, quickly dismissing the notion as he lay back, pulling the covers up under his chin.

He focused his attention on thoughts of Romeo. The young man had seemed content to spend the evening with him, and for more reasons than he had time to count, Piano Man was pleased. He was a fine young man, Romeo was. Any man would have been proud to claim him as his son, Piano Man thought. He sighed, his hot breath warming the air in front of his face.

Lifting himself upward, he reached for the small digital radio that sat on the nightstand. He pushed buttons until the local college station came in clear. The disc jockey was paying tribute to women blues singers, and Piano Man smiled as Rosetta Perry was crying about losing her mind over a man who'd done her wrong. As he lay back, listening to her woes, he could see the piano keys dancing beneath his fingers, the eighty-eight keys bending to his will. If he could have, he would have told her that there was nothing for her to worry about as long as she had the music and let the music have her. When Rosetta was done, the music was interrupted by a commercial for a local Toyota dealership, a man named Marc Jacobs loudly proclaiming to have the best prices in town.

Piano Man's mind raced, his thoughts fragmented. "I've got too much to do and not much time to do it in," he said to no one, just wanting to hear his own voice as it echoed against the cream-colored wall.

Reaching for the clock on the nightstand, he set the alarm for nine-thirty. Switching off the light, he rolled over onto his side and quickly fell into a deep sleep, the faint hint of light outside caressing his cheek, and Billie Holiday whispering in his ear, proclaiming her right to sing the blues.

Taryn rolled over onto her back. Her eyes fluttered open and then closed as she slowly pulled herself out of a restful slumber. She hummed softly, a low guttural purr that rose from deep in her midsection. She stretched her arms up and her legs out. She finally opened her eyes wide and stared around her bedroom. Bright sunshine was shimmering through the window blinds, warm light filling the space. The air was heated, and with the bright blue skies outside, she imagined it was going to be a beautiful day.

Taryn stretched her body one last time before pulling herself up, throwing her legs off the mattress. Rising onto her feet, she moved into the bathroom, her bladder full. After she'd relieved herself she washed her hands and face and brushed her teeth. Staring at her reflection in the mirror, she smiled.

She had rested well, her brief bout with jet lag gone. Her flight home had been uneventful, a pleasant end to a trip that had been long and arduous. The plane had landed in the early afternoon, and by the time she'd made her way from the Raleigh-Durham International Airport to her home, she'd fallen out from exhaustion.

Moving back into the bedroom, she picked up her cell phone and checked for messages. Finding none, she blew a low sigh. She took a fortifying breath and dialed, waiting anxiously until it was answered on the other end.

"Hello?"

"Hey, Roberta, it's me. Did I catch you at a bad time?" Taryn questioned.

She sensed her friend shaking her head. "Not at all. We just finished breakfast. The husband's out in the garage tinkering on his car and I was just about to crawl back into bed to get a quick nap while the baby's sleeping. What's up?"

Taryn took a deep breath. "Do you have Romeo Marshall's telephone number?"

Her friend squealed. "You want Romeo's phone number?"

"I ran into him before I left and promised I'd call when I got back to meet him for coffee. I'd call the club, but I know they're closed today. I figured if you had a house or cell number . . ." Her voice trailed. She took another deep breath.

Roberta laughed. "That's my girl! Hold on a minute."

Taryn heard her drop the phone, her footsteps echoing in her ear. Minutes later Roberta returned, breathing heavily. "Had to find my old phone book." Her voice dropped to a whisper. "You know I had to hide it when I got married."

Taryn laughed.

"You better be glad I did," Roberta said, as the seven-digit number rolled off her tongue. "That's the last number I had for him, but he's got an old-school spirit. He hasn't changed his number. It's the same one he's probably had since he got his first phone," she said with a warm giggle.

"Thank you, I really appreciate it," Taryn said. "I'll catch up with you later."

"You better! I want to know every detail."

Taryn shook her head. "Bye, Roberta!"

After disconnecting the line, Taryn tossed her phone

onto the mattress beside her. She slid her body back beneath the bed sheets, pulling them up around her shoulders. She was second-guessing herself. She'd spent the last week thinking about Romeo Marshall, even going so far as to call in a few favors for a background check on the man. Discovering his record was clean and pretty impressive had alleviated many of her concerns.

Granted, going to such an extreme had been excessive, but Taryn had reached a point in her life where she wasn't willing to invest energy in a man just to discover the relationship had never had a chance of going anywhere. That, and she didn't like surprises. She hated the thought of giving herself to a man to then learn after the fact that he had demons and secrets that she should have been made aware of from the start. She had learned to approach her romantic life much like she approached business, cautiously and well informed.

Taryn had found herself assessing her risks after Romeo's invitation. She had always been efficient at analyzing the pros and cons of every situation and this one was no different. She could have ignored Romeo's invitation, but being honest with herself, that wasn't what she wanted to do. She could wait to call Romeo at the club, but she didn't want to wait. He excited her and she wanted to see how far those feelings might go. But she also wanted to claim control, so calling him on her terms and not his was significant to her. Taking risks and putting herself out there had always been second nature in every aspect of her life—except where her personal relationships were concerned. But after much consideration Taryn had promised herself that was going to change. If she was going to play with fire she was going to make sure she didn't get burned.

And where Romeo Marshall was concerned, she would start by being the pursuer and not the pursued.

The house phone ringing pulled Romeo out of a deep sleep. The shrill chime surprised him since he couldn't remember the last time the device had rung. He grappled with the items strewn across the nightstand, following the sound as the phone continued to ring. Finally grasping the receiver, he pulled it to his ear, mumbling into the mouthpiece.

"Yeah? Hello?"

"Romeo, Taryn Williams. Did I wake you?"

Romeo suddenly sat upright, swiping at his eyes with the back of his hand. "No . . . um, yeah . . . no, it's not a problem. Good morning," he said finally, shifting the phone from one ear to the other.

Taryn laughed softly. "Good morning. I didn't mean to wake you. I actually thought that in your line of work you'd be headed to church to confess your sins," she teased.

Romeo laughed. "God knows my heart. I think he'll give me a pass."

She smiled. "Interesting," she murmured softly.

"It really isn't. So, to what do I owe the honor?" he asked.

"I'm just calling as I promised I would. I was hoping you're still interested in having that cup of coffee."

He nodded into the receiver. "I am. Most definitely."

"Do you have some time today?"

Romeo hesitated momentarily, remembering what he had to do. "I have to take care of some business at the Playground, but I'm available right after. I can pick you up."

"That works for me. But I'll meet you at the club."

"I'll be there at one o'clock," Romeo said. "What I have to do won't take long and we can go from there."

"I look forward to it," Taryn said. "Try to go back to sleep," she added, giggling as she disconnected the call.

Romeo's smile was miles wide. Still holding the receiver to his ear, he couldn't help but wonder where she'd gotten his number.

Piano Man draped his oversized blazer onto the back of the kitchen chair. Dropping onto a padded, floral-printed seat, he lifted a steaming cup of coffee to his puckered lips, sipping noisily. Pulling the morning paper close to his chest, he leafed through briefly until he came to page six and the obituary column. Across the way, Miss Hazel was happily flipping pancakes, tossing them onto a warm plate already piled high with sausage. The ugly black poodle sniffed anxiously at her feet, hoping that a morning treat might drop to the floor.

"You ain't get much sleep last night, did you?" Miss Hazel asked, smiling.

"Don't needs much."

"Uh-huh." She continued, grinning broadly. "I ain't never understood men like you who stay in the streets all night. Can't see what the attraction is."

Piano Man shrugged, twisting the edges of his mouth into a bogus smile. "Well, a sweet woman like you shouldn't be worrying her pretty head over no men like me. We ain't good enough for a fine woman like you, Miss Hazel."

Miss Hazel giggled. "Hush your mouth now and eat up some of this here food."

"I just want to read the obituaries first," Piano Man replied, scanning the list of names of the recently departed. "I looks for my name. If my name ain't here, then I knows I can go on to work." He tossed her a quick wink.

Miss Hazel chuckled again. "You too silly, Mr. Burdett."

Piano Man placed the newspaper back down on the table, reaching for a pancake.

"Now, you needs to eat more than that," Miss Hazel exclaimed, resting her hands on her broad hips. "You needs to fill out some, especially if you gon' run them streets like you do."

Piano Man smiled again. "Now, you're gonna spoil me with all this attention."

Miss Hazel sucked her teeth, flipping her hand at him. Settling into the seat beside him, she speared four more pancakes with her fork and placed them on his plate. After laying a chain link of honey-glazed sausage alongside the fluffy rings of buttermilk dough, she filled her own plate with what was left and proceeded to eat. Piano Man watched with amusement as she ate heartily, stopping every so often to lick the syrup from her fingers.

Inhaling one-third of the pancakes and two sausages, Piano Man finished off his morning meal with the last drop of coffee that had settled in the bottom of the chipped porcelain cup. Wiping his mouth and chin with a yellow paper napkin, he rose from his seat, placing a fragile hand on top of the woman's broad shoulder.

"Miss Hazel, that was a fine meal. I wants you to know that I truly appreciates all you does for me."

Miss Hazel swallowed what was in her mouth, then

grinned broadly. "It ain't nothing, Mr. Burdett. I'm a good Christian woman and I believes in helping folks."

Piano Man nodded, pulling on the navy blue blazer. He looked quite dashing in his matching slacks and pale yellow shirt. His paisley tie was an intricate pattern of blues, yellows, and greens, and although the garments hung loosely over his torso, he stood impressively, his narrow shoulders pulled back straight and tall. "Well, thank you anyway. I needs to be going now before I'm late."

Miss Hazel started to rise from her chair. "Don't get up," Piano Man chimed. "You just sit and enjoy your breakfast." Then smiling sheepishly, he tapped her shoulder one last time before heading out the front door and down the road.

Although it was a short walk to St. Mark A.M.E. Zion Church, the ache in Piano Man's legs made the jaunt seem much longer. As he lifted his tired limbs into the vestibule, his chest rose heavily, his breathing labored. He inhaled deeply, trying to fill his withering lungs with air. It was not long before his breathing returned to normal and the perspiration across his brow had evaporated.

The morning sun was perched precariously in a cloud-filled sky when he finally settled into the sixth pew from the front, the only pew he ever sat in when he attended services. The warm rays peeked eerily through the stained glass windows, casting dark shadows across the highly polished wooden benches, which smelled faintly of lemon oil.

As the morning congregation of overdressed women and blue-suited men eased down the aisles, Piano Man turned about in his seat to bid good morning to his friend Aleta. She had entered shortly after he did and had taken a seat across the way. Piano Man thought her

to be exceptionally attractive seated there in a silk dress
the color of ripened peaches. A straw hat set off by a
spray of satin ribbon was pulled down low over her
brow, angled with much attitude over her eyes. He was
reminded of when they'd been much younger. Aleta
had always possessed an easy beauty, marked occasionally by a faint touch of blush across her high
cheekbones and a light coat of cinnamon lip color to
complement her thin lips. Intoxicating brown eyes still
gazed past dark full lashes, and her skin tone remained
as rich as maple syrup. As Piano Man watched her he
was reminded of caramel toffee with its hard coating
and soft center, a sweet confection that would easily
melt into indifference if left too long in a summer heat.
He grinned broadly as she winked in his direction
before turning away to smile gently at other church-
goers who paused to greet her.

It was the third Sunday of the month and the Men's
Choir was scheduled to sing. Piano Man knew the
morning would go by quickly, not like last week when
the Senior Choir sang. Second Sundays and the Senior
Choir could be exceptionally tedious and required a
patience Piano Man did not possess on this particular
Sunday morning.

The low hum of the large pipe organ filled the inner
sanctuary, its enchanting tones coddling a deep vibrato
that promised salvation for due penance. Doris Gib-
bons, the church's music director, swayed back and
forth along the organ seat, her fingers praying against
the keys. The gold-trimmed choir robe draped over her
shoulders fell elegantly along the bench beneath her,
and Piano Man thought her to be less matronly this way.

He sighed deeply. A mixture of hot pressed hair,
oiled with heavy pomades, impostor perfumes, and
morning kitchen smells filled his nostrils. Cupping his

hand across his mouth, he coughed lightly, attempting to expel the dust he visualized clinging to the delicate tissue along his throat.

As the choir started their parade down the center aisle singing "Glory To His Name," the congregation came to their feet. Piano Man rose, slightly unsteady, then turned his body ever so slightly to watch the procession. His left foot tapped lightly in time to the beat. His fingers played along the back of the pew in front of him, in sync with the music.

Reverend Avery Mayfield and his wife, Juanita, brought up the rear, falling in step behind the six men who made up the illustrious Deacon Board. As they all settled themselves at the front of the church, Piano Man felt content and pleased to be there at that particular moment.

Looking back over his shoulder to the entrance, he eyed the latecomers who would have to stand quietly during the minister's invocation before they'd be permitted to enter. Some of the faces were familiar and Piano Man knew them to never be on time. Turning his attention back to the minister, Piano Man soon found his thoughts interlaced with the sermon. Every so often an "amen" or a "hallelujah" would fall quietly over his lips, dropping like a feather against his ears. At one point even a "praise be to Jesus" tottered across his tongue, fading into oblivion as it eased out of his mouth.

When Reverend Mayfield invited the congregation to kneel at the pulpit in prayer, to unload the burdens they found exceedingly difficult to carry, Piano Man pulled himself from his seat and made his way to the front of the church. On his knees, he bowed his head low, his hands clasped in prayer before him.

Lately, Piano Man prayed frequently. The more time he spent on his knees conversing with God, the better he felt about life in general. He didn't expect total forgiveness for the many indiscretions and odious mistakes he'd committed during his lifetime. He only hoped there would be some understanding of why he'd made the choices he had. When the day came for him to come face to face with his maker, he hoped his own acknowledgment of his actions would ease whatever penance would be bestowed upon him.

His discourse was particularly lengthy this Sunday morning and he suddenly sensed the congregation's eyes upon him as he was one of the last persons to rise. Mildly embarrassed, he whispered a quick "thank you" and an "amen," then struggled to lift his lean frame back upon his tired feet. The struggle was made easier when a young man, his hair cropped close to his head, braced a firm hand beneath Piano Man's arm and pulled him to his feet. Meeting the young man's hazel eyes, Piano Man nodded thank you, then returned to his seat.

As he sat back down for the balance of the service, Piano Man's eyes briefly met Aleta's, skipping past the concern in her face. Aleta continued to watch him from the corner of her eye, but Piano Man's eyes were elsewhere, studying the tall young man who had so gallantly offered his arm to lift the old man from the floor.

Piano Man guessed him to be in his late teens, a faint wisp of facial hair playing along the line of his chin. He sat next to an older man who was obviously his father, the strong resemblance difficult to miss. Every so often, the man would turn to look at the boy and nod his head in agreement to whatever the minister had just preached, and Piano Man envied him. Had things been different for him, he might have had an opportunity to sit in church with his own son and have the boy be proud to be there by his side. Piano Man sighed heavily. "Yes, Lord," he whispered to himself. "If it had all just been different."

The service ended on a jubilant note as the choir bounced back down the aisle, the congregation following. Aleta caught hold of Piano Man's arm and escorted him out of the church, both stopping briefly to say hello to Reverend Mayfield. They continued their walk in silence until they reached the corner of Fairfield Avenue and Spruce Street.

"Where's your car, woman?" Piano Man asked, his voice low and throaty.

"I walked this morning."

He nodded, his arm still wrapped about hers.

"It's been good to see you back in church."

Piano Man laughed. "Knew you'd like that."

"You do it for me?"

"No."

Aleta smiled, shaking her head. "Didn't think so."

"Then why you ask?"

Aleta shrugged. "Woman can't help but hope that sometimes a man will change his ways and do something good 'cause he wants to do it for her. They call it wishful thinking."

"You know me too well to be wishful thinking nothing like that."

Aleta nodded. "Yes, I do."

They continued to walk arm in arm, the morning sounds of a rising city sweeping around them. "So, what brought you back here?"

Piano Man shrugged, purposely avoiding her eyes. "Had me some business to settle is all."

"Does that mean you'll be leaving us again soon?"

Piano Man went silent, grasping her arm tighter.

Aleta nodded again, pressing her lips tightly, then dropped her chin to her chest. She sighed heavily.

"How have you been doing since Irene died?" Aleta asked, her voice dropping to a faint whisper. "Have you finally settled things the way you needed to?"

Piano Man stared straight ahead, his stride slowing as they approached Aleta's front porch. Wrapping his arms around the woman's shoulders, he hugged her closely, leaning to whisper into her ear.

"Irene died knowing that I'd been no good for her while she was alive and that I hadn't changed. I won't no good for her, and I ain't no good for you."

Leaning to kiss her lightly on her cheek, Piano Man lifted her chin to stare into her eyes. "No good," he re-iterated firmly.

Aleta smiled slightly, her face twisted anxiously as though she wanted to cry. "What about the boy?" she asked instead. "What are you going to do about your son?"

"My boy deserve better than me. This is what his mama wanted. I'm just gon' let things be the way they was meant to be."

"You should tell him, James, and let him make up his own mind."

Piano Man stared at her briefly, then kissed her cheek one last time. "Too late for that. I cain't go back and neither can he. What's done is done." Piano Man turned to walk away, his steps slow and heavy.

"Some secrets aren't meant to be taken to your grave, James. He's a good, decent man, and he deserves to know the truth while you're here to tell it. Don't take that away from him. You need to do right by him at least once in your life. You can't keep running away from what you know to be right. Irene died still loving you even though you were always running. I'll die still loving you even though you always running. For once, James, you need to do what's right."

Pausing, Piano Man inhaled her last words, their acrid scent burning his lungs. The ache in his chest intensified. Then, without responding, he continued down the sidewalk.

Seven

Aleta watched Piano Man walk away, wanting to call after him. Knowing that it would be of no use, she pushed her key into the door, twisting it in the lock. Glancing over her shoulder, she watched until he rounded the corner and disappeared out of sight. She shuddered, the midday breeze suddenly feeling cold, then headed inside, locking the door behind her.

Tossing her keys and hat onto the dining room table, Aleta dropped onto an upholstered chair. The tears she'd held back all morning dripped down her face, irrigating the front of her dress. She watched as the dark spots watered the silk fabric, blossoming into large buds against the faille backdrop. Rising, she wiped the back of her hand across her cheeks, the wetness coating her tiny fingers.

Inside her bedroom, she pulled the silk dress over her head, tossing it atop the quilted bedspread. Standing in a full slip and white pantyhose, she reached inside the closet, pulling a large trunk from the back corner. Lifting the lid, she peered inside. A photo of two lovers clasped arm in arm was perched on top. Pulling the heavy brass frame toward her, Aleta wiped lightly at the dusty glass. Irene and Piano Man laughed easily, his arms wrapped possessively around the young girl's teenage shoulders. Aleta's own youth-filled reflection peered back at her, tucked neatly behind the shoulders of the two people she had loved most in her lifetime. She sighed heavily, pulling the picture to her chest.

Beneath the picture lay an assortment of remembrances that whispered secrets many would have said were best left forgotten. Aleta had known better though. Time may have stolen the larger moments, driving away all but the memories, but Aleta had known the keepsakes would one day be important to them all. Her hands brushed against the memories.

"No, sir," Aleta whispered into the empty room, her voice echoing against the backdrop of floral wallpaper. "Some secrets ain't meant to be taken to your grave."

Although the flow of traffic rumbled to the left of him, and the loud screams and laughter of small children playing on the swing sets rang on his right, Piano Man was filled with stillness. Aleta's words had burned like sharp daggers throughout his flesh and the memory of them remained like festering blisters.

His coming back had been a mistake, he thought to himself, pushing the sounds around him up and away as he sank deep into depression, welcoming the dark silence that filled the nether lands of his mind. "I don't need to be doing this," he said out loud, causing more than one mother to eye him cautiously as he walked through Brier Creek Park muttering to himself. "I need to be leaving."

Taking a seat on an empty bench, Piano Man twisted his hands nervously, pinching and pulling at the length of his fingers. His feelings were hurt and he was not sure how to handle the pain that throbbed like a sledge-hammer in his chest. She had told him he needed to do right. "For once, James, you need to do what's right," she'd called after him, stabbing each word into his soul.

Piano Man could feel the warmth of tears rising to his eyes, but he refused to cry. He refused to cry because he knew that he had tried to do right. He had tried for years to do right, but Irene wouldn't let him. She wouldn't give him half a chance to do what he knew he needed to do. And so he had stopped trying. Had ceased all efforts to do what was right. But he had never stopped caring. Had never stopped loving. Had never stopped wanting to do, and to be, what his child had needed.

Irene and her proclamation to keep his son from him had been difficult to deal with, but he had understood. What she had wanted for herself and their child had not been what he'd wanted for himself. Many would have called him selfish, but he had honestly believed to go against the nature of his spirit, to leave the beauty of the music behind, would have been the most selfish thing that he could have ever done. He would have never forgiven himself, or her, if he'd not been able to follow his heart. It would have killed him if life had dealt him a soundless hand, the bitterness of no music hiding behind his woman's wants and that little boy's needs. He had known enough about himself to be certain that he would have blamed them, might even have allowed his love for them both to be tainted by his own anger, and that would have been far more selfish than doing what he had done could ever have been.

He heaved a heavy sigh. His chest hurt. His limbs were heavy and, as he sat on the bench, watching children playing on the swings and parents gossiping among themselves, he knew what he needed to do. The decision had been made for him. Aleta's words had left him with no other alternatives. Hanging his head against his chest, he clasped his hands together in his lap. His body rocked from side to side, the rays of the midday sun painting warmth against his weary flesh. All he wanted to do was will enough energy back into his body to get him to a piano.

Sweat saturated the cotton fabric around Romeo's neck and under his armpits, turning the surface of the pale gray sweatshirt into damp patches the color of charcoal and ash. He swiped the back of his hand across his brow, never breaking his stride as he rounded the track for the eighth time. The half-mile laps were beginning to take their toll, but he was determined to complete a five-mile run. He panted lightly, blowing warm air against his clenched teeth.

Romeo pumped his arms harder, digging his toes against the blacktopped turf. The metal bleachers at the edge of the field were a faint blur out of the corner of his eye. He pushed his body down the length of the track, completing the last fifty feet with little energy to spare. Coming to an abrupt stop, he rested his hands on his hips, gasping for oxygen. The fresh morning air tickled his throat as he gulped large breaths of it, sending him into a fit of coughing. He was desperately out of shape. Operating the Playground now took up a good bulk of his time, intruding upon the regular workouts he had faithfully scheduled and followed so very long ago.

As his breathing eased, he started a slow stroll toward his car. Glancing down at his watch, he realized the morning was rushing by. It would not be long before the afternoon would take control, leaving him helplessly behind. He'd have to hustle if he wanted to make it back in time to shower, change, and straighten up before he had to head to the club and his date with Taryn.

Romeo beamed, his face breaking into a wide grin. His memories of Taryn went back farther than her chance visit to the Playground with Roberta. As he'd thought about her it had dawned on him that she'd attended an event a year earlier—a Chamber of Commerce function hosted by the Playground. Again, she had come in with some associates from her job. She had only briefly caught his attention, serene and regal, with large, round, blue black eyes that had shone brightly. Back then he'd been dating someone else, a woman who'd been a serious distraction from those things he should have been focused on. That relationship had lasted a minute longer than it should have and then, like all his others, she was gone and he had moved on, the memory of Taryn lost until now.

Feeling somewhat foolish for standing there grinning like he was, he looked about quickly to see if anyone was watching. Across the way, an elderly couple walked hand in hand, being led by a large German shepherd just as elderly. They chatted quietly between themselves, occasionally tossing back their silver heads in laughter.

Years ago Romeo could never have seen himself walking in that old man's shoes. There had been no woman with whom he could remotely imagine growing old and cranky. There had never been any woman with whom he wanted to grow flabby and bald and toothless. He chuckled lightly, wondering if a woman like Taryn would still want him when he was flabby and bald and toothless.

As he watched the couple walk off into the distance, a jolt of envy struck him square in the chest. He knew for the first time that he wanted what those two people—with their poor hearing, cataracts, and wrinkled skin—possessed. He knew he wanted an opportunity to walk in that old man's shoes. He wanted a woman by his side who'd be there with him through the best and worst of whatever the remainder of his life had to offer. Wiping the perspiration from his eyes with the lower half of his sweatshirt, he jogged toward the car and headed home.

Romeo was apologetic as he unlocked the door and let Taryn inside. He flipped the lights on and gestured for her to take a seat. She'd been standing outside the door when he'd pulled up. She was wearing distressed denim jeans that had been fashionably ripped across each leg, paired with a black T-shirt, tailored blazer, and stylish heels.

"Really, I just got here," Taryn said. "It's so pretty out I thought I'd enjoy the weather while I waited for you."

Romeo smiled as he pulled up his own chair to the table, taking the seat directly across from her.

"Can I get you something to drink?" he asked, gesturing toward the bar.

She shook her head. "It's a little early," she said, "and it's Sunday."

He nodded. "I'm in the bar business. It's never too early no matter what day of the week it is."

"You've got a point there," she said with a soft chuckle.

Romeo smiled with her. "I'm really glad you called,"

he said. He spun a pencil between his fingers, rolling it back and forth.

"I'm glad you asked."

He took a deep breath. "So how was your trip?"

"Successful."

"What do you do?"

"Sales and marketing for Cooper-Benson."

"The home building company?"

She nodded. "The design division. We're responsible for acquiring and promoting all the finishing touches that make each home unique. I was in Paris learning about a new organic flooring material much like cork. It's a plant-based medium that's great for areas where you might want some flexibility. Like a gym or dance studio."

Romeo nodded. "You like your job," he said, the comment more statement than question.

"I love my job. It's afforded me the opportunity to travel internationally and I've been able to grow and move up the ladder since I've been with them. I'm one of the youngest presidents, male or female."

"So what do you do when you're not working?"

She shrugged. "It's not often that I'm not working. But I'm sure you know what that's like."

He nodded. "I do. I usually only get home to lay my head down for a quick nap, then I'm right back here."

"I hate that I woke you up then."

"I'm not."

She smiled brightly. "So how long have you known Roberta?"

Romeo leaned back in his seat, crossing his arms over his chest. "A few years. How about you?"

"Just since she joined the company last year."

He nodded. "She's been a good friend."

"She says good things about you as well."

Romeo laughed. "I just bet she does," he said, humor tinting his tone.

Their conversation continued easily, both asking questions about the other. Taryn was amazed at how quickly they found a rhythm with each other. Romeo liked how open she was and how his own guard had fallen down in her presence. She made him comfortable and he liked that she seemed at ease with him. Both were looking forward to getting to know each other better.

"Do you play any instruments?" Romeo asked as he suddenly reached across the table for her hand. He studied her fingers as they rested gently against his palm.

She shook her head, the feel of his large appendage heated and teasing. She felt like she'd been burned as she pulled her hand too quickly from his. Romeo lifted his gaze to stare, her own gaze locked on his face. There was a moment's pause before she shook her head a second time. "No. Why do you ask?"

"You have fingers like a piano player. I was just curious."

"No instruments, but I do paint. It relaxes me."

"What medium?"

"Acrylics mostly. Sometimes oils."

"I painted once."

"Really?"

He nodded. "A bathroom. It took me six hours, then I got fired."

Taryn laughed.

"I haven't picked up a paint brush since," he finished.

She nodded, her face bright with glee. Romeo was funny and he made her smile. She was already liking what was happening between them. "So tell me more about you," she said, leaning forward across the table.

When Piano Man entered the club, it was just after two o'clock. Inside, Romeo and Taryn sat across a table from one another, deep in conversation. There was no missing the growing connection that was beginning to bond them together. It wound aromatic links of lavender and jasmine about their bodies, weaving an intricate medley of balsam and myrrh. Piano Man stood off in the shadows, quietly watching. He breathed deeply, remembering a time when he had sat close to the woman he loved, his arms wrapped about her shoulders, the satin of her cheek pressed next to his. Inhaling sharply, the perfumed memories coated his senses, warming his insides.

The elderly figure smiled, the edges of his mouth turned up ever so slightly. They made a nice-looking couple, he thought to himself, admiring the way the two young people flattered each other. Painting a powerful delineation of respect and understanding, they were successfully managing to balance themselves upon an easel of hope, faith, and prayer and it showed without either realizing it. They stood out in their surroundings, their presence a focal point in an otherwise empty room. Piano Man was distracted from his thoughts as Odetta and Sharon rushed in behind him.

"Hey, Piano Man," Odetta said loudly. "What you doing standing in the doorway for?"

Piano Man hugged her warmly. "Make sense a man got to stand in the doorway to get into the room, right?"

Odetta sucked her teeth at him. "Tch."

"Hey, little girl," Piano Man said with a laugh, hugging Sharon also. "How you doing this afternoon?"

Sharon hugged him back. "Just fine, Mr. Burdett."

"Girl, if I done told you a hundred times, Mr. Burdett was my daddy. You call me Piano Man like everyone else do if you want me to be answering you."

Sharon shook her head, a full grin gracing her face. "Yes, sir."

"Hey there," Romeo called out, rising from where he sat. "About time you people got here. Every one of you is late!"

Odetta looked at her watch, ignoring him. "Hey, Taryn girl! What brings you down this way?"

Taryn smiled, standing as well. She pushed both of her hands into the back pockets of her jeans. "Your boss promised to buy me a cup of coffee."

Odetta moved to her side and reached to give her a warm hug. Then she introduced her to Sharon. Their female chatter filled the space.

Romeo shook his head as the three of them feigned disinterest at his presence, more interested in each other. "Excuse me," he said, interrupting the prattle.

Odetta rolled her eyes. "You'll soon learn that this man don't ever do anything but complain."

Piano Man laughed. "Women sure like to stick together, don't they!"

Romeo continued to shake his head, then clasped his hand gently under Taryn's elbow. "Mr. Burdett, I'd like you to meet a very special friend of mine. This is Taryn Williams. Taryn, this is James Burdett."

"It's very nice to meet you, Mr. Burdett." Taryn smiled, extending her hand. "I'm a big fan of your music."

Piano Man pumped Taryn's hand excitedly. "Hey there. Call me Piano Man. Everybody calls me Piano

Man. You calls me anything else and I might not answer."

Taryn grinned broadly. "Yes, sir. Piano Man it will be then."

"What's a pretty little thing like you doing wasting your time with this rusty boy for?" Piano Man asked, slapping Romeo gently across his wide shoulders.

Taryn shrugged. "I'm still trying to figure that out myself," she said, cutting an eye in Romeo's direction. Her smile was sugar sweet.

Romeo could feel himself blushing, his cheeks heating with color. He shook his head. "Can I please get just a little respect around here?"

They all laughed heartily, everyone gathering around a small table in the center of the room.

"This won't take too long," Romeo started.

"Already taking too long," Odetta interrupted, rolling her eyes. "I've got me a pot of neck bones, some macaroni and cheese, and collard greens waiting for me at home."

"Is them smoked neck bones?" Piano Man asked, licking his lips slightly.

"Mixed, smoked and regular." Odetta smacked her mouth.

Piano Man's eyes lit up ever so slightly.

"Do you two mind?" Romeo asked.

"Not at all," Piano Man countered, shifting in his seat. "You got any 'tata salad to go with them neck bones?" Piano Man asked, turning his attention back to Odetta.

"No, but I made some peas and rice, corn bread, and a pineapple upside down cake for dessert. Do you want to come for supper?"

"Thank you kindly. Don't minds if I do. If it ain't no inconvenience, of course."

Odetta flipped her hand. "I have more than enough. In fact—"

"Uh-hum." Romeo cleared his voice. "Hello, we're supposed to be having a meeting here."

Odetta rolled her eyes, propping her elbows up on the table. Piano Man leaned back in his chair, tipping his head toward Romeo. "So what's taking you?"

Behind them Taryn laughed, amusement painting her expression.

Romeo tossed his hands in the air. "Well, all I need to do today is get some photos of you and Sharon out under the marquee. Odetta, you need to start interviewing for another waitress. I think we might be better off with two new girls, but I'm going to leave that decision up to you."

Odetta nodded her head slowly. "I say let's wait and see. Too many girls and we'll just be in each other's way. If it starts getting too busy, then we'll add on another. I know a girl who's been looking for a job. She use to waitress at a restaurant on Capital Boulevard until it closed. I think she'd be good."

Romeo nodded. "I trust you, Odetta. Do what you think is best."

Odetta smiled, brushing the hair from her brow.

Romeo continued. "Sharon, as of next week Friday you will be singing full time. I want you to look the part. I've set up a budget for wardrobe and I want you to go shopping this week and pick out some evening dresses to perform in."

Sharon stared up at Romeo, visibly flustered. "I don't . . . I . . ." she stammered, her voice barely audible. Her eyes widened with nervous anxiety.

Odetta held up her hands as if surrendering. Her head waved from side to side. "Don't look at me!"

Taryn suddenly eased a manicured hand in the air. "I would love to be of some help. I can go shopping with you, if you'd like," she said quietly, her voice soothing. "I know it always helps me to have a second eye along when I need to buy something special." She smiled as she continued. "In fact, I think we should make it a full beauty day. I have a fabulous beautician who would love to give you a makeover, if you're interested."

"Thank you. I'd like that," Sharon whispered, the ends of her mouth tilted up into a faint smile.

Romeo's head bobbed slowly up and down. He tossed Taryn an appreciative smile. The he said, "Piano Man, I'm putting you in charge of the music. You work up a program for you and Sharon. I need to trust you to keep the audience entertained."

"I always keeps the people entertained," Piano Man stated.

Romeo smiled again. "Yes, you do. I wasn't implying that you don't."

"Been entertaining folks since befo' you was born. Ain't never had nobody do no complaining 'bouts my keeping them entertained. I keeps the people entertained now."

Romeo shook his head. "I didn't mean anything by it."

Standing, Piano Man inched his way past Romeo. "I knows that. Why you being so sensitive?"

Romeo rolled his eyes, sighing heavily. "Can we please go take these pictures now? I have someplace I need to be."

"We ain't the ones doing all the talking," Piano Man said over his shoulder as Sharon rose to follow him.

Taryn and Odetta laughed loudly, watching as

Romeo fell in step behind them with his digital camera.

"They're something else," Taryn said, pulling her chair up closer to the table.

Odetta nodded her head. "Piano Man gives Romeo a run for his money. He something else, he is. Everybody like that old fool."

"Sharon's very shy, isn't she?"

Odetta shrugged. "Shy until you get her up on that stage. She's like two different people once she starts singing. It was nice of you to offer to take her shopping."

Taryn smiled. "Why don't the three of us make a day of it? I think we'd have a great time. You up for it?"

Odetta laughed. "Hell yeah! Thought I was gonna have to invite myself."

Taryn laughed with her. "You could have. You know we can hang tight anytime."

Their laughter echoed about the room. Outside they could hear Romeo prodding the two entertainers into place, his voice tipped in exasperation. Odetta sauntered over to look out the window. Pulling back the shade ever so slightly, she peeked out to see what they were doing. Taryn joined her, peering past the woman's shoulder.

"So, what am I getting myself into?" Taryn asked, watching Romeo.

Odetta chuckled, the warmth of it vibrating around the room. "Girl, you don't have a thing to worry about. That's one good man. And I've never seen him looking at anyone the way I've seen him look at you. His nose is so wide open he don't know what to do with himself."

Taryn smiled.

Odetta continued. "He gets a lot of fast women

chasing after him, but Romeo knows a good thing when he sees it. And trust me when I tell you that I will tell him about his self when women like your friend Roberta come in here pressing all up on him. Won't be none of that going on."

Taryn raised her eyebrows questioningly. "It's like that?"

"Oh," Odetta exclaimed, "Romeo doesn't take that mess serious. You've seen how he is. He has no problems sending them packing quick!"

"That's good to know. This thing won't go far if I can't trust him," Taryn said with a quick laugh.

"A man don't do what he don't want to do. I ain't met a man yet who will drop his pants because some woman made him and he didn't want to."

Taryn shrugged.

"Romeo's like any other man. He's either going to resist the temptation or he ain't. If he wants to play around, there's nothing you can do to stop him."

"Well, that makes me feel comfortable," Taryn said, an edge of sarcasm coating her tone.

Odetta laughed. "Girl, don't you start acting crazy about what that man might do. You get crazy after he do it, then you at least got a good reason to be acting the fool."

Taryn wrapped her arms tightly about her shoulders. She thought about Romeo and how he moved her so. She was quickly discovering that he had a devilish sense of humor and schoolboy charms that were drawing her to him. The beauty of his dark complexion and sinful good looks had been overshadowed by his casual demeanor, his ability to engage her in stimulating conversation, and an IQ as impressively high as her own.

She sighed as she turned her attention back to

Odetta. "I really like him," she said. "I'm actually surprised that I like him as much as I do."

Odetta brushed a wide hand across Taryn's back. "Enjoy it and just see what happens. If it works out, all well and good. If not, at least you will have had some fun."

"She's right," Piano Man interrupted, startling both women. "It ain't hard to see that you and that boy got something going on between you," he said as they both spun around to face him.

"Old man, you ought to be ashamed sneaking up on us like that," Odetta fussed.

Piano Man laughed. "Won't nobody sneaking."

Taryn laughed with him, shaking her head. Piano Man smiled at her, grasping her tightly around the shoulders. "Little girl, I think that boy's going to surprise you. You ain't got to worry none. A man don't usually do something stupid to throw away such a precious gift. And something tells me that you are very precious. 'Sides, I will kick his butt good if he hurts a pretty little thing like you." He hugged her warmly as Romeo and Sharon sauntered in behind him.

"What's all this?" Romeo asked, sensing that he had just missed out on something.

Releasing his hold on Taryn, Piano Man cleared his throat, ignoring Romeo's question as he moved to the other side of the room. "Sharon, girl, come sing for me," he instructed, pulling himself up to the piano. "And sing me a love song."

Sharon smiled, settling herself next to the old man on the piano bench. The music was sweet. Her voice was caressing, the throaty tone complemented by the tinkling of keys. The mild reverb vibrated seductively about, teasing ever so slightly, like large, brown hands gently molding warm mocha flesh.

Romeo made his way to Taryn's side. His breath caught when she suddenly leaned into him, brushing her shoulder against his arm as she settled herself comfortably against him. Easing that arm over her shoulder, he relaxed as she nestled into his side, fitting as if she'd always belonged there.

Piano Man's fingers happily skipped against the keys. He watched the new lovers out of the corner of his eye. He marveled at how they reminded him of a time when he had stood strong beside the beautiful woman who'd fallen in love with him as intensely as the two of them were starting to fall in love, neither even aware. He had stood like Romeo did now, wanting to inhale every ounce of her being, relishing the sweetness of her disposition like cool ice cream against the warmth of his tongue.

Piano Man continued to play, wanting to stay locked in his memories for as long as he possibly could. Only Sharon noticed the fine spray of tears nestled along the edges of his dark eyes. When she reached her delicate hand out to lightly stroke the length of his back, only she was aware of the heartache wrapped in the warm breath he blew past his lips.

On the other side of the room, Odetta leaned back against the bar, her arms wrapped around her plump frame. A wry smile graced her face, her expression buoyant. Taryn and Romeo stood absorbed in their own small world, easy caresses being traded back and forth. Each appeared secure in their thoughts as the love song painted itself around the room.

Eight

"Hey, baby! It's me. Again. I had a minute of down time and I was hoping I'd catch you before you went into your meeting. I just wanted you to know that I was thinking about you. Just hoping to hear your voice. Call me when you get a chance. Talk to you soon."

Taryn winced, glancing down to her wristwatch. She'd missed Romeo's calls and she only had a quick minute before she had to be in another meeting. Not enough time to call him back. She stole one last look at her watch.

Since that initial cup of coffee the two had spent much time together. Getting to know Romeo had quickly become the highlight of Taryn's life. The man was engaging and every conversation teased her sensibilities. His humor was dry and teasing and he challenged her in a way she had never before experienced. She loved how he made her feel and couldn't imagine him not being a part of her life.

Taryn was discovering as much about herself as she was about the man who'd managed to wiggle his way into her heart. She found herself excited by the prospect of spending time with him. She would call him without hesitation, seeing no need to wait for him to take the lead in their blossoming relationship. Romeo easily fell into step with her wants, not feeling threatened at all by what she needed and insisted on claiming.

He was a mama's boy and she loved to hear him talk about his mother. It broke her heart to discover that he had no knowledge of the other parent who'd been there at his conception. She could see how that bothered him, the not knowing playing with his psyche. His sharing had opened the conversation to parenting and his thoughts about marriage and children.

They talked a lot, about anything and everything. No topic had been ignored; Romeo was as open as she fathomed any man could be. His willingness to be forthcoming about everything in his life had melted any reluctance she herself might have had. They'd become fast friends and she greatly appreciated everything he offered to her life. From the start, pangs of loneliness were nothing but a memory in both their lives.

Romeo had to be the most romantic man she'd ever known. He lavished her with attention. With him, surprises were routine and he was extraordinarily indulgent as he showered her with gifts and trinkets. She felt special with Romeo and had quickly discovered how much she needed—no, wanted—that in her life. Romeo was a dream come true, everything about the man mesmerizing.

Their last time together had been a point of no return for them both. Like all of their encounters, the conversation was engaging. Their disagreements were not actually arguments but vibrant debates of opinions. As Taryn reflected back, she couldn't even remember the topic, distracted by Romeo and what he had instigated between them.

She closed her eyes as she allowed herself to fall into the memory. He should have been at the Playground but Malcolm had covered his shift because Romeo had wanted to take her to dinner. He'd made reservations at Angus Barn, one of the premier restaurants in the area. Acquainted with the chef, Romeo had arranged a meal, the likes of which paled in comparison to anything she'd ever dined on before. The wine had flowed and the dessert had been decadent.

The evening air had been comfortable in spite of the rain that threatened to chase them from their seats on the brick-paved patio. Sitting beneath the late night sky, they had watched the initial strikes of lightning as they lit up the dark landscape. The rumble of thunder echoed off in the distance.

"I miss you when you go away," Romeo had said softly.

"I wish I didn't have to be away," she responded.

Romeo nodded. "You have my heart, do you know that?"

She lifted her eyes to his as he leaned toward her, clasping both of her hands beneath his own.

"You have my heart and when you're gone it feels like it might break."

Taryn had laughed. "But I always come back. You know that."

"I do, but it doesn't stop me from missing you and it doesn't stop the heartbreak that comes when you're not here."

She didn't respond, not having the words to tell him she felt the same. She could only hope that he could see it in her eyes.

They'd sat together for some time before Romeo stood up, tossing his cloth napkin to the table. He had extended his hand toward her and when she'd taken it, he pulled her from her seat, drawing her tight against his body. He wrapped his arms around her torso and hugged her tightly. In that brief moment Taryn couldn't imagine anything moving her from that space. And then he kissed her, insuring that nothing ever would.

His mouth had captured hers, the gesture possessive. His lips were sweet against her lips. His tongue danced beyond the line of her teeth, frolicking in the warm cavity. He tasted like the sweet wine and berries and the hint of chocolate that had been their dessert. His kiss had been fervent and teasing, his ardor unmistakable. Everything about his touch had been consuming, leaving her breathless. Each inhalation and exhalation of his breath had lingered with her own, nourishing her spirit. He had kissed her in a way that no other man would ever be able to.

A sudden knock on her office door pulled her from her thoughts. Roberta pushed the door open slightly and peered inside.

"Hey, what's up?" Taryn questioned, her eyebrows raised.

"They're ready for you," the woman answered.

Taryn nodded as she blew one last sigh. She wasn't ready, her focus lost as she pondered everything that was good about her and him together. The memory of his lips lingered and she wasn't ready to let it go. Wishing she had time to return her man's last call, she headed for her meeting.

Romeo continued to be drawn to Taryn's vibrant spirit. It possessed and enthralled him. The time they continued to share together seemed to be flying with no regard for his desire to make it stand still, to allow him a few moments to linger in the sweetness of all they were sharing. As he hung up his cell phone, moving back behind the bar, he was excited about the plans they'd made for the weekend.

Romeo's initial advances had been bold, just shy of pushy, and in response Taryn had held him at arm's length, feigning disinterest. But something about her eyes had been all too revealing and so he'd persisted, allowing a beautiful friendship to build between them.

That friendship had left him wanting more, needing to fall headfirst into the promises between them. He had not seen in himself what Taryn had seen in him, but she had wanted him as badly, only on her own terms. He knew only that it had taken weeks of hour-long telephone conversations, romantic dinners, and late night walks before they'd become lovers. Many women had passed between the sheets of Romeo's bed prior to him meeting Taryn, but not once had he considered sharing that space with someone else after.

Once Romeo had let her in, Taryn reaching deep into his spirit, seeing what moved him, he'd been captured heart and soul. When he had finally tasted the essence of her sugar, nourishing his hunger from the fountain of her femaleness, he'd been consumed by his growing emotion for her. Emotion that felt very much like love.

Taryn snuggled close beside him, sleep having taken over her body. She slumbered peacefully, a faint beam of moonlight floating through the window across her cheek. Romeo leaned down to press his lips against hers, running his tongue along the line of her mouth. She smiled in her sleep, pushing her own tongue out of her mouth to lick lightly at her own lips. The subtleness of the movement excited him and he moved his body closer to hers, pressing his hips against her hips, his thigh against her thigh. He could feel the muscles along the lower half of his body tightening, responding as if they'd been commanded to stand at attention.

Romeo marveled at the effect Taryn had on him. He had no control when she was close, the nearness of her taking command over his being. He reached a tentative hand out to palm her naked breast, rolling the lush tissue against the cup of his large hand. Her flesh was warm and inviting, and so he leaned to take the dark nipple into his mouth. He suckled her gently, lapping at her greedily. He felt her hand move to the back of his head, pressing his face against her chest. A low moan escaped past her lips. Peering up at her face, he smiled, noting that she still had not opened her eyes.

Shifting the line of his body, Romeo pressed his hardness against her thigh, pushing himself in slow rotation against her. Responding with her body, Taryn's legs fell open easily, allowing him access to the center of her being. His fingers danced between her thighs, seeking sanctuary in the soft folds of her femininity. The low moan became more intense as he teased her, caressing her steadily against the tips of his fingers, his lips still locked around her breast as he suckled hungrily.

Taryn moaned his name, whispering it into the dark night as she gasped for air. Romeo answered by pulling himself above her, the heat rising from the core of her body guiding him where they both wanted him to be. Wrapping her thin arms around his neck, she pulled him to her mouth, thrusting her tongue between his teeth as she kissed him hungrily. Fully awake, her gaze met his, sleep lost behind the rise of passion that his touch had stirred within her.

Stroke for stroke she lifted her hips against his

pelvis, drawing him deeper and deeper inside her. She felt full and complete. For Romeo, the intensity of the connection was beyond his wildest dreams. He loved her, completely, without reservation, and as he spilled his soul deep into the well of her heart, he told her so.

A loud knock against her front door pulled Aleta from her sleep, moving her to rise from the warmth of her bed. Wrapping a silk robe around her nightgown, she scurried to the front of the house to peer through the door's peephole. Piano Man stood outside, patiently waiting for her to welcome him. She smiled, leaning her forehead against the front door as she unlocked the safety bolt. Pulling the structure open, she stood staring at him, and he at her as he waited to be invited inside.

Neither of them spoke. Piano Man gazed at her intently, knowing there were no words that could convey the emotions sweeping through him. Knowing that if there was anyone who could read his soul, it would be Aleta. The woman had always had the unique ability to translate the language in his eyes.

She pushed at the screen door, allowing him admittance. Locking it behind them, he dragged himself into the bedroom, following closely on her heels as she led the way, pulling him along by the hand. Without uttering a word, the woman dropped her body back against the mattress, tugging the covers up and around her shoulders. She watched as Piano Man stepped out of his clothes, kicking his pants and shirt into the corner of the room. She smiled at the printed boxers that hung to his knees and the bright white T-shirt pulled tight against his chest. He smiled back, a faint rise of blush sweeping heat across his dark cheeks.

Crawling in beside her, Piano Man wrapped his arms tightly around her as she turned to face the wall, the line of her buttocks pressing into his groin. A wave of vibration stirred throughout his body. Piano Man gasped, inhaling sharply as he ran a callused palm down the line of her figure. Her skin was soft, age lost in the folds of darkness that enveloped them. He kissed the round of her shoulder, allowing his lips to draw a damp line along the back of her neck. Relaxing his arm around her waist, his fingers tickled the silk fabric that lay between his hand and her flesh, the outline of her belly button pressing into his palm. She trembled against him and he pulled himself closer, wrapping a protective grip around her body. When the morning sun reached out to kiss the sides of their faces, the warmth of the rays found them still holding tightly to each other.

A storm was brewing off the coast of North Carolina. As Piano Man clicked the off button on the television remote, he thought it prophetic that the weather people had deemed to name the angry swell of wind and rain Hurricane Irene. Lifting his body out of Aleta's bed, he pulled his rumpled clothes from where they lay in the corner, dropping the wrinkled fabric back against his skin. Aleta still lay sleeping peacefully beneath the covers.

As the warmth of a faint sliver of sunlight had pulled him out of his sleep, he'd turned on the television to catch the news. He'd watched with eager anticipation as the newscaster, a young Asian woman meticulously dressed in pale blue cashmere, plotted the storm's pending course. It was predicted that Irene would come raging in their direction by nightfall, leaving a vehement path of tropical anger in her wake. Piano Man shook his head. Prophetic. Even from her grave, Irene was expressing her displeasure, raging at him from wherever it was she lay. He imagined that her eternal peace had been compromised by what he had done. Closing the front door behind him, he didn't bother to let Aleta know he was gone. News of Irene would tell her for him.

Malcolm had unlocked the club's front door earlier than usual. Piano Man and Romeo both entered at the same time, having crossed paths on the sidewalk at the entrance. Their loud chatter preceded them inside.

"This may be a bad storm. We've not had anything like this come through for a while. Not since Fran," Romeo was saying as he held the door for Piano Man to enter.

"Why you think they always name these big storms after women?" the older man asked, his curiosity piqued.

Romeo chuckled. "My mama use to say that the devil had probably pissed off Mother Nature royally. Nothing like a woman scorned. So I guess it's sort of fitting, don't you think?"

Piano Man laughed with him, the two men waving at Malcolm as they made their way toward the bar.

"Good morning," Malcolm chimed. "How are you two doing today?"

"As well as can be expected," Romeo responded. Piano Man nodded his head in agreement.

"Do we need to do anything special?" Malcolm asked, concern rising in his voice. "To protect the place against the storm, I mean."

"I want to board up the office windows out back," Romeo said, nodding his head. "We should be fine though. Are you prepared at home?"

Malcolm nodded his head. "Stopped to get batteries and extra supplies before I came in. Hit the twenty-four-hour supermarket last night before the crowds. Folks were starting to race through the doors as I was leaving."

"Well, if any of you want to bunk here, feel free. This old brick building should fair well."

"I may do that," Piano Man responded, dropping down against the piano bench. "Don't figure I need to go no place anytime soon. Besides, that boardinghouse has way too many trees on the place for my liking. Don't need to take no chances. Know what I mean?"

The duo behind the bar chuckled and agreed.

"What about you, Romeo? Is your house secure?" Malcolm asked.

The man shrugged. "It should be okay. I taped the glass this morning before I took Taryn to the airport."

"Your woman gone already?" Piano Man asked, a look of surprise crossing his face.

"She caught the early flight to New York. She was afraid that if the storm is as bad as they're predicting, she might not be able to get out later in the week, and she has some major meetings to attend in Europe. Figured she'd head to London later today, before the storm got too far up north and she couldn't get out at all."

Malcolm cut an eye in Romeo's direction, both he and Piano Man noting the sad tone that had risen in Romeo's voice. Piano Man's hands ran scales up and down the piano keys, his gray head nodding slowly up and down. Outside the thick rain seemed to grow thicker, the first signs of Irene's diaphanous greeting flooding the air with a veil of harsh wind.

The weather outside was horrendous at best, but for the grace of God, the damage appeared to be minimal. As Aleta peered through the curtained window, watching as the wind whipped debris back and forth, from corner to corner, she thought about Piano Man. She could feel that he was safe, a sixth sense she had only when it came to that man. No other had ever touched her heart the way he had, not even the two husbands she'd married and buried so many years before. She smiled, pushing herself away from the window and dropping down onto the sofa.

The electrical power had gone with the first wave of wind that had blown in their direction. Darkness was starting to fill the outside sky and so she lit the candles that Piano Man had left in a neat row along the top of the coffee table. The flickering flames danced much like her mind, flitting easily from one memory to the other.

It had taken some fifty plus years to get Piano Man into her bed. She had beckoned a silent invitation, the proposal etched in the lines of her face. And he had come. Of his own volition. Time had done that for her. Time, and her best friend's passing, for both she and Piano Man knew, had Irene still been alive, it would not have been her bed he'd have crawled home to. She smiled again, amused that the storm outside came bearing the name Irene, causing Piano Man to run away faster than lightning itself.

She couldn't help but wonder what he'd thought about when he'd touched her, dropping his callused hand against her skin. He had gently stroked the folds of flesh that covered her stomach. His hands had flitted across the breasts that had long since rushed to meet her knees. He had touched her, and his hands had seemed content to hold on, had seemed to enjoy dwelling atop the curves that were no longer girlish. Curves she saw being more matronly than womanly. Curves that had long since been transformed toward another realm. Piano Man had not seemed put off by the changes maturity had made to her body. He had stayed, allowing her to linger beneath his touch, until the rise of Irene had sent him fleeing.

Taryn sat alone at the John F. Kennedy Airport. With the chaos of southbound flights being canceled left and right, she had sought sanctuary in the British Airways executive lounge. After checking her in, an attendant had brought her a refreshing blend of pineapple juice and champagne, and had pointed her in the direction of a well-laid buffet table piled high with fresh fruit, warm baked breads, and other foods.

With access to an electrical outlet, she plugged in her laptop computer, waited for the software to load, then checked her incoming message box. Problems popped up tenfold as she typed quick responses back to the original senders, promising to follow up the moment she arrived back at her London office. Taryn heaved a heavy sigh.

Staring across the room, she took in the plush luxury afforded those with first class tickets and enough mileage points to fly free for a lifetime. The ambience was relaxing, the rich woods and cool fabric tones easy on the eyes. Closing the computer, she decided she couldn't be bothered. They could all wait until she was back, or at least until her physical self

presented itself at the next required meeting. Her mind
would be elsewhere though, still in North Carolina,
lying close to Romeo. The thought of him brought a
smile to her face and Taryn became flush with embarrassment at the perverse thoughts that danced through
her mind.

Bringing her cell phone to her ear, she hit the speed
dial, calling his number. After four rings, the answering machine picked up and she left a message, telling
him she had arrived in New York safely, that she missed
him, and she would try to be back as soon as she could.
She heaved another heavy sigh as the line disconnected.
She thought of calling him at the club, knowing that
was probably where he was. She then figured if she
heard his voice, she might not be able to will herself
onto the airplane to go do what she knew she had to.
She would only want to turn around and go back home.
She dropped the cell phone back into her leather purse.

Lifting the drink to her mouth, she sipped at it
slowly, relishing the taste of the sweet fruit. It was good
and she was glad to have asked for it. The attendant
stopped to ask if she desired a refill, and with the nod
of her head, another sat at her elbow. Across the way,
CNN was tracking the progress of the storm on an
overhead television that played softly for those passengers who were interested. Two businessmen, both in
dark gray suits, sipped their own cocktails as they
stared intently at the screen.

Leaving Romeo had been different this time. Something about their parting had actually hurt. Taryn imagined it had something to do with the look in the man's
eyes. It had seemed as if he'd been pleading with her to
stay, not able to find the words to say as much out loud.
The dynamics of their relationship had changed. Not

only could she could feel it, she could taste it, the sweetness of what they brought to each other, brimming with new energy. As she'd left him standing in the airport waiting area, that energy had surged and now she missed it. She missed him and her wanting hurt. With the announcement of her flight's pending departure, Taryn brushed the feelings aside, gathered her carry-on luggage, and headed toward the gate.

Nine

The weather on the other side of the Playground's brick walls was cruel at best, blowing bitter air in massive swells that shook the structure of the building. Malcolm stood peeking out the window, commenting on the large debris that blew past and down the length of the street. Piano Man sat propped on two chairs pushed together, dozing on and off as the feeling moved him. When the telephone rang, they all jumped in surprise.

Romeo brought the receiver to his ear. "The Playground."

"Romeo? Is that you?"

"Yes, Aunt Aleta. Are you all right?"

"I am. Power's out, but otherwise everything is fine. I just wanted to make sure someone knew where James was, in case the telephones go out. It's bad outside."

Romeo smiled. "He's fine, Aunt Aleta. He's right here. Do you want to speak with him?"

"Yes, please. Thank you, baby."

Romeo passed the receiver to Piano Man, who looked at him with annoyance for being disturbed from his sleep.

"Hello?"

"Why'd you leave?"

He dropped his voice to a whisper, glancing over his shoulder to insure Romeo didn't hear him. "Irene," he said matter-of-factly.

Aleta laughed. "You a fool, James. You could still be in this warm bed with me. Instead you let that storm run you out into the streets."

Piano Man laughed with her. "I saw it as a sign, Aleta. Someone trying to tell us something."

"As long as you're okay. I was worried."

"I'm fine. Everything all right there? House still in one piece?"

"As if you care. You should be here in case I blow away."

"You ain't going nowhere. Who else is going to give me a hard time?"

"You got that right. Don't you leave until Romeo says it's safe. You hear me, James?"

Piano Man nodded his head as if the woman could see through the telephone line, then he dropped the receiver back onto the hook. On the other end, Aleta hung up, still shaking her head from side to side.

"Is Aleta okay?" Romeo asked.

Piano Man grunted. "Ain't nothing wrong with Aleta that I can't fix when this here storm gets finished."

"It's like that, is it?" Romeo said, smiling at the man.

Piano Man rolled his eyes in Romeo's direction. "Woman just need to be checking up on somebody."

In the corner, Malcolm laughed, his gaze catching Romeo's as the two men exchanged a look between them.

The telephone rang for a second time. Piano Man answered it. "Hello? This is the Playground."

"Mr. Burdett, hello. It's Taryn. Is Romeo there?"

"Yes, precious. How are you?"

"I'm fine, thank you. I just wanted to check that you guys were all right."

Piano Man's head bobbed up and down. "We is just fine. Storm blowing up outside. We sittin' here inside. No need for you to be worrying your pretty self."

Taryn chuckled. "You are so sweet. Where's that man of mine?"

"Hold on," Piano Man said, gesturing for Romeo to come take the phone. "Your woman just as bad," he said to the younger man as he passed him the receiver. "They just need to be checking up on somebody."

Romeo laughed as he put the receiver to his ear. "Hey, darling. Where are you?"

"London. We just landed. I'm waiting for my luggage, then I'm headed to the hotel."

"Good flight?"

"Long flight. How's everything there? It looks bad on the television."

Romeo shrugged. "It's nasty out. From what we can tell, the damage will probably be pretty severe."

"Don't forget to check my house, please. Call me if there's anything wrong."

"I'll do that. As soon as it's safe to travel, I'm headed home. I'll swing by your place on the way."

"I miss you."

Romeo's voice dropped an octave. "I miss you too."

"Call me later, when you're by yourself."

"I promise. I love you, Taryn."

The woman on the other end grinned broadly, gesturing toward a skycap to take her luggage. "I love you too, Romeo. Call me soon."

"Bye, baby."

Malcolm chuckled as Romeo hung up. "Lordy!

Lordy!" he said with a wide smile. "Must be something in the water you two been drinking."

Piano Man rolled his eyes as Romeo shook his head and the three men laughed warmly together.

Hours later the men sat huddled over a small card table, rank cigar smoke permeating the room. Piano Man clutched his hand close to his chest, the thin cards brushing against his chin. Reaching for the small stack of quarters on the table in front of him, he picked up two dollars' worth and tossed them atop the large mound of coins stacked in the center.

"I see your dollar and raise you a dollar."

Romeo eyed him suspiciously, a deadpan expression masking his thoughts. Studying his hand one last time, he knew that there was no point in his continuing to bluff his way through. He seriously doubted a pair of eights was going to take him far. "I fold," he said, dropping the cards in his hand down to the table.

Piano Man chuckled as he swept the small pile of coins toward him. "Told you don't come play with the big boys if you ain't ready to get your butt whipped."

The men gathered around the table all laughed. Malcolm rose from where he sat, stretching his limbs toward the ceiling. He yawned deeply, throwing his head back against his shoulders. "I'm done. I got to go get me some sleep. It sounds like the weather has finally calmed down out there."

Jenkins, who had braved the last of the wind and rain to join them, nodded his head, collecting the deck of cards neatly into one pile. "Me too. I guess I need to go home to my wife." He shuddered. "Then again, maybe I should stay here and get me some more to drink first."

Piano Man laughed. "Man, you better take your ass on home. You know you spend too much time away from your woman and she gonna find someone else who'll gladly take your place."

Jenkins shrugged as he slipped on his coat. "You got that man's number so I can call him? Hell, I wish someone would take my old lady off my hands! My woman is a pain in the ass. I'd leave her if it won't gonna cost me a whole lotta money."

Romeo shook his head, tilting his eyes skyward. "Lord, I pray I don't ever feel that way about Taryn."

Malcolm slapped him across the back. "Keep praying. I used to feel that way 'bout my ex-wife too. Now, I just wish the trick would drop in a hole someplace."

"Now, don't be calling no woman out of her name. Ain't right," Piano Man chimed in. He cut a mean eye toward the young man.

"I apologize. You're right, but that's how I feel sometimes," Malcom said. A sudden sadness passed over his expression. Only Romeo knew the hurt Malcolm had endured that had him wishing ill will on all the female sex. The two men exchanged a quick look.

Oblivious, Piano Man continued. "No problem feeling that way, but any woman done give birth to your children don't deserve to be called out of her name. She won't no trick when you was loving her good and making them babies. Means she ain't no trick now."

Malcolm nodded. "You're right. I'm sorry for that. It's just difficult sometimes, especially when my girls are being hurt by her bad behavior."

Piano Man cut his eyes at Malcolm, then toward Romeo, his look still chastising. "Young boys today spend too much time disrespecting our women. And it ain't right. Who birthed you?" Piano Man gazed from one to the other before continuing. "That's right. A woman, and a black woman at that. How you gonna disrespect the creature who done brought you into this world? Don't make no good sense. No, it don't." The old man shook his head from side to side.

Romeo smiled faintly. He tossed Malcolm a look. "You done got him started."

Jenkins buttoned his tattered gray overcoat. "I know I needs me a drink now," he said. "Piano Man up in here preaching."

Piano Man flipped his hand in the man's direction, then swiped his palm across his brow. "Ain't nobody preaching nothin'. Just telling it like it should be."

Malcolm and Piano Man had gone toe to toe on more than one occasion, and Malcolm knew the old man would not back down. He was as opinionated as he was elderly and firmly set in his beliefs. He reached out to shake Piano Man's hand. "I'll see you tomorrow, my friend, and I'll think twice before making that mistake again."

Piano Man grinned a semitoothless grin. "I got too many years on you boys. You two still got stuff to learn yet. Looks like it gon' take an ass whipping or two from me for it to get through to your hard heads."

With a low chuckle Malcolm wrapped his coat around his shoulders and headed for the door. "See you two tomorrow," he called back, pulling the door closed behind them as Jenkins followed closely on his heels.

Romeo lifted his hand to wave good-bye.

Piano Man grunted, lifting his legs to rest his feet up on the table. "So, boy, where your woman done fly off to now?"

"London."

"That little girl sho' spend a lotta time on the road."

Romeo nodded. "Yes, she does."

"You likes having her travel so much?"

Leaning back in his chair, Romeo clasped his hands behind his head. "It's not really my decision. She's got a great career and it's not my place to say whether or not she should travel. She seems to enjoy it well enough though, so I guess that's all that matters."

"Dat don't answer whether or not *you* likes it."

Romeo shrugged. "No. I don't like having her gone so much. I'd prefer to have her home here with me. But what can I do?"

"You ever tell her that?"

"No. It's not my place."

"Your place if you love her and she loves you."

"What's love got to do with it?"

"Everything. Why would you think it don't?"

Romeo shrugged again, not bothering to answer. The echo of Piano Man's breathing filled the room. His heavy breath was clouded thick with exhaustion and a hint of sickness. Romeo studied his dark features. The hardened lines appeared masklike, harboring far too many stories for any one man to remember, let alone share. Piano Man looked up to stare into Romeo's own dark brown eyes.

"What the hell are you staring at, boy?"

"You."

"Why?"

"Why not?"

"Damn, you a pain in the ass. Can't you let an old man rest?"

Romeo chuckled lightly. "I do believe you are getting paranoid."

"No. Just tired of you staring at my black ass. You about to look the color right off me."

"Well, ain't no worry about that. You got more than enough color to spare."

"Now, ain't that some mess!" Piano Man said, sitting upright. "You a piece of work!"

"Me?" Romeo asked with surprise. "What did I do?"

"I think you're color struck!"

"Now, you really don't believe that, do you?"

"Hell no, but I knew it would get a rise out of you," Piano Man said, lifting his legs back up onto the table as he chuckled under his breath.

Romeo tossed a poker chip at Piano Man's head, hitting the cushion behind the man. Piano Man laughed again, then went quiet for a brief minute.

"Color's a funny thing, boy," he said finally. "It scares people."

Romeo leaned forward, listening with a curious ear as the man continued.

"I done lived through it all. Jim Crow, the Black Power Movement, all of it. Even got to see me a first black president of the United States. But trust me, nothing ever changes. Whether we colored, black, Afro-Americans, whatever, there will always be someone out here who gonna have a problem with us black folks. They may come at you wearing white sheets or pinstriped suits, but their feelings will always be the same."

"Do you really believe that?"

Piano Man nodded. "Romeo, there will always be someone who can't be happy unless they can make others unhappy, and I'm not just talking 'bout white folks either. Black folks can be just as bad. Damn, you either got to be light skinned and have good hair to be okay one day or dark skinned and nappy headed the next."

Romeo smiled. "I can remember these two old sisters who used to live upstairs from me and my mother. They spent all of their time rocking on the porch, gossiping about who was better than who. I will never forget the day Miss Ruby said I shouldn't hang around with my friend Otis because 'tar babies don't go nowhere but jail.' When I asked my mother what a 'tar baby' was, she practically knocked my teeth down my throat."

Piano Man laughed.

"Wasn't funny," Romeo said, breaking into a grin.

"You ever play the dozens when you was a boy?" Piano Man asked.

Romeo nodded yes, thinking back to the few times he'd tried to outdo his friends with the streetwise insults.

"Well, what's the first thing a good dozens roller hit you with?"

Romeo smiled.

"That's right. 'You so black—, your mama so black—, your head so nappy—!'"

Romeo laughed, clapping his hands together as Piano Man shook his head from side to side.

"Like I said, people get funny 'bout things that's different, and when they can't find fault with your color, they find fault with your religion, or your sex, or whatever else ain't like theirs. But color crosses both sides 'cause black folks might not care if you pray to God, Allah, Buddha, or the king of Egypt, but if you too light, too dark, or your hair ain't just so, somebody ain't gon' like you."

"Well," Romeo said, "I'm a true believer that when someone goes out of his way to attack someone about something that's not based on the content of their character, it's only because they're not secure in themselves. It's ultimately their problem and nothing we do can change them if they don't want to change. I personally like my color. Kind of Hershey brown, don't you think?"

"I know you proud of your blackness, boy. You can see it in the way you hold up your head."

"Don't laugh. It took me a while to be proud of who I am. I didn't always like being black."

"Why not?"

"Spent too much time listening to people tell me that as a black man I wasn't good enough to be respected. I've seen the few black men I could look up to be ripped violently from this world simply because of the color of their skin. And, too many times, too many doors have been slammed in my face because I didn't shine as bright when the lights were out. There was just a point in my life when I viewed the color of my skin as more of a hindrance than an asset."

"I can understand that. I can remember a time when I was called 'nigga' so much I use to think it was my name," Piano Man stated.

"I remember the first time someone called me 'nigger' to my face. I'd gotten into this debate with this fair-haired, blue-eyed white boy in school. We were arguing politics. When he didn't like what I had to say he told me that he didn't expect a 'wanna be nigger' to understand the true American way. I was so shocked that by the time I thought to react it was too late. Mark Turner Johnston was his name. He's now the vice president of one of the largest engineering firms in the country and married to one of the most beautiful black women that I have ever had the pleasure of bedding." Romeo shook his head over the memories as he continued. "The second person to ever call me a 'nigger' to my face was Diane Berry. That woman had a long list of names she called me that night."

"Well, you did good then, if that was the first time someone had called you 'nigga.' Hell, when I was coming up that was all we were to the white man and sometimes to each other. My daddy taught me that when a white man called me 'nigga' it was because he was afraid of what he knew I could become. When a black man called me 'nigga' it was because he was afraid of what he had not become."

"I think your father was right," Romeo said, nodding his head. He paused briefly. "Hell, when I think about all the time I've wasted trying to prove myself to people who really didn't give a damn one way or another, I could kick myself. I use to work for a man who got a perverse thrill out of telling racial jokes. He was Irish and he thought that as long as he threw in a few Irish slurs with the Italian, Polish, and black jokes, that it was okay. I think about it now and I guess you can't expect someone like that to respect you when he didn't even respect himself."

Piano Man nodded in agreement as Romeo continued. "I guess I finally came to value my own self-worth when I first opened the Playground. I knew then that I could do anything I wanted and I didn't need any man, black or white, telling me how, when, or why. At that point, I knew that my mother had raised me to be the best I could be and had showed me that I was loved no matter what. I accepted that my being black had made me better because it made me stronger. My blackness forced me to fight harder and to appreciate everything more. It's just too bad there are too many black men out there who haven't learned that yet."

"You right about that," Piano Man said, yawning again. Yes sir, boy, you right about that. That's why some black women turning to white men. Ain't enough of us out there for them to lean on."

Romeo thought for a moment, raising an eyebrow. Thinking of all the interracial couples he and Taryn knew and socialized with, he interjected. "Hell, I've had black women complain to me that too many brothers are turning to white women, and they're not far from right. Explain that."

Piano Man shrugged again, shifting in his seat. "Well, I sure as hell can't say nothing. I've had more than my fair share of white women."

Surprised, Romeo clasped his hands in front of him. "So what was it? The pursuit, the conquest, or the prize?"

"No, won't none of that," Piano Man said, shaking his head. "I guess it was just 'cause they let themselves be had. Hell, if you put candy on the table and tell a child he can have it, he's gonna take a piece and eat, right? It won't much different. Playing in clubs all the time, I saw women as just candy ready to be taken. Yellow, black, red, and white. It didn't matter much what color they was as long as they was sweet."

Piano Man shrugged. "If I could do it different, I think I would, but I can't go back now so I don't worry about it."

"I guess you're right," Romeo said. "I know there have been white women that I've been attracted to, and more than my share of women, black and white, who have made themselves available to me. I have just always compared the women I've been with to my mother. I wanted a woman whose beauty was like hers and who had the same qualities she did. I've only found that in other black women."

Piano man smiled. "A man just wants a woman who's gonna support him and help him to feel like a man. Just someone who's gonna love him without all the bullshit. Just like that sweet little girl does for you."

Romeo smiled back. He missed Taryn. Missed holding her, missed her smell, the way her bottom lip quivered when she laughed.

Piano Man continued. "Too many young boys today

spend too much time fighting each other instead of fighting for what they can become. It don't leave our women much to choose from after a while. It's a damn shame too. Need to go back to the basics. A good ass-whipping is what most of 'em need."

"Old fashioned values wouldn't hurt," Romeo said, "but what we used to know as discipline they call child abuse today. Hell, these kids will turn your behind in at the drop of a hat just for raising your voice at them if they think they can get away with it. Or worse, kill you."

Piano Man laughed. "My granny used to tear my behind up. My father never hit me, but do something wrong, Granny would wear herself out whopping your butt." Remembering, Piano Man smiled widely. "The best was when we used to go south. She would send you outside to break off one of them switches from a tree and don't come back with no little stick either. She would sting the hell out of my legs with that damn switch, but you can bet I never did whatever it was I did wrong again. Shoot, not like that today," he said, shaking his head.

Romeo laughed with him. "Same thing in my house, but my mama used a belt. It was this thin, black strap she used to call 'Mr. Jones.' When I acted up, she used to tell me to go get 'Mr. Jones.' I used to think I was slick and try to hide it, but she'd always find a new one to take its place. I was fifteen the last time she spanked my behind. I thought I was a man. Too big to get hit. I jumped up in her face real big and bad and she slapped me right down. Mr. Jones wore me out that night." Romeo snickered.

Piano Man sighed, nodding his gray head. "It's hard to raise our kids today and it don't help when fathers are stuck in jail serving time over some ignorance or just not there period. Can't make young boys today understand why it's so important for them to be decent, God-fearing men."

Romeo nodded his head in agreement. Glancing at his watch, he yawned deeply. "Mr. Burdett, I need to go home and get me some sleep."

"Yeah, it do be that time." Pulling himself up, Piano Man adjusted his clothes, resting a frayed straw hat on top of his head. "Personally I'm going over to see my friend Aleta."

"How is my Aunt Aleta doing?"

"She gon' be much better once I gets there," Piano Man said with a sly wink.

The younger man laughed. "You better watch yourself. Miss Bowen don't play like that now."

"I sure knows that!" Piano Man exclaimed. "She done put me in my place more times than I like to count."

"You in love?"

Piano Man paused, then buttoned his coat jacket. "There are things I love about Aleta. She always been a special friend to me."

Romeo watched as Piano Man opened the door to exit.

"Special friends don't come 'long but so often," the old man finished.

Rising, Romeo nodded his head. "Have a good night, Mr. Burdett," he said softly. "Don't let that wind out there blow you away."

Piano Man smiled. "You too, boy. You too."

Ten

Aleta pulled the heavy wool covers up and tucked them around her and Piano Man. Curling the length of her body against his, she pressed the bottoms of her feet against his lean legs.

"Damn woman, your feets is cold," Piano Man stammered, wrapping his arms about her waist. "They's like ice."

"Sorry." Aleta smiled, rubbing them briskly up and down the length of his lower legs.

Piano Man nuzzled his face into the back of Aleta's head, the length of her hair caressing his cheek. He'd forgotten how comfortable it was to wrap himself around a woman, intent on nothing but holding and being held. Easy hands gliding for no other reason than to relish the warmth of touching and being touched. It felt good.

Just as sleep was tiptoeing across his brow, pulling him into its seductive embrace, Aleta's voice drew him back.

"So, what brought you back here tonight?"

Piano Man sighed deeply. "You want me to leave?"

"Didn't say that."

"Sound like you complaining."

Aleta sucked her teeth. "Why can't you just answer a question without getting all testy?"

Piano Man shrugged. "Won't nobody getting testy."

They lay together quietly before Piano Man broke the silence. "I missed your company. Just wanted to be with you is all."

Aleta nodded her head, pulling his arms closer around her. "I missed you too."

Piano Man rolled over onto his back, one arm curled over his head, the other still wrapped around her shoulders.

"What are you thinking about?" she asked.

"Nothing really. Just seem funny how things turn out is all."

Aleta nodded. "You thinking about Irene, aren't you?"

Piano Man shifted, slightly pulling his body away from Aleta's. "Just thinking that if she was still alive you and me wouldn't be here like this now."

Aleta said nothing, inhaling sharply.

"It bother you that I still thinks 'bout Irene, even when I'm with you?"

"Sometimes. It's hard being second behind a ghost."

"I ain't never lied to you 'bout my feelings, Aleta. You knows how much I cares about you, but it won't never be like it was with Irene. I won't never love nobody that much again."

Aleta nodded. "I have never asked you to love me, James Burdett, never."

"No, but you wanting it."

"Woman has a right to want, doesn't she?"

"Don't make no sense wanting what she know she ain't never gon' have."

Aleta bit her bottom lip.

"You wants me to leave?"

"You leave 'cause you don't want to be here, James. If I didn't want you here I wouldn't have let you in."

Piano Man kissed her cheek, cradling her gently in his arms.

"I don't means to hurt you, Aleta. I just can't be the man you wants me to be. I can't. It ain't fair to you either, me pushing to be close to you knowing I ain't never gon' be what you want me to be. But there's only two people left in this world who keeps me going. You and my boy. You two is all I have left that mean anything. I ain't ready to let you go yet. It's selfish, but that's just how it is. Can you understand that?"

Aleta nodded, pulling her body up closer to his. "I remember when we was younger and you and Irene use to sneak off behind that old building used to be down on Commerce Street. Irene would swear me to secrecy, making me promise that if her mama ever asked I would say she was with me. I would have lied through my teeth for the two of you. Irene was my very best friend and I loved both of you. I would have done anything just to keep the two of you close to me."

Piano Man smiled. "Yeah. Irene knew that too. She knew she could depend on you no matter what. But both of you knew not to do no depending on me."

"Yeah, you got that right. You was trifling, James. No good trifling."

Piano Man laughed, hugging her tightly. "You the only person know how much I loved my Irene. The only one can understand. What you and me share is special too. She was your best friend and I think she'd be real happy that me and you are close now."

Aleta shook her head. "I don't know about all that now. Irene may have loved you when she passed away, but she was still angry as hell at you for all you'd done to her. And I don't think she'd be real happy 'bout my being with you."

"She'd be happy that you was happy. She'd be pissed as all hell that I was getting something out of it," he said with a laugh.

Aleta laughed with him.

Piano Man rested a wrinkled hand atop her breast. "How come you ain't never come after me when Irene was alive? I knows you wanted me."

Aleta moved his hand down to her waist. "There are lines you don't cross, no matter what. As long as Irene was alive I couldn't cross that line, even when she'd written you off. No matter how I felt about you. Now that she's gone and the two of us are way past old, it doesn't make much sense to be wasting a whole lot of time not being happy."

Piano Man caressed her breasts one more time, brushing his lips down the length of her face. Lightly tracing the line of her ear with his tongue, he whispered, "I cain't promise my 'quipment gon' work. My body don't cooperate like it used to, but I can still make you feel good if you wants me to." His hands fell against the curve of her hips, dancing down the length of her thigh.

Aleta kissed him tenderly, her palms pressed against his face. "Don't worry 'bout your equipment," she whispered back. "Just hold me tight, James. I don't need you to do nothing but hold me."

Piano Man smiled, nodding his head. "I can do that. Yes, ma'am. I can sure do that."

They cuddled closely. Piano Man's hands lightly stroked the silk of her skin. Long black fingers tickled the bend of her elbow, rested easily against the arch of her back, sometimes tracing the round of her small bust line. He felt a mild tremor in his loins, the flicker in his manhood ever so faint. He took a deep breath, pressing his face into Aleta's neck. He could barely remember the first time impotence had taken hold of his manhood, recalling only the acute embarrassment blamed on an excess of drink. Piano Man had stopped anticipating more long ago, only expecting as much from his body as any man his age would want to expect.

The warmth of Aleta's body embraced the dark, limp flesh, teasing slightly. Closing his eyes tightly, Piano Man pressed his face against her breasts, the beat of her heart tapping at the brown of skin against his cheek. He sighed heavily, then drifted off into a deep sleep.

Taryn greeted Romeo at the door, a chilled glass of orange juice in her hand.

"Welcome home," he beamed, folding his arms around her.

Nuzzling her nose into his chest, she leaned up to be kissed, melting into his embrace.

"Mmm, thank you," she murmured.

He brushed his lips gently against hers. "You're home early. I didn't even get a chance to straighten up the mess I made."

Taryn shrugged, moving out of his arms. "Don't worry about it. How was your run?"

"It was good. I am so bad at keeping up with any kind of exercise. At least it doesn't hurt anymore."

Taryn patted his abdomen, laughing. "The things you have to do to keep an eye on this baby."

Romeo laughed with her, downing the glass of freshly squeezed oranges. "Thank you, that was good."

Taryn padded back into the kitchen, Romeo on her heels. "So, how long before you're off again?"

"I'm only home for the week, then I have to be back

in London and Berlin for two weeks. Do you think you can stand it?"

Romeo shrugged, a grimace gracing his face. "If I must."

Taryn wrinkled her nose. "You need a shower."

Romeo lifted his arm, sniffing the hollow of his armpit. "What are you trying to say?"

"You stink."

He laughed, pulling her to him again. "You don't like me au naturel?"

"Your au naturel doesn't bother me, it's your body funk that's about to kill me."

Kissing her cheek quickly, Romeo bounced up the stairs.

"What's on your agenda today?" she called after him, pausing at the bottom of the stairwell.

"Whatever you want to do! Now are you coming to wash my back for me?"

Taryn smiled teasingly as she headed up the stairs behind him. "Maybe. Maybe not."

She followed Romeo into the oversized bathroom, lowering herself onto the floor by the tub as he turned on the faucet, flooding the white porcelain container with warm water. She watched as he stepped slowly out of his clothes. He pulled his T-shirt up and over his head, flinging the garment to the floor. As he pulled at the waistband of his running pants, he smiled, then licked out his tongue, running the appendage slowly over his lips. Taryn smiled back at him, then rolled her eyes mockingly. Romeo gave her a quick wink, then flexed the muscles across his chest and arms. He smiled seductively and she could not help tossing her head back to laugh, the beauty of him shining in her eyes. He grinned, then lowered his naked body into the tepid flow.

"You getting in?"

She shook her head. "No."

He shrugged, bemusement painted on his face. "Suit yourself."

Reaching her hands into the warm water, Taryn filled the small cups of her palms and ladled the water down the length of Romeo's body. With his eyes closed, he lay back under the liquid blanket and enjoyed the patter of fluid against his skin as it trickled between her manicured fingers.

Taryn slowly painted the brown of his skin with a thick lather, brushing his flesh with a heavy coating of soap. Romeo welcomed the warmth of her fingers against him as she kneaded his flesh teasingly. As she traced the lines of his face, he pressed his lips against her palm, kissing the soft flesh. Leaning toward him, Taryn lowered her mouth to his. The embrace was slow, the two of them relishing their intense emotions. Reaching for her, Romeo pulled her down into the tub with him, the watery cloak saturating her fully clothed body. Taryn laughed heartily, the wet fabric quickly feeling uncomfortable.

Eager to feel her against him, Romeo pulled anxiously at her soaked shirt, ripping the cloth from around her. Taryn struggled slightly, freeing her lower body from the knit shorts that squeezed her hips. Hugging her tightly, Romeo pressed his chest against hers. The sensation of flesh against flesh was electrifying as desire surged between them.

Romeo could find no words to illustrate the emotions cascading through his body. There was no sense of control as his firmness sought the pliant crevice of her being. Romeo felt possessed as he gave in to the sweeping stimulation of her body against his. When their loving became too much to bear, when he no longer held dominion over the flexed muscle penetrating the satin of her inner lining, he heard himself cry out her name, the lilt of it embracing them both.

Romeo clasped Taryn as tightly against him as he could, conscious not to cause her any hurt. He lay spent beneath her, the warmth of the water lapping against their naked bodies. They lay together for some time, the fluid cooling around them.

Taryn lifted her body from his, extending a hand to him as she stood. Rising to his feet, Romeo reached behind her, turning on the shower overhead. Stepping into the heat of the fine spray, he shook lightly, the warm water tingling against his skin. As they soaped and rinsed each other, Romeo suddenly felt vulnerable; never before had he wanted to spend time with a woman as he now wanted to with Taryn. He smiled slightly, his dimpled cheeks rippling in the lines of his face.

"What?" Taryn aked. "What's so funny?"

Romeo shook his head, his smile stretching into a grin. "Nothing."

Taryn smiled back, her eyes twinkling. "Yeah, right."

"No really. It's nothing. I was just reflecting."

Taryn lifted her chin slightly, eyeing him curiously. Passing him a large towel, she watched as he stepped into the middle of the room, wrapping the plush sheet around himself.

"How long do you think it will last?" Taryn asked coyly, not looking directly at him.

"What?"

"The great sex."

Romeo stopped, dropping the towel to the floor.

"I would hope forever."

"I don't know," Taryn said, still focusing on wiping the moisture from her skin. "They say when two people are with each other for a very long time that the sex starts to get monotonous, routine, oh so boring."

"You're not complaining, are you?"

"Not me. Of course not." Taryn smiled, heading into the bedroom. "But it's different for women. I mean, most fake orgasm to begin with."

"Oh, hell no!" Romeo exclaimed, following behind her. "Now you're telling me you fake your orgasm with me?"

Taryn laughed. "You're being too sensitive. I was just generalizing."

"Sensitive my behind. I'm trying to figure out what the hell you're talking about."

Taryn fell to the bed, sprawling across the pillows. "I was just wondering out loud how long it would be before sex with you became boring."

"Why?"

"Planning ahead is all. You never know when it'll be time to move on."

Romeo dropped to the bed alongside her. "Now you're making plans to leave me?"

Taryn laughed again. "You worried?" she asked, rolling her body up against his, kissing his cheek.

Romeo shrugged. "Not really. I know I'm the best thing to ever happen to you."

"Do you now?"

"Uh-huh. Haven't you heard? I'm the catch of the town. Women are standing in line waiting for me."

"Are they?"

"Yes, ma'am."

"And why is that, sir?"

"The word's out that not only am I incredibly good

looking, phenomenally intelligent, and financially secure, but I'm also very well endowed."

Taryn laughed, tears rising to the edges of her eyes. "Really," she gasped.

"In fact, I have it on good authority that you were the one who started the rumor. That's how I know I'm the best thing to happen to you. You're talking about me. You go, girl!"

Taryn shook her head. "You need to stop."

"So, why are you trying to mess with my head, woman?"

"I'm not doing anything."

"You know exactly what you're doing. You've got my head so messed up now I probably won't be able to perform anymore, worrying about whether or not you're faking it."

"Well, even if I was, you wouldn't be able to tell."

"That makes me feel better," Romeo said with a laugh, wrapping his arms around her.

Taryn kissed him again. "I love you."

Romeo smiled, his eyelids suddenly heavy. His dreams would be sweet now that Taryn was home. Brushing his brow into the softness of her hair, he murmured lightly, then dozed off, Taryn still wrapped within his arms.

Eleven

Taryn's voice called out to him from the answering machine, the lilt of her voice tearing him away from the sleep that held him hostage. Romeo struggled to roll across the mattress, knocking the telephone from the nightstand as he reached for the receiver.

"Hello?"

"Hey, baby."

Romeo inhaled, taking a deep gulp of air as he gathered his senses. "Where are you?" he asked, yawning into the palm of his hand.

He could hear her giggling lightly on the other end. "I'm in Paris. I'm at the office," she responded.

Romeo reached for the alarm clock on the other side of the bed. It was quarter to four. Outside, it was still dark, no hint of the moon to be found. Then he remembered the time difference between the two countries.

"When are you coming home?" he asked her, rubbing the sleep from his eyes. "I miss you."

"I miss you too. I should be done here tomorrow and be home by the weekend."

"Taryn, I hate the fact that you have to travel so

much," he blurted out, surprising himself as the words spilled over his lips. "I mean—"

"I know," Taryn interrupted, cutting him off. "I hate it too. And I'm about ready to give this up. I hate being away from you."

"Do you mean that?"

"I do," she responded. "I don't know how we're going to work this, but I figure we can just take it day by day as we try to figure it out."

Romeo beamed, his wide grin spreading across his face. "I love you."

He could see the smile painted across her face. "I love you too. I'll see you soon."

After hanging up the receiver, Romeo sat upright against the headboard, wide awake. Thoughts of Taryn danced through his mind. She was coming home, and if he was lucky, maybe to stay for good.

Rising from where he lay, he eased himself into the bathroom to relieve his bladder. Minutes later he peered into the inner cavity of his Jenn-Air refrigerator. With its built-in mahogany overlay, the appliance blended seamlessly into the other cabinetry of the oversized kitchen.

With Taryn's help he had remodeled and updated his kitchen and bathrooms. He'd sought out her input when he and the decorator had bantered back and forth over the interior. He had wanted Taryn's influence, needing her to plant a bit of herself into the house he was breathing life back into. He knew that he had wanted Taryn to be a permanent part of the home he hoped to build.

For weeks now Taryn came and went at her leisure. He'd pressed keys into her palms without thinking twice and had been offended when she'd refused to sell her own four-bedroom Tudor to come live with him

full-time. Fiercely independent, Taryn was a woman
who insisted on having her own, insuring that he understood they would share whatever they agreed upon
the day he put a ring on her finger and made her his
wife. He had loved her even more for that, but still
had not moved himself to formalize their relationship.
Romeo heaved a heavy sigh.

Everything Taryn had chosen for his house had been
carefully selected, the woman insistent about the
makes, models, and styles, detailing specifically how
such would enhance the retail value of his home if he
ever opted to sell. Both he and the interior designer had
been impressed.

The cold cavity of the appliance was sparse, hosting
nothing but a bottle of Evian water, a Tupperware container of something that needed to be tossed into the
trash, and an assortment of condiments, too many jars
in varying degrees of empty. Romeo closed the door,
reaching into the cabinet behind him to pull a crystal
glass from the enclosure.

Walking into the den, he moved behind the large bar,
searching for the last bottle of scotch that he'd hidden
on one of the lower shelves. He made a mental note to
replenish his personal stock before the week was out.
Uncapping the bottle, he poured himself a drink, swallowing it quickly. Before replacing the cap, he refilled
his glass a second time, then headed back to the bedroom, drink in hand.

Back in his bed, he pulled a cotton sheet up over his
legs, then leaned back against the padded headboard,
his arm bent up and over his head. Drifting back to
sleep would be easier with the hint of scotch to lead
him in that direction. He wished that Taryn had not
been in the office. Had she been alone, in her hotel

room, she could have whispered him to sleep, her seductive voice helping to ease the tension that pressed taut through his groin. He palmed his hand across his crotch, his body quivering as his manhood strained for attention. Reaching for his glass, he downed the last of the bitter spirit.

Thoughts of the old man suddenly swept through his mind. He and Piano Man had lingered briefly after he'd closed the club, talking comfortably with each other. Romeo liked the old geezer. Piano Man had told him about his travels, enthralling him with stories of being on the road and playing with musicians many could only ever dream of hearing play. The man had lived his art, allowing it to lead his every move and action. Romeo admired his fortitude, the wealth of sacrifices he must have made to follow his passion. Romeo didn't know many men who would have done what Piano Man had done without regrets. Romeo had asked him if there had been anything he would have done differently. As he lay there he remembered the look that crossed the old man's face. The look that conflicted with the words that eased out of his mouth.

"No," Piano Man had answered, his eyes shifting from Romeo's face as if he wanted to avoid the younger man's scrutiny. "But it don't matter much if I wished I'd done something differently, 'cause I sure can't go back and do it all over. Life happened for a reason. God moved me where he wanted me to go. Ain't my place to question why or ask what if," he'd concluded.

Romeo sighed. There had been something in the old man's eyes that had told him otherwise. He'd sensed that Piano Man had been asking God a number of questions that hadn't been answered.

* * *

Piano Man tiptoed about quietly. Struggling with the buttons on a freshly laundered shirt, his hands shook as he fought to push the tiny alabaster stones through the small holes. His large fingers fumbled awkwardly as he grappled with the small closures. When he'd successfully closed the last button and had tucked the neat white shirt into the waistband of his dark gray slacks, he sighed deeply, the simple act of dressing himself now exhausting.

Aleta lay sleeping, oblivious to his presence. Piano Man smiled down at her, wanting to run his palm across her cheek, but not wanting to wake her. He'd been calling her small cottage home for almost a month, ever since she'd pressed her spare door key into his hand and had told him to come and go as he pleased.

Up most of the night, he'd been unable to sleep. His mind had been racing aimlessly about and he knew that whatever he hoped to accomplish would have to be done soon. His body was no longer as compliant as it once was. An inner voice now told him that it would not be much longer before he would have to eventually succumb to his decaying bones and withered muscles.

He had successfully pushed himself even farther and harder than he could have ever imagined being able to, but his time was running out and there was none that he could borrow. He'd been surviving on borrowed time far longer than most, but the end was drawing near and he would not fool himself into thinking otherwise.

Sliding his thick tongue across the back of an envelope, he folded the flap down and sealed its contents firmly inside. The two letters he'd written earlier lay side by side and he looked upon them proudly, stroking the paper as a sculptor might stroke a work of art.

Dropping them both into the top drawer of Aleta's bureau, he nodded his head, content with his work.

Piano Man eased himself out the front door, closing it quietly behind him. Inhaling deeply, he washed his lungs with crisp, fresh air. Morning dew clung heavily to thick blades of vibrant green grass and the early dampness felt intoxicatingly refreshing. Piano Man gulped hungrily, nourishing his body with oxygen. Making his way down the street, he strolled along slowly. Strangers walking their dogs greeted him warmly and he stopped every so often to say hello to a familiar face.

The walk was taxing, but as he rounded the corner and caught a glimpse of the large marquee that hung over the Playground, he smiled. Although it was early, he knew that Romeo would be inside and that he could hover over the piano keys for as long as he wanted without anyone disturbing him. There would be no questions about his plans or advice offered about what he should or should not be doing. Within those walls he was permitted to be who he was, doing as he pleased, with no questions asked. Also, if he asked nicely there was always a shot or two of scotch to help pass the time and sedate the gnawing pain in his joints.

Inside, Romeo sat at the bar, pouring over a mountain of paperwork. Quarterly taxes would soon be due and he needed to reconcile the inventory sheets Malcolm had meticulously completed for him. When Piano Man shuffled through the rear door, Romeo looked up momentarily, greeted the man warmly, then focused his attention back on his work. As Romeo balanced numbers, deciding what needed to be included and what could be ignored, he could feel Piano Man staring at him before turning his attention to the piano keys.

Music filled the empty room, pushing the quiet into a far corner.

Romeo had grown comfortable with their routine. Neither had any need for conversation. When they were ready they talked, but during the early morning they were most at peace with their own silence. Silence that sat nicely against the backdrop of the old man's music. Piano Man didn't ramble on unnecessarily, nor did he search for conversation Romeo didn't have time to be bothered with.

Romeo sauntered to the other side of the bar and poured himself a cup of hot coffee. After carefully taking a sip of the hot brew, he filled a tall glass with water and ice. As Piano Man danced a cha-cha with a pair of chords that would not bend and dip like he wanted, Romeo set the glass on the piano top. Piano Man nodded his thanks and watched as Romeo returned to his seat and his paperwork. This is how their mornings had gone for weeks now and how it would end on this particular day. Almost simultaneously they looked in each other's direction and smiled, each warming the other with a fountain of internal sunshine.

As the clock struck one, Piano Man's stomach growled loudly, the rumbling rising from the empty pit of his belly, vibrating throughout his intestines. He rose from the piano bench and stretched his limbs outward, cracking his knuckles. Pulling his fingers through his coarse curls, he scratched his head and yawned.

"Hey, boy, what you want for lunch?"

Romeo looked up from his books, glancing over at the clock behind the bar. "Didn't realize it was so late."

"I wants me some roast beef. You wants some roast beef?"

Romeo licked his lips, pondering what he had a taste

for. "Not really. I think I'd like some fish. I haven't had fish in a long while."

Dropping his body onto the stool beside Romeo, Piano Man shook his head. "Had me some fish the other night. Aleta fried me some porgies. They was real good too."

"And you didn't bring me any?"

"Won't nothing left. Hell, don't nobody have no left-overs when you got some fresh fried porgies. Nobody who got some sense at least."

Romeo chuckled, shaking his head. "Why don't we call over to Sunny's Diner? I can order fish and chips and you can get your roast beef."

Piano Man nodded. "You calls it in and I'll walk on over and gets it."

"Don't they deliver?"

Piano Man shrugged. "I needs to walk. My legs done got stiff."

"How do you want your roast beef?" Romeo asked.

"Order mine with mayonnaise and a touch of horse-radish."

Romeo lifted the telephone receiver to his ear.

"Add some french fries with that too. And a vanilla shake."

Romeo laughed. "Is that it or do you want to add the rest of the farm with that side of cow?"

Piano Man flicked his hand in Romeo's direction. "It should take me 'bouts ten minutes to get over dere. Tell 'em I'm on my way now."

"Do you need money?" Romeo called after him.

Piano Man waved good-bye, not bothering to respond, and headed out the door. As a heavy voice answered on the other end of the telephone, Romeo placed both of their orders, including two slices of peach pie to complete their meals. Standing, he gathered up the last of his papers. In his office he dropped the ledgers onto the desk, then stared out the window, leaning against the frame. Warm sunlight flooded the room and the heat penetrating through the window felt good against his skin.

Although it had been a slow morning, a prelude to an even slower day, Romeo enjoyed Piano Man's companionship. He had never realized how alone he sometimes felt going through his daily routine with no one else present. Malcolm usually arrived between two o'clock and two-thirty, and it would not be long after that Odetta would come strutting in. Piano Man's presence had become a welcome diversion from the mundane duties that were a necessary part of Romeo maintaining so successful a business.

It didn't take too long before Piano Man returned, his arms laden with bags that smelled of heavy cooking oil and spicy sauces. Romeo rushed to give him a hand as he struggled with the door.

"Thanks," Piano Man sputtered, resting against a wall. "Thought I was gon' have to stop and eat my half back at the corner. Dem bags is heavy."

"I told you to let them deliver."

Piano Man shrugged, pulling a stool up to the bar and his sandwich out of the bag. "Ain't no never mind. What done is done."

Romeo shook his head, rolling his eyes upward. "My fish is probably cold."

"You got a microwave back dere in that office. What you complaining for?"

Romeo laughed as Piano Man clamped down on the corner of his sandwich, his thick lips locked tightly against the bread and meat.

"You weren't hungry, were you?"

Piano Man flipped his hand at Romeo, responding only with the smack of his lips. Swiping his tongue across his mouth, he laid a trail of spittle and bread crumbs over his top lip, which was quickly brushed along the back of his hand, then wiped against his pant leg. Romeo rolled his eyes again, shuddering ever so slightly.

Drawing up a stool to sit beside the old man, Romeo proceeded to eat his own lunch. The fish was good, filling the emptiness in his midsection nicely. Every so often he'd look over at Piano Man gnashing his teeth and smacking his lips. He smiled a faint smile as the elderly figure pushed a forkful of flaky crust and syrupy fruit past his lips.

"Good pie, huh?"

Piano Man nodded. "Uh-huh. Taste 'bout good as my granny used to make. Apple pie was her favorite though."

"My mother's favorite dish was sweet potato biscuits. They would melt in your mouth they were so good."

Piano Man smiled, nodding his head vigorously. "Sweet potato biscuits. Mmm, mmm, mmm. Now that brings back some memories."

Romeo smiled with him. "Women don't cook like that anymore. At least Taryn doesn't."

"Aleta can still burn a pan, but you right. Ain't like it was."

They sat in silence, quietly reflecting back on memories that had not surfaced in a very long time. Retrospections of sweet kitchen smells that wrapped you in warm aromas of cinnamon and vanilla. Romeo was mystified at how quickly remembrances, stashed away years before, could suddenly dance across your senses, rousing sensations and impressions long laid to rest.

Thinking of his mother's biscuits brought a warmth across his brow and down his back that he'd not felt for a very long time. He could almost feel his mother's fingertips as they tiptoed against the nape of his neck, could almost smell her faint perfume and feel the brush of her lips sliding down his cheeks. He could even hear the soft lilt of her voice calling his name as she admonished him to finish the plate of food and not just the sweet potato biscuits he was so fond of.

Piano Man sat beside him, lost in similar memories. Then shaking the daze from his head, he cleared his mess from the counter and headed for the piano. Tapping lightly at a string of keys, he shook his head again and said, "Piano needs tuning."

Romeo stared as Piano Man pointed at the large black instrument.

Piano Man continued. "I'd do it myself, but my ear ain't as good as it used to be. I knows a boy who'll do it for real cheap and he'll do it good too."

Romeo nodded up and down. "I trust you. Take care of it and let me know what I owe."

Piano Man pulled at his pants, the waistline hanging off his hips. "I needs me some sleep. Gon' go lay down on your sofa in dere, if you don't mind?"

"You know you don't need to ask. Make yourself comfortable."

Piano Man slowly eased his way toward the office, then stopped abruptly, turning to face Romeo. "Your mama ever make you cheese eggs and homemade sausage to go with them biscuits?" he asked.

"Yes, sir. In fact, that was her favorite breakfast. Only thing I didn't like was the sautéed okra and

tomatoes she'd make to go with the sausage and eggs."
Romeo shuddered. "I hated the okra."

Piano Man laughed. "Me too. Couldn't never stomach
no okra no matter how it was cooked." Turning back to
continue his slow stroll, his whole body nodded in
agreement and you could see the kitchen smells pulling
him toward his dreams.

Twelve

The crowd was boisterous, reeling from one side of the room to the other. Piano Man held command over the masses, holding court from his throne up on the stage. Women in black, black, and more black swayed lean hips in soft shimmies and wide behinds in hardcore gyrations. It was almost too good a time for any one individual to absorb.

Romeo mingled with the clientele, strutting back and forth like a proud peacock. The women were excited by his presence, wanting to at least brush a soft breast or firm behind against him, feigning innocence at such brazenness. Laughter clung to the edges of full, wide lips that held promises of wet, wicked kisses. The vibe hanging in the air promised them it was going to be a night of unholy decadence, not suitable for the faint of heart or those with a Christian calling.

"Whoa," Odetta called out over Romeo's shoulder, bouncing up and down. "There's a party in here tonight!"

Romeo nodded, pearl white ivories shining brightly behind his wide smile. "I'm having me a good time," he exclaimed.

"Everybody having a good time," Odetta said, laughing. "Damn good time!"

Malcolm nodded behind the bar, passing a tray of drinks toward Odetta. "Piano Man is hot tonight. He's playing like the devil done got hold of him."

Odetta and Romeo nodded in unison. Romeo looked down at his watch. "Miss Sharon almost ready to go on?"

Malcolm pointed toward the dressing room door and they all looked over just as Sharon sauntered out. An expensive silk dress, the color of yellow mist, clung hungrily to her thin body; against her porcelain complexion it looked stunning. Romeo smiled, nodding his head ever so slightly, as Odetta poked him in the side.

"I done her hair. It look nice, don't it?"

"Very nice," he answered.

Sharon blushed as she caught them all staring in her direction. Her hands raced quickly down the front of the dress, smoothing the fabric against her thighs. She looked briefly over her right shoulder, her eyes darting about behind her. Her friends laughed.

"You look incredible," Romeo said, smiling and reaching out to hug her.

Sharon blushed again. "Thank you," she whispered.

Odetta giggled. "You go girl. You looking hot."

"These brothers in here aren't going to know what to do with themselves," Malcolm chimed, each of them lauding her with support and encouragement.

Sharon shook her head with disbelief, wringing her hands nervously.

"Go sing for these people and sing sweet. This crowd wants a lot tonight." Romeo kissed her lightly on the cheek. "Sing real sweet."

Sharon smiled. "Yes, sir."

Romeo placed her hand in the bend of his arm and

escorted her to the stage. Pulling the black microphone from its thin metal stand, he brought it to his lips and raised his hand for the crowd's attention. Piano Man rippled a line up the piano keys, then dropped his hands into his lap. He grinned broadly, reaching to caress Sharon's manicured fingers.

"Ladies and gentlemen, put your hands together for the Playground's very own diva, the stunning and talented Miss Sharon Wallace."

Romeo passed Sharon the microphone, leaning to kiss her one last time. Thick applause filled the air. As Romeo stepped off the stage, Piano Man started his dance atop the piano keys, pulling Sharon onto his dance floor. The crowd went wild. Romeo inched his way back toward the bar, stepping past hands and bodies reaching out for partners to swing and shuffle.

Malcolm and Odetta raced to keep glasses from being empty for too long, passing liquid spirits in every conceivable direction. Romeo picked up a tray to give them a hand. Up on the stage Piano Man and Sharon wove a heavy blanket of chords and lyrics, wrapping it around everyone present. Pausing briefly, Romeo stopped to stare up at the entertainment. The sight before him caused his breath to catch tight in his throat. Sitting in front of the piano was a man possessed.

There was madness in the old man's eyes, an all-consuming vengeance that had taken him above and beyond the wrinkled, decaying flesh that housed his spirit. His fingers raged deliriously, a bittersweet battle with Sharon as his supporting troop. He effortlessly fought against the silence, filling the room with his own personal battle cry, and as Romeo stood watching, his eyes transfixed upon Piano Man's face, he found the man's expression almost frightening. Romeo couldn't help thinking that it was as if the old man had made a pact with the devil and Satan himself had come to lay his claim.

The club was finally still. Malcolm had escorted Odetta and Sharon home an hour earlier and only Romeo and Piano Man remained. Romeo had closed himself away in his office, whispering over the telephone with Taryn. Piano Man smiled. It pleased him to know Romeo was as happy as he was, that life had blessed the young man with much love.

The old man lifted himself up from the piano bench. He'd not left the seat since he'd first sat down earlier in the evening and it had only been a brief minute or two since the Naugahyde-upholstered bench had begun to press uncomfortably against the back of his weary legs. Standing beside the instrument, he ran his palm across the wood, tracing the lines of the sleek design.

It was a Baldwin, their grand model, and it was a beautiful specimen. The craftsmanship of the polished ebony was impeccable. It had an elegant presence, reminding him of a sensuous, well-dressed woman who fit into a man's arms as if they'd been molded especially for her. And the tone was pure power, its sound extraordinary. Piano Man likened it to a musician's wet dream when it was played perfectly. He couldn't have chosen a better model if he'd picked it out personally, he thought to himself as he peered under the lid, examining every square inch of the instrument with his index finger.

Years ago he'd told a woman that he only loved two things, her and the piano. There was nothing in him that could have chosen one over the other, and his honesty about such had sent her running as fast and as far from him as she could manage, taking with her the only other thing in his life that he would ever love as deeply. His love though, had increased tenfold and he couldn't help but marvel at the capacity of the thoracic muscle pounding its own beat in his chest. It was expansive, filling him whole as he'd opened himself to the possibility of loving someone or something else, as well. Piano Man had discovered an abundance of love for Romeo and this new family of friends that had welcomed him with open arms, asking for nothing in return. It was great love.

Taking a slow stroll across the room, Piano Man stood at the entrance to Romeo's office, his ear pressed against the door. On the other side, the man was still laughing heartily, lost in the moment with his woman, and Piano Man smiled again. Pulling on his jacket, he eased his way to the rear exit and outside, then headed in the direction of home.

Hours later, Piano Man tossed and turned about, trying to find some comfort atop the soft mattress. Aleta had not found her way home yet and he was lonely. He'd grown used to her company. He now sought out companionship, wanting to spend each waking moment in someone's company.

As he pulled a pillow close to his chest, twisting his body around the soft cushion, he exhaled heavily, blowing stale breath past his dry lips. Anxiety swept through his veins, feeding the tension across his brow. The darkness was beginning to close in around him.

It was a curious chain of events, this growing old. He remembered as a young boy thinking that it would never happen to him. He had always insisted that he would beat the dark monster that lay waiting for everyone else. The obscene creature looking for the ideal moment to sneak past the door of good times and besiege one's youthful flesh with poison and decay. Piano

Man chuckled to himself, staring at the backs of his hands.

Old age had not only crept in, but had clearly jumped on his back, taken control, and was riding him like he was a wild horse needing to be broken in. He now did old age's bidding, no longer able to maneuver and control like he had some twenty-odd years ago.

His heavy fingers shook, an uncontrollable quiver of chocolate pudding. The ripened flesh was dotted with brown spots much like dark chocolate chips pressed into chocolate cookie dough. You could play connect the dots if you were so inclined, easily able to create a myriad of patterns.

Rubbing his hands together gently, Piano Man feared the day they'd no longer allow him to play the piano. The mere thought that the swelling in his joints would soon take away his one and only pleasure wrapped the tissue of his heart with a desperate sadness that he found too unbearable to even consider. He was nothing when he could not play the piano. Nothing that anyone could possibly want to care about. He twisted his body in the opposite direction.

Everything hurt. He'd not known it possible to experience so much pain for so long a time. "Lord, Lord, Lord," Piano Man cried out loud. "How much longer, Lord? How much longer?" Piano Man knew the answer though, knew it as surely as though he'd picked the date and time himself. He had one more thing left to do, one more goal that needed to be met. Then and only then could he close his eyes and sleep in peace.

The party was still going on at Amber House. Aleta swayed from table to table making conversation with old friends who were more family than acquaintances.

She looked up briefly to see Romeo enter the small room and take a seat at the bar. Making her way to his side, she wrapped her arms about his waist, giving him a swift hug.

"Now, I know you're lost, baby boy! What in the world has brought you here this time of the morning?"

Romeo smiled. "Couldn't sleep, so I thought I'd come by and hear the old man play." Romeo looked toward the stage and the empty piano bench. "Where is he? On break?"

Aleta shook her head. "No. He hasn't looked well lately, so I told him to go straight home tonight. I told him if he showed up here I was going to have him thrown right out. He's wearing himself out not getting any kind of rest, and the alcohol isn't helping much."

"I'm glad you could get him to slow up a bit. He doesn't listen to me at all."

"Trust me. James doesn't listen to anyone. He does exactly what he wants to do. No more, no less. He went home because he was tired and it had finally caught up to him."

Romeo nodded, his eyes drifting off into the distance.

Aleta watched him for a quick moment, marveling at the reflection of familiar faces painted in his eyes. He was a wonderful blend of both his parents, having claimed the very best of both of them. Romeo caught her staring and raised his eyebrows as if to ask why.

"You okay?" Aleta asked, concern kissing the edge of her words.

Romeo nodded. "Yes, ma'am. Missing Taryn is all."

Aleta hugged him again, not needing to say anything else. Her attention was diverted to the other side of the room and she politely excused herself to go resolve an arising problem. Romeo sat quietly, waiting for her return. Every so often a familiar face would wave a hand in his direction and he would respond politely but with little enthusiasm. His heart was not in it.

Aleta pulled up a stool and sat down beside him. "So, you and James have been spending quite a bit of time together lately. He's really enjoyed it."

Romeo twisted a paper cocktail napkin between his fingers, his head dipped ever so low. "So have I. He's a nice guy."

"Well, he thinks you're something special too."

Romeo looked up, studying Aleta's expression. Gulping the shot of alcohol before him, he wiped his lips, then turned about in his seat. "Who is he, Aunt Aleta?"

"Who?" Aleta's body stiffened slightly.

"Piano Man. Who is he?"

"Just an old man who has no idea how much people care about him. He's special and he doesn't even realize it."

Romeo shrugged. "Do you know anything about his history, his family? Anything?"

"We are his family, Romeo. Everyone who has ever gotten anything out of his music, we are his history. Anything else doesn't make much difference." Aleta rose to her feet, her gaze flitting back and forth to avoid Romeo's. "But why are you going on like this? It's late and you should be home getting some rest."

Sighing, Romeo laid a crisp twenty-dollar bill alongside his empty glass.

Aleta swatted her hand at him. "What do you think you're doing? You know your money is no good here."

Romeo smiled. "You are not going to turn a profit if you keep giving it away."

"Trust me, baby boy. I can count on one hand the

number of people I give it away to, and you two won't break me."

Romeo nodded. "Well, tell your bartender it's his tip."

Aleta shook her head as Romeo reached back into his wallet and said, "Do me a favor please?"

"Anything," Aleta responded.

Romeo counted off a row of green bills. "Slip this into Piano Man's pocket when you get home. He hasn't asked for anything, but I know he could probably use some money."

Aleta rolled the cash into the palm of her hand, nodding her head. "I'm sure he'll thank you personally tomorrow." She leaned up to kiss his cheek. "Stop fretting so much," she whispered into his ear. "You are too young to be worrying as much as you do."

Romeo kissed her back. "Good night, Aunt Aleta."

"Sweet dreams, baby boy. Sweet dreams."

As Romeo swung about, heading for the door, Aleta called after him. "Baby boy."

Romeo looked back over his shoulder.

"He's someone who needs us now more than ever. He's not used to staying in one place for any length of time, and I imagine he'll be leaving us real soon. Just let him know you're here if he needs you."

Nodding, Romeo took his exit as Aleta stood watching him, wanting nothing more than to be able to cry.

The sun was just beginning its ascent into the sky when Aleta eased through the front door of her home. In the bedroom, Piano Man lay face down on the bed, his naked backside framed by the ivory duvet cover. Aleta shook her head, amusement adorning her face.

"What are you doing awake?" she asked, moving to the head of the bed to stare down at him. "And where are your clothes?"

The man grinned, a wide expanse of happy painting his expression. "Couldn't sleep and it was hot up in here."

"You should have turned on the air conditioner."

Piano Man shrugged. "You home kind of late, ain't you?" He rolled onto his side as he watched her stripping slowly out of her black pants and white blouse. She stood in a Playtex bra and matching panty still staring at him.

"You keeping tabs on me now?"

He smiled again. "Do I need to?"

Aleta shook her head from side to side, the gesture slow and easy.

"Come here," Piano Man commanded, patting the bedside with his palm. "Let me rub your back for you."

Aleta hesitated for just a brief second before easing herself next to him, lying against the mattress. Piano Man shifted his body upward to kneel over hers. He began to slowly massage the width of her shoulders and her upper arms. As Aleta allowed herself to relax into his touch, she could feel her muscles reacting on their own accord.

Piano Man leaned to whisper into her ear. "A good lover, like a good musician, knows how to play his woman to get the best out of her that she has to offer."

Aleta smiled. "Oh, really?"

He nodded, his fingers lightly kneading the upper part of her back. "You got to know how to improvise the moment." His lips followed his fingers, damp kisses pressed against her skin.

A low murmur eased past Aleta's lips.

"That's right," Piano Man whispered. "Got to be slow and easy with her, let the music build up on its own."

Aleta giggled.

Piano Man continued to manipulate her flesh, skating lower with each pass of his fingertips. "Gots to have just the right amount of rhythm and, just like when I play the piano, gots to know just the right amount of pressure to use. Good loving, like good music, can't be but so quick. You want it to last just the right amount of time."

Aleta purred softly as he palmed the round of her buttocks. When his fingers skated down the length of her thighs, his hands teasing the insides, she jumped ever so slightly.

Piano Man laughed, a low chuckle that rose from his midsection. "Hit the right note that time!" he exclaimed.

Aleta burst out laughing. "You a fool, James Burdett!" She rolled over onto her back, tapping him against his bare chest. Piano Man laughed with her as he lay down beside her, easing his body up against hers. They lay quietly, easing into the warmth of silence that revolved around them. Aleta closed and then opened her eyes, turning to stare at the man who was watching her closely.

"Romeo came by the club tonight. Was asking a lot of questions about you."

"What kinds of questions?"

"Wanted to know if I knew anything about your past or your family."

"You didn't tell him nothing, did you?"

"You know I didn't."

The two went quiet for a second time, both falling

into their own thoughts. Aleta broke the moment. "You need to tell him, James."

Piano Man shook his head. "No, and don't start with me, Aleta. Ain't no point in stirring up a mess that don't need to be started."

The woman heaved a deep sigh. "I don't agree. He has a right—"

"No," Piano Man said firmly, lifting himself to the side of the bed, turning his back to her. "Just leave it alone, woman. Just leave it alone. Please. It's too late to change things now."

"It's not too late."

The man tossed her a quick look over his shoulder. "Look, it's time I went on my way. I wasn't planning on staying this long and I'm about ready to move on. Why bring him any sadness before I go? That's what Irene was always afraid of anyway. I won't do that to him. He don't deserve that."

"He needs to know that you love him, James."

Piano Man came to his feet, heading into the bathroom. "He'll know," he said softly. "He don't need me to say it for him to know."

Thirteen

Romeo's cell phone was ringing as he entered the house, pushing at the keypad to still the alarm. Racing into the kitchen, he dropped his bags onto the counter and pulled the device from his coat pocket.

"Hello?"

"Hey, handsome."

"Where are you? I miss you."

"I'm sorry, baby. I'm still in London. I've been delayed."

"Woman, don't tell me that! I need you home. I need you badly."

"How badly?"

"Badly. I'm hurting without you."

"I wish I could do something for that problem, but I'm stuck here for another day or so."

Romeo moved up the flight of stairs as he pulled at the collar of his shirt, loosening his necktie. He kicked his shoes off at the top of the landing. In the bedroom, he fell back against the mattress, pulling the pillows under his head.

"Are you still there?" Taryn asked.

"What are you wearing?" Romeo asked, his voice low.

Taryn giggled. "A suit. That red one that you like so much."

"No. What are you wearing under it?"

"Black lace. A thong with a matching camisole."

As Romeo closed his eyes, imagining Taryn bedecked in black lace, he could feel the line of an erection rising. His body responded to the imagery before he even thought to touch himself. He moaned softly as his hands fell against the waistband of his slacks and then dropped down against his thigh. He shifted his buttocks against the bed, finally palming the front of his pants with his hands. The telephone lay propped between his ear and the pillow.

"Where are you?" Romeo asked, still stroking himself through his clothes.

"My hotel room."

"Take off your suit," he commanded, "and tell me about it. Take it off slowly."

"Romeo, be for real," she said, and giggled.

"I am, baby. Do it. Take it off for me. I want to see you naked," he said, his sultry tone lighting a fire in Taryn's midsection. "I want to touch you. I want you to touch yourself for me," he said softly.

Taryn's breathing quickened. "I'm unbuttoning my jacket," she said softly, "and I'm laying it across the bed. Now I'm undoing the zipper to my skirt. I'm pulling it down slowly." She paused. "It just fell to the floor."

"Do you have on stockings?"

"No. Bare legs. Bare legs and black lace."

Romeo could feel his blood pressure rising. He struggled to release himself from his pants. "Lay on the bed," he said, his voice barely a whisper as he struggled with his own breathing. "I want to see you on the bed," he said, repeating himself.

"Can you see me, baby?" Taryn whispered over the phone line. "Can you see me lying here waiting for you?"

"Oh, yes," Romeo moaned. "Oh, yes, girl."

"Can you see me touching myself?" Taryn said, falling into the moment with Romeo. "My hands are caressing my breasts."

"Squeeze them," Romeo said, "just like that. Very nice. Your nipples are hard, baby," he said, his hand still pulling at his own flesh. "I want to taste them," he said, imagining the round of her flesh pressing at his lips.

"Ohhh, Romeo. You feel so good," Taryn cried out softly.

"I'm touching that spot, baby. Can you feel my hands?" Romeo asked, the pace of his breathing quickening.

"Ohhh, yes, Romeo."

"Right there, baby. Feel my hands. They're at your knees, stroking your thighs. I'm touching that special spot, baby. That's my spot. Feel me touching it."

Taryn groaned, her hands dancing against her body. Chills radiated from her fingertips, moving across the brown of her skin. Thoughts of Romeo's touch blew a cool breeze against her body and she shivered with anticipation.

Images of Taryn's body quivering alongside his flashed through Romeo's mind. He craved her, desperate to have her near him. Tension pulled anxiously at him, shaking the length of his torso as he maneuvered to bring himself to a climax. "Talk dirty to me, Taryn," he said. "Please, baby."

Taryn whispered into the receiver, fueling the fantasy

washing over Romeo's spirit. It wasn't long before she heard him scream her name, the rush of his excitement stimulating her own. When their moment of ecstasy passed, they both were breathing heavily.

"Come home. Soon," Romeo managed to finally say as he reached for a tissue on the nightstand.

"Before you know it," Taryn responded, still breathless. "I love you."

"I love you too. Call me later, okay?"

"I will. Bye, Romeo."

After pushing the room service tray and its empty plates out into the hallway, Taryn shut the room door behind her and locked it. Her briefcase lay at the foot of the bed, its contents untouched since she'd walked into her room and had thought to call Romeo. Her red Tahari suit still lay at the foot of the bed where she'd discarded it hours earlier, its wrinkled presence a reminder of the intimate moment she and Romeo has shared over the telephone line. She blushed at the memory. Romeo had a way of moving her like no other man. He engaged her to do and try things she might not otherwise partake of, but he was always with her, holding her hand, making her feel safe and secure when she did.

Dropping down across the bed, Taryn was still thinking of Romeo. The flux of confusion over her spirit had resurfaced and she knew she was well past ready to go home. Although she loved her job, and loved the opportunities the position had afforded her, home lay miles across the ocean, where Romeo laid his head at night. She would sleep alone tonight. Tomorrow would be a whole other story.

* * *

Romeo stood in front of the refrigerator, cool air blowing up his shorts and across his bare chest. Pulling a package of sliced baloney and two slices of yellow American cheese from the shelf, he heaved a deep sigh. Dinner would be meager tonight, the emptiness of the cool appliance rivaling the emptiness in his stomach. Pressing the meat and cheese between two slices of bread, he tossed the sandwich into the melted butter that sizzled eagerly in a heated frying pan.

His thinking of Taryn caused his heart to pulse in rapid succession, and the muscle below his waist to twitch with anticipation. Sweat saturated his brow, and if Romeo didn't know better, he would have thought the temperature in the room was excessively hot. That's what Taryn did to him. That's what not having Taryn did to his body when he thought of her. When he'd heard her sensuous voice over the telephone, he'd lost control. The sultry lilt to her tone had excited every nerve ending in his body and he had craved her like a thirsty man craves a cool drink of water.

With his grilled cheese and baloney sandwich, and a glass of Pepsi cola, Romeo retreated to his bedroom. She had promised she would be home soon. He'd sleep alone tonight, temporarily satisfied, holding tight to what tomorrow might promise.

It was late. Neither man had any inkling what the exact time was, but both knew it was late. They'd worked hard, the club filled to capacity just hours earlier, and now they were easing into the space on terms that didn't involve either of them being polite to each other or anyone else. Reaching under the bar, Romeo pulled a bottle from the shelf, cracked the cap, and poured a drink for himself and one for Piano Man. It was their second bottle since they'd locked the doors for the evening. The vintage scotch burned lightly as he downed the shot straight, then poured himself a second. Sitting down on the bar stool beside Piano Man, he brought the glass up to his nose, savoring the pungent aroma.

"Tonight was something else. After last weekend, I didn't think it could get any better, but you and Sharon keep outdoing yourselves."

Piano Man nodded, grinning. "Thank you. Now, tonight is how it's suppose to be. People was happy. A man doing something right when people get happy like that."

The second shot of scotch didn't burn quite so much. Romeo watched Piano Man out of the corner of his eye, noting the tired lines settling in his dark face. His eyes were growing heavy and his breathing no longer seemed easy.

"How are you feeling, Piano Man? You don't look good lately."

"Look good, feel good," he said sarcastically. "What's it matter anyway? I'm old. I ain't got but so long left in this world, then I can play my music whenever I wants. That's all that counts. Ain't nothing as good as the music."

Romeo shook his head. "You been to see a doctor at all?"

"Don't like medicine men, Romeo," Piano Man answered, his words slurred ever so slightly. "They ain't nothing but a pack of lying cheats charging you too damn much to tell you what you already know. I ain't got nothing that a bottle of scotch and some good cootchie won't cure."

Laughing, Romeo asked, "Well, I know you've been getting the scotch, old man, but what about the cootchie?"

Piano Man raised his eyebrows slightly. "Probably been getting too much. My heart might just give up if I keep going the way I am."

"You are so full of bull." Romeo laughed loudly.

Piano Man laughed with him, reaching for the scotch bottle. "What about you, Romeo? When's the last time you stroked some cootchie and stroked it good?"

"It's been too damn long, old man," he said, sighing heavily, his hand palming his crotch.

"Then you the one should be seeing the doctor, boy. All these pretty girls who be throwing themselves at you and you ain't had no cootchie. Don't make no kinda sense to me."

"Must be love, I guess. I just don't want anyone but Taryn, and when she isn't here, I wait. It's easier to do sometimes than other times, though."

"I loved me a pretty brown skin gal once. We was gonna have us a yard full of pretty butterscotch babies and cootchie whenever we wanted," Piano Man said, drifting back in time, a drunken stupor leading the way.

Romeo interrupted his thoughts for a brief moment. "What happened to her?"

Piano Man shrugged, shifting uncomfortably in his seat. An uneasy pause followed as his mind raced back to a time long since laid to rest. Recalling the warm flow of sanguine fluid passing from her soul, he felt himself shiver, contained emotion flooding throughout his body. The flashbacks remained too vivid in his memories.

He thought back to the cold ivory porcelain violated by the harsh crimson splatter of her pain, and the piercing scream wrenched from the murky depths of

his own heart. The skeletal figure torn from her uterus
had borne no resemblance to the predilection that had
laid its foundation. It had been crudely discarded by
the aged hands that had minutes earlier poked and
prodded at the core of her being. With hunched shoulders and henna-coated hair, the old woman had admonished them both, then told them to never tell.

"Forget," she had muttered, her putrid breath hot
against his ear. But his unborn child had forever remained a faint whisper upon his lips and a reverberating void within his thoracic walls.

On the train ride home, he had wrapped his arms
protectively about her, cradling her gently against his
firm chest. Although he tried to shield her from the re-
flective stares she thought to be all knowing, he could
not hide either of them from the guilt sweeping through
their souls.

The stench of urine in the elevator of the housing
project where she lived had greeted them at the doorway, the vile odor stroking his nostrils, reawakening his
numbed senses. Inside the small apartment she shared
with her mother and two younger sisters, he had sat
with her until she fell into a pensive sleep. Finally
making his way past the contemptuous stare of her
mother, he had muttered a soft "I'm sorry" as he'd
rushed out the door.

Home, within the confines of his own apartment,
he'd met his father's brooding gaze with frustrated
anger, then had wept like a baby into the robust bosom
of his paternal grandmother.

His father's words had rung heavily in his ears and
he was awed by the clarity with which he could now
remember the conversation.

"So it's done?"

"Yes, sir."

"How is she?"

"She's okay."

His father had nodded his head slowly, purposely, his index finger moving in sync as he'd pointed in his son's direction. "This don't make you a man. You remember that. It don't make you a man. When you can hold your son in your arms and wipe away his tears, and when you can teach him right from wrong and watch him grow into all that you want him to be, then you can consider yourself a man. Just getting your woman pregnant ain't nowhere near being a man if you can't support them and respect them the way they deserve. Don't you ever think otherwise."

The words had stung, slapping him across the face as though his father had raised his arm and struck him with the back of his hand. He knew though, that what his father said was true. The mere act of procreation had not bestowed upon him the status of manhood. It had only affirmed the repercussions of his yielding to the innate yearnings of his phallus.

Piano Man had been seventeen. Irene had only been fifteen. Her mother had cursed them both when she found out. She had made big plans for her daughter and giving birth so young wasn't one of them.

Many angry, tear-filled discussions between his father and her mother had preceded their decision, and when all was said and done they had placed the young girl into the care of Grandma Goody.

Grandma Goody, with her toothless grin and high-pitched cackle, knew how to "cure" her "ailment." She had "cured" many a girl with this "condition." Grandma Goody was safer and cleaner than most back alley baby butchers, but more importantly, she was cheap.

After wiping away his tears, he had changed into a pair of worn sweatpants and had gone to play ball with the rest of the boys, hoping to escape the haunting memories of that day.

"What happened?" Romeo questioned again, disrupting the old man's memories.

Shaking, Piano Man shrugged again, meeting Romeo's brown eyes, then dropping his gaze to the floor. "Time just sort of passed us both by, I guess. We was real young and went through some hard times too soon, then we just went our separate ways for a while. She passed away a couple a' years ago."

Romeo nodded his head, easing once again into the silence that followed.

They both sat quietly, each lost in his own thoughts. The scotch had finally eased the tension of the long day and they both relaxed comfortably, coddling the precious bottle between them.

Stirred by emotions that had not touched him for some time, Piano Man tapped his fingers nervously against the wood. Taking the last swig of the alcohol left in his glass, he cleared his throat, his body shaking.

"She always smelled so good."

"Who?" Romeo asked curiously.

Ignoring the question, Piano Man continued.

"Like flowers, real sweet and fresh. She had real pretty hair, long down her back, and she would rinse it with rose water. I use to love to just smell her hair," he said, his voice trailing.

Refilling both glasses, Romeo listened intently.

"I still remember the first time I touched her. I mean really touched her. I was taking her home and we had to walk up nine flights of steps 'cause the elevator was broke. We had just gotten up to the fifth floor and she kinda trips and falls backward against me. I just wrapped my arms around her little waist, spun her around, and pulled her real close. Man, she had the sweetest lips. They was full, like ripe berries just ready to be picked.

"I kissed her real hard and then my black ass got bold. I reached right on up and grabbed one of the littlest titties I have ever touched. My hand felt like it was burning her flesh and I couldn't breathe, the girl felt so good." Piano Man laughed. "Then she slapped the hell out of me. Had my ears ringing for days."

Still laughing, Piano Man rose from his seat, swaggering to the piano. Heartache suddenly danced lightly about the room as he penciled his emotions across the ivory.

As Romeo pictured a much younger Piano Man groping the virginal body of his first love, he thought of Taryn.

Just as quickly as he had started to play, Piano Man stopped.

"That bottle empty yet, boy?"

"Not yet," Romeo answered, filling the empty glass and passing it to the old man. As Romeo watched him sip from the glass, quenching his thirst, he realized how little he knew of Piano Man's personal life. Tonight though, Piano Man seemed to want to speak freely. Before he had always been very reserved, even somewhat cautious.

"You got any kids?" Piano Man asked quietly, his eyebrows raised.

Romeo shook his head no. "At least none that I know of."

Piano Man nodded, understanding like only another man could possibly understand having a child that he did not know of.

"You never had any, right?"

Piano Man shrugged, shifting his gaze away from Romeo's. "Actually I did. I had me two babies."

"Oh. I thought you said you and your wife didn't. . . ."

"That's right. Beulah and I didn't have no kids together, but when I was seventeen, my girl got pregnant the first time. Since we was planning on getting married anyway, we figured it was okay. Her mother, on the other hand, wouldn't have none of it. Insisted we get rid of it. She and my daddy found some old witch to do it. Couldn't go to no clinics like you can now. That broke my baby's heart.

"Won't nothing the same after that. Not her, nor me. She didn't even look at me the same. That broke my heart. We finally just stopped seeing each other and then one day she was gone. We caught up to each other again a few years later, but by that time I was a very different man." Piano Man paused, briefly shifting his body in his seat before continuing. "We had us a baby boy then." Piano Man nodded to himself. "Yes, sir, a mighty fine boy, and . . . well . . . I let them both get away from me." Piano Man sighed heavily. "That was a long time ago."

"I'm sorry," Romeo said sympathetically, conscious of the tears pressing at the man's eyes.

Piano Man shrugged his shoulders, took a quick sip from the short glass, then coughed loudly, dropping the glass heavily onto the piano top. He began to play again, a light, even tone quickly reverberating about the room. He stopped suddenly, overcome by a fit of coughing that shook his chest violently, the harsh waves vibrating down his body.

Romeo rose anxiously, but stopped when Piano Man lifted his hand, gesturing at him to stay where he was. As the coughing subsided, Romeo sat back down, hesitant. "You okay?"

"Yeah, yeah. It ain't nothing."

Their eyes locked momentarily, until Piano Man

broke the gaze, returning to his playing. Romeo settled back into the cushioned seat, spinning his own scotch-filled glass between the palms of his hands. He sighed, exhaling deeply, enjoying the light serenity of the music, which brushed soothingly across his brow, massaging the tension in his shoulders and neck. As he closed his eyes, the music whispered to him through the darkness, its silvery touch calming.

He thought about the women who had shared moments in time with him. Women who'd danced in varying shades of brown like autumn leaves swaying in a warm breeze. Shades of brown that had melted against the backdrops of glistening sunsets, clear morning skies, and starched white sheets. Each shade of brown stood out vivid in his memory, sweet against his taste buds like a rich chocolate confection. Melting into his memories, the syrupy sweetness blended into a mixture of cocoas and caramels. So absorbed was Romeo in his own thoughts that he barely noticed when Piano Man stopped playing.

Quiet again enveloped the room, disrupted only by the clock behind the counter that hummed softly and the wind outside that tapped lightly against the windows. Shaking himself back to reality, Romeo watched as Piano Man sat engrossed in his own thoughts, anxiety skipping across his face. As Romeo observed the man's complacent expression transform to one of anguish, the beat of his heart quickened. "Hey there. Are you okay?"

The lengthy pause that followed only heightened Romeo's own anxiety. "Piano Man, are you okay?" he asked again, emphasizing each word slowly.

Piano Man finally responded, his tortured gaze once again meeting Romeo's. "I coulda been a good daddy," he whispered softly. "If I'da been man enough to stand up for what I believed in, me and my girl woulda raised lotsa pretty butterscotch babies like we wanted, and I woulda been a good daddy. My boy's a grown man now and he don't even know how much I love him. All he knows is that his daddy won't nowhere 'round when he needed 'em." With that proclamation, the tears spilled from the old man's eyes, rolling over his flushed cheeks.

Rising, Romeo sat down on the bench beside Piano Man, draping his arm over the man's hunched shoulders. They sat together for some time, Piano Man's sobs resonating off the cream-colored walls. The heat had finally eased down, replaced by cool fresh air.

As a chill crept slowly up Romeo's spine, his eyes scanned the room, now made larger by its emptiness. Behind the bar, assorted bottles sat neatly upon oak-tinted shelves, and glasses in varying sizes hung neatly in drying racks. Romeo counted each bottle slowly, fighting to keep from crying himself.

It had been years since he'd last shed a tear for anything of any real importance. He'd been twelve years old, maybe thirteen. His Little League baseball team had just played the final game in the city championships. The score had been four to three with two outs in the bottom of the seventh inning. Bases had been loaded and the opposing team's biggest hitter was at bat. A line drive past third base had hit Romeo's outstretched mitt, nestling comfortably in the oiled leather. As he pulled the prized catch into his chest, the crowd's cheers exploded around him, the roar pleasant to his ears. His teammates had slapped him about the shoulders and back as kudos echoed in his heart. Parents were hugging and kissing them for a game played well, and it wasn't until he had watched the last father lead his son home that his tears fell. They had continued to fall as he made his way home alone and greeted his mother at the door when she arrived home from work.

He had cursed the father he didn't know for never having been there, his mother for always having to work, and his tears, which would not stop falling from his dark eyes. His mother had held him, rocking him against her breast. His teardrops had soaked the front of her worn blue sweater. Her own tears had rested cautiously at the edge of her eyes. "You can't force a man to be what he don't think he can be," she had said of his father. "A man makes his own path toward right and wrong." Romeo had wept one last time for the man whose only contribution to his existence had been to water the seed that had given him life.

In the distance, water dripped lazily from a spout, each drop bouncing against the metallic sink, then rolling down the drain. Romeo hugged Piano Man closer, the sobs shaking the man's weakened body. Quivering as though cold, Piano Man fought to regain his composure, suddenly embarrassed by his display of emotion. With a wrinkled hand, he wiped roughly at his bloodshot eyes, moisture falling into the ebony creases.

"Look at me," Piano Man gasped. "Blubbering like a damn baby. Black man ain't got no business crying like that."

"Why not? A black man is entitled to show his pain like anyone else."

Piano Man shook his head. "Different world you and I come from, Romeo. Ain't no man black or white suppose to show his weaknesses, and if a white man not suppose to do it, you can sure as hell bet a black man better not even think about it."

"Same world, Piano Man. We just look at it from different angles." Leaning over the bar, Romeo reached for a third bottle of scotch. Twisting the cap easily between his long fingers, he twirled it slowly, pressing the metal closure against the glass. Stroking the cool amber glass, he searched his heart carefully for the words that rose anxiously to his lips.

"I used to cry a lot for my daddy."

A pained expression crossed Piano Man's face. "Why?"

"Because he was never there. Because I didn't know anything about him. For as long as I can remember it was just me and my mother. When she died, it was just me."

Piano Man closed his eyes, inhaling deeply. Opening them again, he focused on the ground before him, scuffing the toe of his shoe along the wooden floor. "Lotsa boys grow up with no man around. Doesn't mean they daddys didn't want to be there though. Sometimes that just how it has to be. I knows 'cause if I could've, I would have been there for my boy.

"Personally, I thank the good Lord every day for making our women strong like he done. Ain't no woman like a black woman who gots to raise her babies alone. My boy was lucky 'cause he had a real good mama. I ain't never loved no woman the way I loved her."

"Amen to that," Romeo cheered, nodding his head in agreement. "My mother's probably the only reason I made it. She worked three jobs to raise me with a roof over my head, food on the table, and clothes on my back. I didn't appreciate it then, but now I wish I could give back one ounce of what she gave to me. I can never repay her for all she did and I just hope she knew I loved her. I always wondered, though, if he ever thought about me. I could never understand how any man would not want to at least know his own child."

Piano Man looked at him pensively, shrugged his aching shoulders, then hung his head. "Sometimes a man can't do what he wants to do or even what he should do. It don't make him a bad man though. It don't mean that he didn't care about you either. He probably had his reasons for not being there."

Romeo shrugged. "My mother once said that he didn't think that I was his. I use to be real angry about that. Who the hell was he to doubt me or what my mother told him? My mother was a good, decent woman and he had no right to doubt my paternity, especially knowing how much she loved him."

Piano Man grunted. "What else did your mama have to say?"

"Nothing really. I don't think she really knew what to say to me about him. I don't think she truly understood what happened herself." Romeo dropped his head into his hands, thinking about his mother.

Conversations between them about his father had been few and far between. She'd always changed the subject when Romeo asked about him, telling him that there had only been one resurrection and if he needed to call upon his father, then he should drop to his knees in prayer to God. The most information she had ever volunteered about the man was that he'd been a wanderer, never able to settle down in one place. He'd gone searching for something, she'd once said. Something neither one of them had to give him.

"You ain't never seen your daddy at all?" Piano Man asked quietly, staring over Romeo's shoulder.

Romeo shook his head no. "My mama would never even show me a picture of him. In fact, up until the day she died she even refused to tell me his name. It's not even on my birth certificate. She used to say that I was better off not knowing. That what I didn't know couldn't hurt me."

A tear slid down Romeo's cheek, falling onto the piano. "It did hurt though. It still hurts, although I keep telling myself that I'm too old to let it bother me." Clasping his hands tightly together, Romeo laid his forehead against the cool keys, a dull cord vibrating against his skin.

Piano Man poured a shot into his glass, stared at the contents, then pushed it away, saying, "I drink too damn much." He sighed, staring past Romeo's broad shoulders. Looking back down at the keys under his shriveled hand, he pushed lightly at the ivories. Slowly he played scales from one end of the piano to the other, pushing Romeo out of the way as he did.

"My grandmother taught me to play the piano," he said, adding a soft chord with his left hand.

Romeo smiled, lifting himself up to watch Piano Man's crinkled fingers skate along the keyboard.

Piano Man continued. "Every day she'd make me sit down at the piano and practice. Every day. My father would just sit back and read while I practiced, then when I was done my granny would play. She'd play these old spirituals that reminded me of church smells in the summertime. She taught me to love the music." Piano Man stopped playing.

"Each summer we'd go south to this small dirt road town in South Carolina. We'd drive down in this big black Buick she had. She always chose revival week at her old home church to go visit her people. I swear, we used to sit in church half the day and most of the night, just so my granny could play. Watching that old woman make that piano sing was what got me hooked. It'd be hot, and the water would be pouring down her face, but she was so happy. No matter how bad things was, she was happiest when them old spirituals was dancing out of that piano."

Piano Man smiled, reminiscing about his grandmother and those sojourns south. He could remember cornfields stretching for miles, the tops of the stalks reaching high up into the sky, crying for rain. Off in the distance, tall oak trees would loom eerily, peeking strangely over the corn stalks, seeming out of place in a small boy's mind. The heat would hang uncomfortably in the air, drawing the moisture from his small body, and with each hot breath, his lungs would burn, crying for a cool breeze.

He remembered the dust that swirled under his bare feet, up about his head, leaving an ashy film atop his skin, and the incessant swarms of mosquitoes, flies, and bees that buzzed about.

He also remembered his grandmother telling him that whatever he played should come from that part of him that was too deep for anyone else to reach. That one spot within his soul that only the music and the good Lord could reach without effort. She had played for her God. Rich, warm tunes that started out slow and easy, rising to an impassioned praise of all that was good and honest. Back then, in his young mind, all this was well beyond his comprehension and nowhere within the realms of his small reach.

Piano Man resumed playing. Romeo recognized the tune, but couldn't remember all the words: *"Steal away to Jesus . . . steal away home. . . . I ain't got long to stay here. . . ."* He knew his mother had played it every so often on a Sunday afternoon when she could find a quiet moment to herself. She'd play gospel records while rocking on the front porch, the smell of freshly fried chicken and hot peach cobbler wafting from the kitchen. He would go sit at her feet, leaning his head into her lap so that she could stroke his brow. They'd talk about her dreams and aspirations for him, her hopes for the future, and those old records would play over and over and over again.

His mother and Piano Man's grandmother had been cut from the same cloth. Like many black women, they'd been nursed from the same bottle of hope, had been fed off the same plate of expectation, and had loved like many black women struggling to raise proud black men out of scared brown boys.

The tune suddenly changed, a crisp, clear tantalizing syncopation of past and present meeting like two old friends. Rising from the piano, Romeo slow-danced across the floor, his arms wrapped about an invisible partner. He pulled her close, pressing his cheek against hers, wrapping his arms around the curve of her waist. He envisioned a long frame gliding along with him, a manicured hand gently stroking the small of his back.

He suddenly longed to hold Taryn in his arms, to hear the sound of his name brushing across her lips as she pressed herself into him. He imagined himself sweeping her up into his arms and laying her gently across an unmade bed, feeling her shapely legs wrapping tightly around him, the eve of her crotch pressed anxiously against his rising erection. Allowing the fantasy to consume him, Romeo could feel the tightness of his third leg straining against the front of his gray wool slacks.

He spun his ghostly partner, dipped her gently, and then pulled the mirage close to his chest again. They swayed easily from side to side, then danced a slight two-step from one side of the dance floor to the other.

In his mind's eye he saw himself pausing at Taryn's navel, moist and sweet from the glistening perspiration rising on her skin. He was pulling excitedly at her denim jeans, slipping the confining fabric from her hips past her quivering knees. Easily plying her legs apart, he ran his tongue along the insides of her thighs, inhaling the sweet aroma of her passion. She tasted of sweet cream and he pressed his nose into the brown bush of bristled curls to taste of her honey.

He pulled his dance partner closer, the front of his slacks pushing at the zippered seam. He twirled her lightly about the room, easily gliding from side to side. They moved in perfect synchronization and he marveled at how light on her feet she was.

Romeo thought again of Taryn, dreaming of lapping greedily at her juices until neither of them could wait any longer. He then ripped his own clothes away from his taut frame and pushed himself easily into her, the muscles across his buttocks pressing him tightly against her. Her legs would fall lightly across his back and she would meet him stroke for stroke until there'd be nothing left but the essence of his manhood pouring deep within her.

Drenched in perspiration, Romeo dropped to his knees, his arms falling to his sides. He watched silently as the phantom dancer blew him a kiss, then floated quietly out of the room, now lost within the realms of his imagination. He shook slightly, then rose back onto his feet. Turning toward Piano Man, who had finished his song, he watched as his dear friend reached for the full glass of scotch and pulled it to his aged lips.

Fourteen

"What you got to eat in that office back there, boy? I'm hungry," Piano Man stated matter-of-factly, standing gingerly on his arthritic legs. His ill-fitting clothes hung loosely on his thin body, the black cotton shirt and slacks nothing but folds of limp, worn fabric. He scratched his head briskly, then yawned loudly, stretching his arms high into the air. Smacking his parched lips, he grinned broadly, revealing tar-stained teeth.

"You hear me, Romeo? What you got to eat? I need something to soak up some o' dis liquor or I ain't gonna be no good tomorrow."

Romeo grinned broadly, adjusting the bulge in his crotch. "You're in luck tonight, old man. Odetta brought me some fried chicken and sweet potato pie."

"Well, what you wasting time dancing with yourself for when we coulda been eating. You knows I love me some sweet 'tata pie," Piano Man said, smacking his hands and his lips together in anticipation.

Disappearing into the next room, Romeo went to prepare two plates. Hesitating just briefly, Piano Man reached for the bottle of scotch, then replaced the cap. Returning it and the used glasses to the bar, he turned up the lights, then sat himself comfortably at a side table, suddenly famished.

As he waited patiently, he thought about Romeo. "Good boy he is," he said aloud to himself. "A real good boy."

He had liked Romeo the moment he'd found him. Not many would have opened up so warmly to an old man with no job, no home, and seemingly nothing in his future but hopes for a quick and painless death. But Romeo had treated him with kindness and genuine affection. And most important of all, respect. Romeo made him feel like a man of worth, something within himself he had come to doubt. Something he didn't think he deserved from Romeo.

With Romeo, Piano Man was reminded of his own father. Knowing there had been no man for Romeo to turn to while growing up ripped through his heart like a warm knife slicing through butter. It tore up his insides because Piano Man's own father had been his lifeline, his source of strength and guidance, and to see that his own son had never known such security made him sick to his stomach.

Romeo had endured his growing up alone, with no male presence to guide and support him. Piano Man's pain came raging at him, the tempestuous emotions bullying the goodness dwelling within his soul. When he was reminded of not having been there for his son, he felt the tide of self-hatred propelling him back toward the doors he'd long ago tried to leave closed behind him. He had failed his son, and repeatedly since the day he'd walked through the doors of the Playground, he felt as though God had given him yet another chance at redemption. And he was once again failing Romeo.

Wrapping his arms tightly about his shoulders,

Piano Man hugged himself closely, fighting the urge to start crying all over again. He sighed heavily and suddenly wondered about Irene. Forgiveness had not been in her heart, her love replaced by something that surely wasn't loving. Clearly she had not been able to forgive him, wanting to fuel the void between him and his child with half-truths and lies. And Piano Man had let her, refusing to step up and do what he should have done. Irene had not forgiven him for that, and Piano Man couldn't help but wonder if Romeo would ever be able to.

Piano Man couldn't understand when or even why things had gone south for the two of them. He had loved Irene with every square inch of his heart, and he had earnestly believed that loving her as hard and as deep as he had was enough to get them through anything. His music hadn't made him millions, but he'd done reasonably well for himself. They could have had a comfortable life together if only she could have understood his need for the music. He had never asked anything from her other than to share him with his piano, and that one request had been more than she had been willing to oblige him. And despite it all, he had never stopped loving her or hoping that the two of them could have reconciled for the sake of their child. He heaved a deep sigh, his thoughts suddenly disrupted by the noise coming down from the other room.

Romeo returned with a tray piled high with cold fried chicken, deviled eggs, slices of buttered bread, and a pie plate filled with a creamy confection of whipped sweet potatoes, praline nuts, and a light, buttery crust.

"Good idea, old man," Romeo said, setting the dishes down on the table.

Piano Man nodded, reaching for a chicken breast. "I know. Hell, any man know when you got some woman on your mind and your Johnson won't go down thinking about her, that all you's got to do is think about putting some food in your belly."

Romeo looked up from his own piece of chicken, suddenly embarrassed. "Damn, old man, you don't miss anything, do you?" he said, blushing profusely, the flush of color rising in his cheeks, peeking past the brown of his satiny skin.

"What?" Piano Man spewed, bits of food falling down his chin. "Oh hell, boy, I was talking 'bout me. My Johnson been up since Odetta leaned them big titties on my arm tonight. You know a man my age can't take but so much."

Romeo laughed loudly, choking on a mouth full of food. Pounding his chest to help clear his airway, Romeo sat doubled over with laughter. As he gulped for air, tears rose to the edges of his eyes.

Piano Man sat coolly, gnawing hungrily on the fleshy meat fried in a crisp coating of seasoned flour and buttermilk. "You gonna live?" he asked casually, picking a large wedge of meat from between his teeth.

Romeo gasped, still chuckling. Nodding his head brusquely, he coughed to clear his throat. "That hurt."

Piano Man grunted, dabbing at his plate with the crust of bread. "Dis some good food, boy. You gonna eat that chicken on your plate?"

"Get your eyes off my meat, old man," Romeo whispered hoarsely.

"Just asking."

Piano Man reached for the plate of sweet potato pie, sliding a large wedge off onto the chipped ivory coaster in front of him. Spooning a generous portion into his mouth, he savored the creamy sweetness, the rich dollop gliding along his tongue.

"You're right. This food is good," Romeo agreed, licking the tangy spices from his fingertips.

Piano Man responded by shoving another fork full of pie into his mouth. The two men ate in silence, punctuated only by the sounds of their slurping tongues, smacking lips, and gnashing teeth. When nothing remained on their plates but the polished chicken bones and flecks of piecrust, they both sat back, resting their hands on their heavy stomachs.

"So," Piano Man asked suddenly, "when you gonna marry this girl of yours?"

Romeo shrugged his shoulders, a pensive look etched on his face. "I don't know. I'm almost afraid to ask her. She's so damn busy with her job that I'm not even sure she'd say yes if I did ask her to marry me."

Piano Man raised his eyes slightly. "You know. Men know. Women have this look about them. When they want you, you can feel it burning deep down inside you."

"Well, we've talked about it, but I guess I've avoided anything definite. She knows I love her and plan to spend the rest of my life with her, but we've never said when or how." Romeo leaned on his elbows, resting his chin against his clinched fists. "It just seems so damn final. I've never known anyone who's been married for any length of time or who was happy after the first few years. I just don't want to make any mistakes." He sighed heavily.

"Marriage like anything else. You got to work at it if it's gonna be right. Down in South Carolina where my granny's people lived, lotsa folks stayed married. They'd be rankled and irritable with one another, but they never stopped working at loving each other right. "Yup, just takes a lot of work," he repeated.

"Were your parents married a long time?"

Piano Man nodded his head yes. "They married young. My mama was fourteen. They had seven kids before me, then came my brother Willie Ben and my sister Ruth. I was nothing but a baby myself when mama died. By then, she and Daddy had been together some twenty-six years. When she died, Willie Ben and Ruth went to live with my older sister, Kitty. I stayed with my daddy, and my grandma moved in to take care of us. They's all gone now. Every one of 'em. Ruth died last year from the cancer."

Romeo stared out into space, hugging his arms about his torso. "Your daddy never married again?"

"No. My daddy used to say no woman could ever take Mama's place in his heart 'cause he loved her so much. They had promised till death would dey part and even then, she was still his one and only wife. Now, he didn't go givin' up on women all together or nothing like that, 'cause I knew when he used to go round to Miss Nettie's house for a little cootchie, but he ain't never brought her into my mama's home or my mama's bed."

Romeo smiled. "Folks just don't stay together like that anymore. It's become too easy to get out when things start getting tough."

"Ain't that the truth," Piano Man exclaimed in agreement. "But you knows when it's right, boy. And you knows when it ain't. Just follow your heart and it will work out. Besides, chasing cootchie all the time ain't no good for you, no matter how I might joke."

"You're right about that, old man. Hell, these days you can die from too much sex. Definitely ain't like it used to be," Romeo responded.

"Uh-huh, you can say that again," Piano Man echoed. Sitting back in his chair, he licked each of his fingers, wiping away the oils and seasonings with his tongue. As his shriveled fingers each disappeared slowly past his chapped lips, Romeo noted how bent and knotted they appeared. "That arthritis bothering you much lately?" he asked with concern.

"In my legs and hips mostly."

"What about your hands?"

Looking down at the appendages stained with age spots, Piano Man wiggled them slightly. "I can still play if that's what you're asking."

"Stop getting defensive. I just want to be sure your playing isn't causing you any pain."

"Well, it ain't," Piano Man answered testily. "And don't you go being a nuisance about it. Odetta and Sharon already give me a hard enough time. I don't need you mothering me too."

"Keep it up, old man, and I'm going to tell Taryn. If you think those two mother hens are giving you a hard time, you wait. Taryn will show you what a hard time is," he stated matter-of-factly.

"Now, don't you go starting no trouble between me and Taryn. I like that pretty little thing and I won't let you go spoiling it."

Romeo laughed. "Just keep it up then and see if I don't unleash her on you."

Piano Man tossed a bone at Romeo, missing his head by inches. "She hear you talking 'bout her like that and you the one she gonna give a hard time to. Taryn don't play like that. I seen how she puts you in your place," he said, nodding his head.

"You right there—she doesn't fool around. I think that's what I love most about her. Taryn is probably one of the few women I've ever known who doesn't waste her time trying to play mind games with me. She lets me know where she stands on everything so there are no misunderstandings."

Nodding, Piano Man slumped down low in his chair. "Well, don't mess up waiting around to marry her. Do it soon too, 'cause I ain't never played at no wedding before." Piano Man burped loudly, the reflux of chicken and pie bitter in his mouth. "'Scuse me. Feels like I done made some more room."

"Well, it won't do you any good. That's the last of the food."

"Then pour me another drink."

Romeo shook his head. "Bar's closed, partner. We've both had too much. Besides, the sun'll be up soon and you know we'll have a full house tonight. I don't want you to fall asleep at the piano. And I need to keep Sharon on track. I can't have her on stage singing cold."

"Pretty voice that baby girl got," Piano Man said. "Sent right from heaven, she was."

"So I've heard before," Romeo said with a slight smile, thoughts of Malcolm crossing his mind.

Piano Man nodded. "Yup, she's an angel from heaven."

"Piano Man, if I didn't know better, I'd think you were sweet on our Miss Sharon," Romeo said coyly.

Piano Man fidgeted slightly in his seat. "She just reminds me of my girl. You don't know how much you miss something till you know you'll never see it again. Anyways, no—I ain't sweet on Sharon, at least not like that. I just know what it's like to need someone and she needs people right now. Besides, a man can go to jail for messing with young girls like that."

Romeo laughed. "Now, Sharon isn't that young. At least she better not be."

"No, no," Piano Man exclaimed. "She's not that young, but she still way too young for me. Cootchie that young would definitely hurt my heart."

Both men laughed heartily.

"We are truly blessed," Piano Man said, rising.

Romeo nodded his head as he also rose to clear away the dishes on the table. "Sometimes, old man, we forget just how much."

Piano Man ambled slowly over to the piano, the effects of too much whiskey and the pain of his swollen joints slowing his progress. Dropping awkwardly onto the bench, he pulled himself into a seated position and adjusted the bench beneath him. His breathing was heavy and labored, and as he struggled to pull his shoulders back and sit up straight, Romeo resisted an urge to run over to him to ease his hurt.

Romeo watched Piano Man, astounded to see him age so quickly right before his eyes. The creases etched into the old man's brow had deepened, the dark furrows bordered by weathered skin. As he sat hunched heavily over the piano keys, his limp body seemed void of life and emotion.

Romeo was suddenly reminded of an old rag doll his mother had when he was smaller. It had been sewn from old sack cloth and scraps of gingham fabric. Heavy yarn had graced its small head and its slight body had been stuffed loosely with old scraps of rags and straw. A single black button sat where an eye should have been and faded wisps of red string hung in place of its mouth. It had been his mother's one and only doll as a little girl and she had long stopped nurturing it with her childlike goodness. Romeo remembered how it had sat limply atop an old dresser, its ghostly form peering lifelessly out into space. He could remember thinking then, as only a young boy could, that if he held it and loved it, it would sit straight and tall and watch over him as his mother had taught it to.

Sitting back down, Romeo watched as old age washed itself over Piano Man, clouding the man's vision and impairing his hearing. It swarmed about him like small gnats on a hot summer's day, hovering on the edge of all his words and thoughts. Romeo suddenly hated what the passing of time had thrust upon his new friend and detested that he could do nothing to turn back the hands on the clock.

Piano Man sat stiffly, succumbing to his exhaustion and the drunken numbness that wallowed through his system. He shook his head as it suddenly felt heavy on his shoulders. Coughing to clear his lungs, he swallowed back the tainted phlegm, too weak to spew the vile spittle past his lips. He struggled to ease the tension in his aged muscles, hoping to stretch life back into his limbs. He was tired and he hurt and he was old, and at that very moment he didn't want to give a damn about anything.

He could feel Romeo's eyes upon him and he suddenly wished the younger man would fade from his sight and leave him alone with his misery. He suddenly felt truly unworthy beneath Romeo's kindness and he did not want the man to see him so low. The alcohol was gaining control and Piano Man had to fight to regain his equilibrium. Inhaling deeply, he mustered a small amount of energy from deep within himself and began to play.

The music was passionate and emotional, its intoxicating warmth tranquil and serene. Romeo rose and sauntered over to Piano Man's side, not wanting to disturb him from his playing. He bobbed his head in time to the music, his broad shoulders twisting slightly to and fro. He snapped his fingers easily, the subtle tune flooding deep within him. It was unusual, yet mesmerizing. He knew he had never before heard this music, but it was comfortably familiar. He leaned easily against the piano, the dulcet vibrato seeping deep into the marrow of his soul.

"Real nice, Piano Man. Real nice. I don't think I've ever heard that song played before," he said eagerly.

Piano Man shook his head, invigorated by that which he loved most. "No. This was something I wrote a long time ago. I almost forget about it. I call it 'Brandy.'"

"Brandy?"

"Yeah. I once knew this woman who used to read stuff to me by some guy named Shaw. I don't remember much of what she read, but I remember that he wrote that music was the "brandy of the damned." Well, if that didn't apply to me, I don't know what else did. This song came from that man's thoughts 'cause I could feel what he was saying."

"It's good, damn good. Why haven't you played any of your stuff before?"

"There ain't nobody want to hear the ramblings of an old man like me."

"I do."

"Well, you ain't all together there in your head no way, boy."

Romeo smiled slightly, shaking his head from side to side. "I can't believe that I have all this talent under my roof and you don't want to share it."

Piano Man shrugged his shoulders, painting a picture with the music. "Some things ain't meant to be shared with just anybody."

Romeo eyed him with growing curiosity. "Did you

ever think about recording some of your music? That might be something you want to consider while you still can."

Piano Man pondered the younger man's comments as he thought about the pages of sheet music that filled the large suitcase beneath Aleta's bed. He'd been blessed with many opportunities to showcase his talent. He'd drawn his inspiration from talented pianists like Tatum and Basie and had played alongside the likes of Davis, Hancock, and Jarrett. There had been days when he'd been privileged to sit in on jam sessions with Blake, Monk, and Corea, and had talked shop with men like Hines, Strayhorn, and Mingus.

One of his peers had told him once that until he'd sacrificed his whole heart for the music, he'd never know the fame and fortune that was waiting for him. The man had claimed Piano Man's heart was too divided, caught between the devil and a woman, he'd said with a wry laugh. He'd been right, and even before the words had left his friend's tongue, Piano Man had known the man had been right. But he'd been happy playing and writing for himself. It had been enough to just love the sound of the keys as they tickled the tips of his fingers.

Sensing that Romeo was waiting for him to respond, Piano Man tossed the man a quick look. "Things ain't like they used to be, son. Back in my day musicians could spend some time on their records. You could play the way you wanted until you got the music right. Nowadays they want it fast. Musicians are expected to record stuff quick, make a song like folks be making instant grits. Pour some water on it and it's done. A few quick notes and be finished. I can't play like that. My music is what it is and when I play I just do it until it feels right. I might have to play it for years before I can get the notes right."

Watching Piano Man, Romeo understood, and as his eyes met the old man's neither needed to say anything further. Piano Man suddenly stopped playing.

"What's wrong?" Romeo asked.

"Nothing. My bladder's just about to burst is all. Time to get rid of some of this water," he said, shuffling to the men's room.

Romeo laughed, his deep chuckle echoing about the empty room. He suddenly found the intense vibrancy of his own voice out of place, the silence alarming. He had always reveled in his aloneness, but suddenly found himself apprehensive and fearful of the unknown. Feeling out of control and attributing it to the alcohol, he tried to shake the sensation, the coldness dancing across his vertebrae.

Realizing that there were still empty dishes left on the table from earlier, Romeo set out to clear away the last of the mess. Scraping what remained of the chicken carcasses into the trash, he dropped the plates into the sink. Turning on a spray of warm water, he left them to soak until Odetta or Malcolm came in to wash them up. He paced impatiently, wondering if he should go check on Piano Man, then thought better of it. He was determined not to start hovering over the old man, not wanting to drive him away. A man's pride had a funny way of sending him in the opposite direction if he felt the least bit threatened, and Romeo did not want that to happen.

Lowering the lights, he sauntered into his office and sat himself behind the mahogany desk cluttered with piles of invoices and orders. A computer terminal sat perched on the top left corner, the keyboard lost under the mounds of paperwork. A picture of him and Taryn stared up at him from an ornate gold frame, their smiling reflections telling of a laughing, loving moment.

Glancing down at the Rolex on his wrist, he was surprised by the time. "Time flies when you're having fun," he muttered under his breath.

"What you say, boy?" Piano Man asked, entering the room.

Romeo looked up with a start. "Just wondering what was taking you so damn long. I was beginning to think that I was going to have to send in the troops."

Piano Man raised his eyebrows slightly. "Well, I would have pitied the soldier who walked into that men's room looking for me tonight. That call of nature would have watered his eyes."

Romeo shrugged, grimacing at the thought. "I hope you sprayed."

Piano Man laughed. Settling himself comfortably on the printed sofa positioned against the wall, he stretched his lean body out, resting his heels on the armrest.

"Don't ever let Taryn see you do that. She'd have a fit if she saw you with your shoes on that couch. Do you know what she put me through finding just the right piece of furniture for this office? She had to have 'Hamburg Teal' in just the right cut. Took weeks to find that damn sofa."

"Your woman sure do like things to be in they place. But don't worry about it. She'll get over it soon enough."

"Well, if she don't, I sure as hell will have to."

"Boy, you pussy whipped! That sweet little thing done whipped you big time."

Romeo laughed. "I prefer to think of it as trained."

"As long as you know it." Piano Man laughed with him, suppressing a yawn behind a clenched fist. "Boy, you see that sun starting to come up? I can't believe you kept me up all night."

"Me? Old man, you got some nerve."

They both sat in silence for a few minutes. As Piano Man drifted off to sleep lightly, Romeo watched the sun peeking lowly beneath the open window, searching for its throne in a cloudy sky edged in varying shades of blue. Despite his lack of sleep, he felt more rested than he had for some time. He turned to watch Piano Man, the man's chest rising lightly with each breath.

In the dimly lit room shadows flashed across the dark of their skin. Romeo enjoyed the silence between them almost as much as he enjoyed the conversation. It was as comfortable and easy as their laughter, possessing a natural ease he welcomed. He inhaled, then pushed the warm breath past his lips. Piano Man turned onto his side, then rose to a sitting position. Their eyes met and locked within the depths of Piano Man's face, a man could have found his own reflection if he had only known how to search for it.

Romeo broke the silence, cautiously asking the question that had been lingering in the back of his thoughts. "Where's your son now?"

Unable to immediately respond, Piano Man held his head in his hands, his elbows and knees supporting the weight of his upper body.

"Why did you leave him and his mother if they meant that much to you?" Romeo pressed on. He waited, watching as Piano Man struggled to focus, gathering his thoughts.

Minutes passed before the old man could finally respond. "I was in my thirties when my girl and I got back together. I'd gone back home for my daddy's funeral and she was back visiting with her mama, who won't doing so well herself. She was still the sweetest thing I'd ever seen and I wanted her real bad. But like I told you before, I was a very different man then. The streets had gotten a hold o' me. I knew she woulda been better off without me, but I couldn't let well enough alone. No sir, I had to try and get back what we had when we was real young."

Piano Man's voice dropped slightly, his tone barely audible. "I loved her, but I couldn't do right by her. She needed a man who could be home nights to hold her and who'd work during the day, and that won't me. I wouldn't let it be me. When you young like that and you think you got it all just 'cause you wants it, you sometimes stop thinking straight. Anyways, I didn't do right by her because after so long I didn't know how.

"One day I gets this opportunity to go play with dese big boys in Harlem and I won't gon' pass that up for nobody. Not even for my girl." Piano Man shook his head slowly from side to side. "See, the streets had made me selfish. All I could see was me and what I wanted—nothing else. I was running big time and I thought I had it all.

"What I didn't know, though, was at that time she already had our baby in her belly. She didn't tell me. She just told me that if I had to go, then go. She didn't want me to be staying if I wasn't doing it for me. I tried to get her to go with me but she wouldn't. She knew she couldn't live her life on the road like that. She had a lot of pride, my girl did. So I packed my bag, kissed her good-bye, and left, telling myself that she was better off. She was a strong woman by then and she didn't need no man to take care of her. Dat's what I wanted to believe."

Ringing his hands together, Piano Man continued, his lean body quivering ever so slightly. "I gots myself lost in Harlem. Didn't know where to find me. I didn't pray to nothing but a scotch bottle and some reefer and didn't want nothing but a good time with a no good woman. I was what my daddy woulda called worthless." He paused, brushing his hand across his brow. "I guess I must've been there 'bout two, maybe three years before I found out about my boy. A good friend was the one who came to tell me. Gave me a picture of him and everything. In fact, I been carrying it 'round in my back pocket ever since." Hesitating momentarily, Piano Man reached into his wallet and pulled a tattered black and white snapshot from its folds, staring at it proudly as he continued.

"When I finally broke down and called, her heart had gone cold toward me. She told me the boy won't mine, that he belonged to some man she was with before I'd come back to her. Now, I knew she was lying. And I knew she was lying 'cause she couldn't trust that I'd be there for her if she let her guard down. But I just told her okay and went about my business like it ain't never happen. Everyday, though, I'd look at this here picture 'cause deep in my heart I knew he was my boy. Right here, I knew." Piano Man patted his chest heavily, tears beginning to fall in heavy drops from his eyes.

Romeo leaned forward intently. "Why didn't you do something? Why not go and see?"

Piano Man shrugged. "I did, eventually, but it was too late by then. She was gone and my boy was all grown up. He didn't need me and I didn't think he woulda wanted me. Besides, look at me. It ain't like I had something to give him. I ain't never had nothing of any value to give him so he could be proud o' me."

Romeo stood up. "If he wanted to know you as much as I wanted to know my father, he would have been happy to just have your love. That's all I ever wanted from my old man."

Piano Man nodded, staring off into space, then lay back against the soft cushions.

"May I see his picture?" Romeo asked, disrupting the old man's concentration.

A look of distress passed quietly across Piano Man's face as his fingers, which held the small square of paper, shook. Romeo rose and walked toward him, his hand outstretched. Piano Man inhaled sharply, panic cutting through him with nowhere to run and hide. As Romeo stood over him, Piano Man dropped his head, hunching his shoulders forward as the photo fell from his grasp onto the floor. Bending before him, Romeo leaned down to retrieve the image. The faint gray likeness of a small child standing before his mother stared back at him. As he pulled the picture toward him, studying it closely, he gasped, the familiar reflections laughing up at him.

Staring at Piano Man, he stepped backward, throwing the photo back to the floor. Spinning quickly about, he rushed back to his chair and sat down sharply. Leaning his chest atop his knees, he inhaled deeply, fighting to fill his lungs with air.

"Damn you," he gasped, the anguish saturating his voice. "Damn you."

Piano Man clutched his head, tears raining down his face, relieved that the secret he'd harbored for so long was out for all to know. And on the other side of the room he could feel his son's rage rising as quietly as the sunshine outside.

Fifteen

In the brief moment that it took for Romeo to comprehend all he had just learned, an eternity passed. Cycles of life and death swept through his hungry soul, preying on his sanity. In that short span of time the emotions that rolled across the spirit of his being were all too consuming, amassing into a battalion of childish rage.

Trying to speak, his lips sputtered open, then closed. His tongue felt thick, like dry cotton pressed tightly into a too small container. As a young boy, he had dreamt of this moment, playing out every possible scenario he could imagine, carefully rehearsing each and every line. He had never prepared himself for this scene, though. He had never truly believed that this day would come to pass. He sat back in his chair, his large hands clasped in prayer in front of him, and decided to say nothing at all.

Piano Man lay back down across the sofa, his lanky legs stretched straight before him, crossed at the ankles. His arms were folded across his chest.

"When your mama died, I wanted to die too. In the back of my mind I think I truly believed that she would always be there for me when I was ready. That if anyone coulda made things right for me and you, it woulda been Irene. Your mama was a good woman. There's not a woman around—"

"Don't tell me about my mother. You weren't there for her. You don't know how good she was." Romeo spat the words out.

Piano Man nodded to himself, biting on his lower lip. He continued talking, not bothering to respond to Romeo's outburst. "It took me a long time to find you—in fact it only happened by accident. I'd come here for my brother Maceo's funeral. Seems like I was always catching up with folks at somebody's funeral." He paused. "Anyway, you was here, selling off that house you'd bought for your mama. Folks was just a gossiping 'bout you. Talking 'bout how you'd come here and was opening up this club with the money you was getting from selling that little piece o' property. Hoping that you might take an interest in one of 'em's daughters. Yeah, boy, you were news 'round these here parts then.

"Well, after that it won't hard to track you down. Aleta helped me too, when I finally started being honest with her. Then one day I just decided to come meet you for myself. I needed to know that . . . well . . . that you was the man I knew you was gonna be. I needed to know that you was more like your mama than me, 'cause I knew I won't no good." Piano Man swallowed hard.

Romeo was suddenly conscious of the fact that he had not moved since he'd sat down. He shifted uncomfortably in his chair, unable to look directly at the aged figure before him. "Why didn't you tell me when you first started working here? Why didn't you tell me you were my . . . my . . . my father?"

Piano Man swallowed again, his throat parched. "Boy, I ain't never been no father to you. I know that better than anybody. I know'd what it was to have a daddy, 'cause your granddaddy was a strong man, and I know that I ain't never been there like that for you. I didn't want you to know how weak I was. I was hoping that in your mind you'd made me into something good and decent and that you was going on living not wondering 'bout me and why I was the way I was. I didn't tell you 'cause I didn't want to have to own up to all the wrong I'd done before I went to meet my maker. I thought it would just be easier facing the good Lord, who done heard my prayers and thoughts every day, than it would be to face you."

"Then why come at all? I don't understand that."

"Romeo, I'm an old man. I just didn't want to die not having ever loved you up close. Didn't care if you ever loved me back or not. . . . I just needed to be with you up close even if it was only for a real short time. I didn't never 'spect to be around as long as I been and I sure didn't 'spect to ever be here with you like this, right now."

Romeo nodded, a small part of him understanding, a larger part of him not wanting to. He sighed heavily, trying to dislodge the anger that was trying to consume him, eroding at the already delicate tissue of his being.

"So why tell me now? Why now?"

Piano Man sat up straight again, rubbing at the ache in his knee joints. Rising, he walked over to stand beside Romeo. "'Cause whether I planned it or not, it was the right thing to do. You deserved to know the truth and there ain't nothing like too much scotch to bring out the truth. Sure can't hide your soul behind a liquor bottle."

Piano Man paused, the two men still staring at each

other. "Romeo, if you want to hate me for not being around when you was growing up, then you need to hate me for the whole truth and not the one you done imagined. Boy, I ain't got no excuses for what I done. I can't take it back and I ain't gonna worry myself trying.

"You now know everything about me. Me, Piano Man. Me, James Burdett. The good and the bad. I didn't change into somebody else ten minutes ago. I'm the same man you took in and fed and clothed and have talked to on a daily basis for all these months. I'm the same man who done shared a bottle of scotch with you every week for the last I don't know how many weeks. I ain't no different now that you know who I am, and you needed to know that. That's why I told you."

"Do you really believe that nothing has changed? That you and I can just go on like nothing is any different?" Romeo stared up at him, his expression disbelieving.

Piano Man cracked a semitoothless grin, spraying a fine thread of spittle down his chin. "Romeo, you tell me right now to get out and never come back and I'll go, but I'll go happy. I'll go happy 'cause I know my boy—*my boy*—is a far better man than I ever was. Otherwise I'll wake up later, eat me some food, and come back here and play just like I do any other night, and I'll play happy 'cause I still know my boy is a far better man than I ever was." Piano Man nodded his head, still smiling. "Now, if you think I'm gon' be sitting 'round waiting for you to call me daddy or something, you wrong. I don't deserve it and I'll be the first one to tell you so. So you do whatever you think you need to do, 'cause I'm too damn tired and almost too damn drunk to care."

Piano Man's stupid grin still graced his face. Romeo shook his head, incredulous. The rage that had threatened to burst forward moments earlier would not be easily dispelled, no matter what Piano Man thought.

As Romeo studied the dark figure before him, he wanted to be angry. He wanted to revel in the bitterness of it. He wanted to relish the taste of the hateful phlegm, allowing it to fill the empty pit that had been hollowed out all those years with a child's longing and a mother's tears. No matter what Piano Man wanted to believe, everything had changed between them.

Perhaps if Romeo had known he'd had a father in Piano Man before, if it had been a quiet understanding between just the two of them, then maybe now having the commonality of their bloodline painted boldly before him would not be so painful to accept. Despite Piano Man's hopes, this knowledge had not served to further cement their bond.

While Piano Man made his way back over to the sofa, Romeo shook his head, infuriated by the turn of events. He watched Piano Man settle himself comfortably on the sofa. The man's eyes fluttered slightly, opening and closing as he tried to fight the sleep straining to possess him.

"Enough talk," Piano Man grunted. "I'm tired. We can talks about this more later if you wants, or I can leave. It be your choice." Happy to give in to the slumber that quickly enveloped him, Piano Man rolled over onto his side, burying his face into the back of the sofa. A haunting silence filled the room, touched only by the old man's deep wheeze. His heavy breathing was mildly alarming, though Romeo wanted desperately not to care.

Finally, giving in to the goodness his mother had

instilled within him, Romeo rose from his seat. Pulling a warm blanket from the closet, he tossed it over Piano Man's body. Staring down at him for some time, Romeo wallowed in that part of himself that had reached out to a stranger and had found the father he'd longed to know since he'd been two years old.

Finally, turning off the lights, he closed the window blinds, shutting out the morning light fighting to shine inside. Pulling his trench coat over himself, he leaned back against the padded chair, laid his long legs across the desktop, and drifted off to sleep.

The loud ring of the telephone startled Romeo from a sound sleep. Jumping, he knocked a pile of papers from his desk to the floor and searched for the phone. Pulling the receiver to a numb ear, he mumbled an incoherent hello into the mouthpiece.

"Good morning. You don't sound like you're up yet," a soft voice responded into his ear.

"Hey, sweetheart. No, I'm not." Romeo stretched, arching the kinks out of his back. "Piano Man and I pulled an all-nighter and I'm paying for it now," he said.

"Serves you right. You should have been home. You had me scared to death when I got in this morning and you weren't here."

"You're home?"

"Yes, and all by myself."

Romeo smiled across the phone line. "I'll be there in fifteen minutes."

"Make it ten and I promise to still be awake."

"Don't worry. I know how to wake you."

Taryn laughed, her tone low and seductive. "I know you do. See you soon."

"Taryn . . ." Romeo said, pausing. "I love you."

"I love you too."

As the line clicked dead in his ear, Romeo continued to hold the phone against his cheek, inhaling deeply. Across the room, Piano Man had not stirred, still consumed by his dreams. Romeo watched him, his chest rising and falling heavily. The blanket had fallen from around him and he lay with his body hanging partially off the sofa. Romeo rose, placing the receiver back on the hook, and made his way over to Piano Man. Gently rolling the man back onto the couch, he rewrapped the blanket around him. Lightly brushing his hand across the old man's cheek, he marveled at the softness of his skin. Skin that was suddenly more like his than he could have ever imagined.

Stretching his long limbs again, Romeo made his way to his private bathroom to relieve himself. Staring at his reflection in the mirror, he was not amused. His hair was matted tightly in the back, a thin crust of film had dried down his chin, and his eyes were bloodshot. His clothes were wrinkled and he found his own body odor offensive. Struggling to revive some life into himself, he turned on the shower and stood waiting for the water to flow hot.

As the small room slowly filled with steam, he reached for the toiletry bag Taryn kept packed for him. Finding a new toothbrush, he unwrapped it, spread a thick layer of paste across the bristles, and proceeded to polish the pearly formation within his mouth. When he was finished, he gargled with a capful of mouthwash and immediately felt better. Dropping his clothes to the floor, he stood naked, studying his body. He was beginning to lose the slight paunch around his midsection since he'd started exercising again, and he made a mental note to continue to work on it. As he flexed the muscles in his chest, the rich brown tones of his skin rose and fell, rippling like a vat of melted milk chocolate. Cupping his testicles in his hand, he noted that his genitalia weighed heavily in his palm. Thinking of Taryn, his organ twitched slightly, yearning for what lay waiting for him.

As he stepped into the flow of water, his body shook, the wet fountain warm and relaxing. Leaning his head into the downpour, he let the stream fall across his face and over his shoulders. As he passed the soap across his body he thought of Taryn's hands and felt his erection rising. Rinsing himself quickly, he stepped out of the misty cubicle and shivered as cool air blew against him. Rubbing himself briskly with a fresh towel, he felt desire surge throughout his body in anticipation.

Pulling on fresh clothes tucked neatly away in a closet, he dressed quickly. Back in his office, he tiptoed past Piano Man, who still lay sleeping, a low whistle blowing past his lips. Romeo shook his head, his mind still numb. "What am I going to do about you?" he whispered as he pulled on his trench coat and glanced down at his watch. After pulling a tortoiseshell brush through his hair, he slipped into his shoes, the charcoal gray leather wrapping snugly around his feet. Studying himself once more in the mirror, he smiled, now pleased with the reflection that stared back at him. Wrapping his coat tightly around himself, he ventured out into the cool morning air and headed for home.

Reaching over the visor, Romeo pushed the remote button to the two-car garage and sat patiently as the large door rolled open on its track. Easing the car into the remaining spot inside, he rested it beside Taryn's, a pearlescent Cadillac XLR that contrasted brightly alongside his own luxury vehicle.

Closing the garage door behind him, Romeo entered the four-bedroom structure, skipping up the flight of stairs to the main level. The aroma of freshly brewed coffee and hot glazed coffee cake greeted him as he entered the doorway. He dropped his keys onto the cedar table in the foyer, tossed his coat over a chair by the door, and called out to Taryn.

"In here," she responded, calling out from the kitchen.

Rounding the corner through the dining room, Romeo found Taryn peering into the oven, the sweet aroma of cinnamon and nutmeg floating through the air. She stood barefoot, an oversized T-shirt hanging loosely on her body.

"Hi there," she chimed, pulling a pan of fresh baked pastry from the oven.

"Hi yourself," he responded, leaning back against the counter to watch her as she set the hot pan onto a cooling rack, then twisted the oven knobs to off.

Smiling, she pulled the quilted oven mitts from her hands, dropped them onto the countertop, then stepped eagerly into Romeo's outstretched arms.

Pulling her against himself, he held her tightly, nestling his face into the softness of her hair. She was even smaller than he remembered, her petite body lost within the enclosures of his massive arms. Sliding his hand through the mass of curls along the nape of her neck, he tilted her head back gently, pressing his lips onto hers. She tasted of ripened strawberries coated in sweetened cream. He pushed his tongue lightly past her full lips, brushed against the bite of her teeth, then traced the line of her tongue with his own. As he kissed her harder, their tongues entwined like vines of grapes, his breathing quickened and his heart beat loudly inside his chest. Neither of them had any inclination to stop.

Her small hands gently caressed the length of his back as he held her tighter, not wanting to let go. Slowly he planted light kisses across her face, tasting first her chin, her nose, her forehead, then her cheeks. Gasping lightly for air, he nuzzled against her ear, pulling at the lobe with his lips.

"Damn, woman, I missed you."

"Good, because I missed you too," she whispered breathlessly. "You hungry?"

"Uh-huh," Romeo said, nipping gently at her neck.

"The coffee cake is hot."

"Don't want coffee cake," Romeo said, chewing lightly at her chin.

"I could scramble you an egg."

"Don't want an egg."

"What do you want?"

"Mmmm," Romeo cooed, brushing her cheek with his own. "You," Romeo stated, lifting her up into his arms. Wrapping her arms about his neck, Taryn kissed him again, her lips trembling with anticipation. As he carried her across the length of the living room and up a second flight of stairs, her hands skated across his chest, undoing the buttons on his shirt.

Upstairs in the bedroom, he sat her on the bed, pulling the T-shirt she wore over her head. Pushing her back against the pillows, he stood watching the rise of her breasts as she inhaled deeply, the dark aureole of her nipples pushing out to him. Without any hesitation, he pulled the clothes from his body, releasing his swollen sex. His protruding member stretched toward her, its bulbous head crying hungrily for her.

Crawling toward her, his mouth struggled against hers, as his hands anxiously searched the cavity between her legs. As he pressed his fingers into the moist passageway, her body quivered, her knees falling apart to welcome him.

Cupping him gently, Taryn pulled him into her, trapping him deep within. He filled her and she held him tightly. Arching upward, she accepted the weight of him, gasping for air as he pushed the full length of himself deeply into her. His whole body tensed as he slowly rotated his pelvis, pulling at her hips with his own.

Time stopped. As the convulsions rocked through him, the beating in his heart exploded, the bright flash of light before him radiating throughout the length of his body. He heard himself cry out, his nerve endings trembling with pleasure. Tears misted his eyes as he clung to her, his embrace just shy of suffocating.

They lay together quietly, neither wanting to be the first to break the magical spell that had encompassed them. Rising only slightly, Romeo pulled her erect nipple into his mouth and sucked on it lazily, his hands exploring her body.

"Mmmm," Taryn murmured, twitching beneath him. "What's this? Afterplay?" she asked softly.

"No, baby. Foreplay. I haven't gotten started yet."

Taryn giggled.

"Don't laugh. I've got to make up for lost time," Romeo said, smiling up at her, her breast resting against his lips.

Taryn stroked the side of his face gently as he moved within her teasingly. Hugging her closely, he rolled over onto his back so that she lay spread over him, snuggled closely into his chest.

Rising up onto her elbows, Taryn rested her chin

onto her hands and stared into the dark depths of his eyes. She kissed his chest, the familiar scent of soap and sweat pleasing to her.

"So what have you been up to since I've been gone?"

"Working too hard. Spent most of my time down at the club."

Taryn nodded. "What was up with you and Piano Man hanging out all night? Did I miss a good party?"

"No," Romeo said, shifting slightly. "We just put down a bottle of scotch and talked."

"Just the two of you?"

Romeo nodded yes, his dark eyes clouding.

"Well, I wouldn't want to have your head this morning and I definitely wouldn't want to have Piano Man's. Is he okay?"

"Yeah, I guess. He was asleep when I left. He's probably crawling to the bar right now for his breakfast drink."

"You shouldn't encourage him to drink so much."

Romeo shuddered. "I don't. Not really."

Taryn shrugged, then pulled herself off him, lying down beside him.

"He didn't look good the last time I saw him, Romeo. I worry about him."

"Everybody does," Romeo said, stroking her hair. "But he's ready to die and he wants to go happy. That means being able to live his life the way he chooses."

"Did he say that?"

"Not in so many words, but he probably said more last night than I was prepared to hear. But I'm not interested in talking about Piano Man right now." Romeo went silent, thinking back to all that he and the old man had shared.

Focusing his attention back on Taryn, he studied her

intently. "Taryn, marry me," he said finally, breaking his silence.

"What?" Taryn asked, pleasantly surprised.

"Marry me," Romeo repeated, his tone more of a command than a request. Rising onto his elbow, he leaned over her, grasping her chin in his hand.

"I love you and I want you to be my wife. There is nothing in this world I wouldn't give you and I want to give you the best of myself that I have to give."

Taryn sat upright alongside Romeo, who wrapped his arms protectively around her as he continued. "I want to take care of you. I want us to spend the rest of our lives together, and I want you to say something before I continue to babble like a damn fool and embarrass myself."

"Yes." Taryn smiled, looking deeply into his eyes. "I love you too and I would love to be your wife."

Romeo laughed with joy, the hearty vibrato rising deeply within him. Wrapping himself around her, he pulled her down on top of him and thought of all the pretty butterscotch babies they would make together.

Hours later, they sat at the kitchen table sipping iced coffee and nibbling on room-warm coffee cake.

"So, what all did you and Piano Man talk about last night?" Taryn asked, noting that Romeo was deeply lost in thought.

Pausing for a brief second, Romeo gathered himself. "He told me last night that he was my father."

Taryn stopped chewing, a look of surprise crossing her delicate face. "What . . . ?"

Romeo nodded. "He told me he's my father," he said, repeating himself, the words sounding as strange to him as they did to her.

Reaching over to grasp his hand, Taryn pressed her palm heavily against his. "This is unbelievable." She shook her head in disbelief. "After all this time he now decides to tell you he's your father? Are you positive he's telling the truth? I mean, are you sure it's not something he's just imagined because maybe he wants it to be true?"

Romeo nodded his head. "He showed me a picture of me and my mother when I was younger. He's had it for years. It's true."

"Are you okay? I know this must have been a shock for you," she said, rising to go refill both of their coffee cups.

Romeo lifted his elbows onto the table, dropping his head into the palms of his hands. "Taryn, I'm so angry. I would have never thought that I'd be this angry. All I wanted to do was grab him and shake him. It took every ounce of strength I had in me not to lose control. I still want to hurt him."

Taryn stroked the width of his back with her palm. "But what do you plan to do instead?"

Romeo met her eyes, angry tears seeping out of his eyes. "Nothing. Why the hell should I do anything at all?"

Taryn wrapped her arms about him, pulling his head against her chest. "Romeo, if you want to be bitter and angry about this you can, but it's not going to do you any good. You have to be honest with yourself. Before last night, Piano Man was someone you respected and trusted. You cared about him and what happened to him.

"Today he's your father. But he's still the same man he was before he owned up to that fact. You just need to decide what's more important to you—being angry and keeping him out of your life, or being accepting and working through whatever happens with him from this point forward."

Romeo shrugged. "I don't know if I can be as rational about it as you seem to be."

"I'm not touched by it as personally as you are. I can understand you being angry. Hell, you've been angry with him all your life. I just know that you won't be able to live with yourself if you decide not to have a relationship with your father. Now that he's walked into your life, like it or not, you have to play by a whole different set of rules."

Romeo nodded his head slowly.

Taryn smiled. "I think you really love that old man, whether you're willing to admit it to yourself or not."

Romeo raised his eyebrows, a pregnant silence following. "Maybe I do," he answered finally, brushing his cheek against the warmth of her breast. "Or maybe I just need to."

She stood holding him for some time, lightly stroking his brow. The warmth of her skin dried the dampness across his cheek, stopping the flow of tears wanting to trip across the borders of his eyes.

"So what do you plan to do today?" Taryn asked, turning to clear the dirty dishes from the table.

"We need to get dressed. I need to go talk to Piano Man."

Leaning against him, Taryn bent down and pressed her lips to his cheek, the kiss ever so soft on his face. "I love you. I hope you know that."

Romeo smiled, affirmation gleaming from his dark eyes.

"Piano Man made me do a lot of thinking last night. I guess sharing someone else's experiences makes you evaluate your own. I know, if nothing else, that if we are going to make it, you and I are going to have to work at it. I know that I want to do that with you, so half of our battle is already won."

"Yes, just like I believe that there is a reason you and I have come together and not you and any of the other women you've known."

"Do the other women who have been in my life bother you? I mean, they still come down to the club and I am still friends with many of them."

"Not really. I trust you and I know you would never do anything to hurt me. Do the men who've been in my life bother you?"

"Hell, yes," Romeo responded without hesitating, "and I don't like it."

Taryn laughed. "You're too much." Reaching over, she kissed him. "Well, let's get you back to the club."

Grabbing her from behind, Romeo pulled her close, grasping her breasts with his hands. "Don't you worry about that," he whispered into her ear, his breath hot against her neck. "Right now you need to worry about paying me what you owe me."

"Owe you?" Taryn asked as she felt his rising bulge pressed hard against her back.

"Yes. I made a list. A really, really long list."

"Uh-huh. Really long?"

"Yes," Romeo said, pushing her up the stairs. "Come on and I'll show it to you."

"I thought we had to go to the club."

"We do, but my list is much more important."

"I just bet it is." Taryn giggled, racing him up the stairs.

Sixteen

As Romeo entered the front door of the Playground, his arm wrapped lovingly around Taryn, Malcolm waved at them from behind the bar.

"Hey, boss. Hey, Miss Taryn. How's it going?"

"Hi, Malcolm," they both called back as they made their way over to where he stood taking inventory.

"Everything going okay?" Romeo asked as he pulled off the lush fur jacket from Taryn's shoulders.

"Yes, sir. Just finished inventory and I need to go down to the storage area to restock some of these bottles. Odetta called and she and Sharon should both be here real soon."

Romeo nodded. "Do me a favor, Malcolm. I forgot to call Forresters' yesterday about that glass order. They promised to have that delivery here last Thursday and I meant to call to find out what happened. Jot yourself a note to do it tomorrow for me, please."

Malcolm nodded his head as Romeo studied the ledger he had passed to him to inspect. Pleased, Romeo passed the green sheets back, his hand quivering ever so lightly. "Where's Piano Man?"

"Asleep on your sofa. Scared the crap out of me. I

went in there thinking I was by myself and there that fool was laying up on the sofa snoring."

Malcolm and Taryn laughed. Romeo smiled faintly, the ends of his mouth barely curved upward.

"We need to put a bed in there if you and Piano Man are going to make this a regular thing," Taryn interjected, rubbing her hand down Romeo's back.

Kissing her gently, Romeo replied, "Won't be a regular thing if you stay home and be a good wife like you promised."

Taryn laughed. "Now, I promised to be your wife. I didn't say anything about staying home."

"Hey, is this official?" Malcolm asked, looking from one to the other.

"Sure is," Romeo responded. "In fact, we are going to slip out right after Odetta and Sharon get here so I can go look at an engagement ring my baby here wants."

"Don't let him fool you, Malcolm. He's the one insisting I want a ring."

Malcolm laughed. "He's not fooling me, Taryn. I know he just wants to make sure everyone gets that you are officially off limits." Extending his hand out to Romeo, Malcolm hugged him warmly, then leaned over to kiss Taryn's cheek. "Congratulations you two. I'm real happy for you."

"Good," Romeo said, "because we both want you to be in the wedding. I'm going to need me a best man."

Malcolm nodded his head, grinning. "I'd be honored."

"What's going on, everybody?" Odetta beamed, rushing into the room with Sharon on her heels. "Hey, Taryn, how are you doing, girlfriend?"

"Doing just fine, Odetta. How are you? Hi, Sharon."

"Real good now that I don't have to keep my eye on

your man for you. Girlfriend, this brother's so boring I'd rather watch my stories."

They all laughed loudly as Romeo tapped Odetta lightly on the back of her head.

"Romeo and Taryn are getting married," Malcolm announced, eager to spread the news.

"No kidding?!" Odetta asked, stunned.

"Oh!" Sharon exclaimed. "That's great."

Taryn nodded, beaming as Romeo wrapped his arms around her. "Yeah. She finally got that rope around my neck. I guess I don't have a choice."

Taryn punched him playfully. Screaming with glee, Odetta rushed to hug both of them. "This calls for a special celebration," she gushed. "Malcolm, what we got to celebrate with back there?"

Romeo nodded. "She's right, Malcolm. Break out a bottle of something. I'll go wake Piano Man and we'll toast this thing right."

As Romeo headed for his office, the three women and Malcolm chattered enthusiastically, their excitement warmly filling the room. Entering the office, Romeo called out to the aged figure lying across the sofa. "Hey, sleepyhead. You planning on joining us today?"

He flipped the switch on the wall, flooding the small space with light. Staring toward the sofa, he was surprised to find it empty, Piano Man no longer there. He moved to the desk. Piano Man's keys rested on top, on the original key chain that Romeo had given him. Beside it was two hundred dollars in bills, and Romeo knew instantly it was what remained of the old man's cash advance.

Tears rained down Romeo's cheeks as he dropped into the leather executive's chair, rocking his body back and forth like he used to do as a small child. "Damn you, old man. Why now? Why did you have to leave me again? Why now?"

Not since his mother's death had Romeo's heart felt so heavy. When he could bear no more, the rush of tears flowing abundantly, he stood up and crossed over to the window. He lifted the shade to let in the last ray of sunlight peeking from behind a gray-edged cloud.

Exiting the room, Romeo stood staring out into the small club, his expression pained, his heart aching. With their noisy chatter broken by his entrance, his friends stared as he walked over to the large black piano and seated himself on the bench. Malcolm and Odetta gave each other an uneasy stare, confusion washing over both their expressions.

Taryn moved to his side, dropping down on the bench next to him. She stared into his eyes, the pain he cried filling her gaze. She pulled his head down onto her and held him close as he sobbed into her shoulder.

Above Romeo's sobs and Odetta's cries, a low hum rose in the room, filling the darkness around them. *"Blessed assurance, Jesus is mine. . . . Born of his spirit, washed in his blood."*

As Sharon stood with her head held high, her arms reaching out to heaven, her voice cried out to Piano Man, cried out to him as Romeo had cried out to him that first day the old man had walked into the Playground.

Looking up into Taryn's face, Romeo pressed his wet cheek against hers and whispered into her ear. "Son of a bitch is gone," he sobbed, patting his chest gently. "My father has left me again."

Tears rose to Taryn's eyes as Romeo's body shook angrily, his fist beating against the piano. And, as Romeo sat listening for the tinkling of music, the blues swelled thunderously in his head.

* * *

Toying with an unopened bottle of scotch, Romeo rested the container heavily in his lap. On top of the piano, his glass sat empty. As he sat lightly stroking the closed cap, he was tempted to crack open the seal and fill the crystal to the brim, but he couldn't.

He sighed heavily. A knock on the club's front door interrupted the silence, intruding upon his thoughts. He cursed under his breath. Although the closed sign sat prominently displayed in the window, patrons had still knocked incessantly, hoping to gain admittance. He ignored the harsh tapping.

Rising from his seat, he rested the full bottle next to the empty glass. Darkness had filled the room hours earlier. It had settled itself around Romeo's shoulders like a heavy blanket. He had eased into the comfort of its warmth as his friends had searched the whole of Raleigh hoping to discover where Piano Man had disappeared to. Sharon and Odetta had both wept inconsolably until Romeo had hugged them tightly, then sent them home to rest.

Taryn had left with Malcolm, both promising to check the bus and train stations one last time. She had wanted to come back to get him, but he'd needed some time to himself and had told her to go home. They had left him there alone with his memories, understanding his need to confront his ghosts. As he sat contemplating that bottle, he thought about his father's long absence from his life, the loss of his mother, and the bond he had shared with Piano Man.

It was funny to him that he could not associate Piano Man with the male figure he had detested for so long as a young boy growing up. The man who had missed his ball games and school plays, who'd not been there to teach him to drive or to discipline him for running with the wrong crowd was embodied someplace other than the pith of his spirit, where he'd embedded the essence of Piano Man.

Romeo was numb. There were no more tears and his spirit had chilled like a fine wine set on ice. He was stunned by how quickly things had changed for him. Every facet of his existence had turned on a dime. He knew that he would go on, but things would not be the same. He thought again about that scotch bottle and how familiar its contents would be and how different his drinking it would be from the drinks he had shared with the piano player the night before. Taking a deep breath, he tripped his hand across the piano keys, the dull tone harsh against his eardrums.

In his office, he studied the pale walls, backdrops for framed degrees and citations with his name engraved boldly in black. The promotional photo of him and Piano Man sat eerily over the sofa that had hours earlier shouldered Piano Man's slight frame. The sofa's thick cushions now lay strewn around the small room.

Romeo studied the black and white photo, thinking back to that Sunday he had to force Piano Man to stand still in front of the club's billboard to have his picture taken. Piano Man had cursed him, and they had laughed, and just as quickly, it had been over. Romeo sighed.

The pile of papers Romeo had knocked to the floor earlier that morning still lay scattered about, having been kicked and trampled upon. Romeo kneeled to retrieve them, shaking the dust from the glossy sheets. As he sat himself in his chair, he threw the pile on top of another.

Advertisement copy lay in one neat stack, inventory sheets in another. Romeo fanned the papers, shaking his head. The work waited, not knowing that things were very different, oblivious to how Romeo had been changed. The payroll needed to be completed and there were orders to be placed; Romeo pushed the pile to the side, not caring.

A light knocking at the rear door of his office disrupted his thoughts. He rose slowly, sliding the dead bolt back and pulling the door open. Aleta stood in the doorway, her small body quivering, streaks of mascara running in dark streams down her face. Romeo pulled her inside, hugging her close. Neither spoke. Aleta wept against Romeo's chest, his cotton shirt absorbing her stained teardrops, the dark residue settling in the fabric.

"He loved you very much," she finally whispered, pulling her small body out of the embrace.

Romeo reached behind her to close and lock the door. "Yeah," he said faintly, wiping at his eyes with the back of his hand. "Yeah."

"I know you don't believe it, but it's true. You can't imagine how much you meant to him," Aleta continued, dropping onto a chair.

Romeo pushed his hands deep into his pockets. "Did you know he was my father?"

Her gaze locked with his. After a moment Aleta hung her head, nodding ever so slightly.

"Why didn't you tell me?"

"Swore to your mother and him that I wouldn't. Your mama didn't want you to know anything about Piano Man."

Romeo headed back to sit behind his large desk. "Guess Mama knew best, huh?" he said sarcastically.

"Now," Aleta said sharply, "your mama knew the kind of man Piano Man was and she just didn't want you to get hurt. She did what she thought she had to do." They stared at each other, Romeo's anger sweeping through the air.

"When did you find out?" Aleta asked, her voice low and consoling.

Romeo folded his arms in front of his chest. "He told me last night."

Aleta nodded her head slowly. "He really did love your mother. Nobody can ever take that away from him. He may not have done right by her, but he surely did love her."

Romeo rolled his eyes. "I suppose he loved you too—her best friend?"

"No. Not like he loved your mama." The tears rose and fell from Aleta's eyes again. "I loved him, but he never loved me like that. If your mother were still here, he wouldn't have given me the time of day. Neither one of us would have done anything together that would have disrespected your mother. Even after she passed it wasn't like that between us. It's only been that way since he came back this last time."

"Nice of you two to have waited."

"Boy, don't you dare speak to me like that." Aleta stood up, anger lifting her voice an octave. Her reprimanding tone was stern and cut right through him. "I couldn't help how I felt about that man any more than your mother could. I don't owe you or anyone else any apology for being in love with Piano Man. Loving him wasn't wrong. In fact, your mama loving him is why you are here. Your mama loved him more than life itself and he loved her almost as much. No matter what you think, he also loved you."

Romeo inhaled sharply, dropping his chin to his chest, contrition painting his expression.

Aleta reached into the pocket of her woolen blazer, pulling a pale blue envelope from the folds. "This belongs to you. When you can stop being so angry there's more that you should see. When you're ready you know where to find me."

Dropping the letter onto the desktop, Aleta walked behind the large wooden structure and wrapped her arms about Romeo's shoulders. Hugging him closely, she pressed her lips against his forehead, kissing him gently. Romeo clasped her hand beneath his palm, then rose quickly to let her out. He watched as she walked swiftly to her car, got inside, and pulled off, tears once again streaming down her face.

Back inside he fingered the blue envelope, afraid to read its contents. He recognized Piano Man's shaky scrawl and noted that it had been addressed to him just a few weeks earlier. As his hand shook he slipped a metal letter opener beneath the seal and opened it. Peering inside, he frowned as he pulled out a short stack of hundred-dollar bills, all the money Romeo had paid in advance. Easing the lined paper from its slim container, he unfolded the letter, smoothing it flat against the desktop, and read. The words *Dear Son* were written along the top of the paper in dark blue ink.

Romeo wept as he read the two pages repeatedly, his tears marring the dry ink into blurred spots. When the words were carved in his memory he refolded the damp paper and pushed it back into the envelope, then dropped it into the desk drawer. Piano Man's one and only request of him was simple. The words clearly defined what he wanted from Romeo. Asking as only a father would think to ask his son.

Wiping his eyes, Romeo gasped for air, filling his lungs. Outside the wind blew gently, lifting fallen leaves and scraps of trash in an intricate dance. It all flitted about aimlessly, seeking a quiet cranny to settle between and cling to. Romeo gazed out the window,

into the dark sky hovering behind a half-full moon.
Azure and turquoise striations touched by luminescent
topaz curtained the clear sky. Its crispness seemed out
of place to Romeo and he found himself wishing for a
pattern of pale charcoal clouds to muddy up the darkness. He stood there for some time not wanting to
move and not knowing what he should be doing.

Could he find an ounce of forgiveness in his heart to
do what Piano Man had asked of him? Was there some
secret place where he could tuck away his anger or
perhaps lose it for good, or would it forever possess
and control him? Romeo shivered, wrapping his arms
about his body. As he wrestled with the challenge
before him his heart raced rapidly. The noise swirling
through his head was reminiscent of a torrential rain-
storm. Romeo struggled to hear the clarity of the
music.

Standing there for some time, he felt the warm tears
falling off the round of his chin, drying somewhere
along the neck of his shirt. Inhaling deeply, he suddenly wished his mother were there to whisper the answers in his ear. If only she could wipe the salty water
from his face and warm the cold racing up and down
his soul. A breeze seemingly rose out of nowhere,
dancing past the window, tapping against the panes.
Romeo blew his warm breath out slowly. Closing the
blinds, he sat back down behind his desk.

Piano Man had asked for his forgiveness. He'd apologized for leaving but hoped Romeo would understand
his reasons. *Don't know if we'll ever meet again*, he'd
written, *but if our paths should ever cross someday, I'll
be the man who loved you, your mother, and my piano
more than anything else in this world.*

Romeo blew a deep sigh. He marveled at how that
old man had touched him like a summer storm that had

blown in as quickly as it had blown out. The ghostly memories swelled thick and full around him.

She had left the bed unmade, the imprint of his body still etched against the wrinkled sheets. Aleta stood staring at the outline of his torso, reaching a shaky hand out to caress where his head had lain the last night they'd been together. Her tears consumed her as she sobbed, the hurt of his leaving lining the walls of her heart.

Lying atop the covers, she could still smell him, the scent of his cologne and body odor clinging like a faint film against the bedding. Pulling the covers to her nose, she inhaled deeply, then wiped her tears against the pale yellow sheets.

He had known, and in some ways so had she. He had welcomed her home wrapped only in his birthday suit, a wide grin gracing his face. As she'd leaned to kiss his cheek, he'd pulled her down to the bed beside him, tugging anxiously at her clothes. She'd scolded him, slapping at his hands as they'd both giggled like school kids caught up in the fun of the moment.

His kisses had been sweet, light caresses along her face, her neck, down the length of her arms. She'd felt young, and his exuberance had excited her. She had melted under his touch and when she'd reached for the rise of nature between them, he had pushed out his chest like a peacock, pride shining all over his face.

He'd loved her slowly, reveling in his masculine prowess, fearful that it would be gone from them too soon. When the moment passed, his chest had heaved heavily, his lungs fighting for air. Concern had crossed her brow, but he had kissed her again, and had joked about catching his breath so he could do

it again the next night, and the one after that. They'd
giggled and laughed and then he had held her as they
both drifted off to sleep.

The next morning he was gone, the two blue letters
lying against the mattress beside her. She had held
them both in her hands for some time before finding
the courage to open the one addressed to her, and as
she'd read the words, she'd known. Piano Man wasn't
coming home. Running her hand against the bed-
clothes, she sighed heavily, wondering if she'd ever be
able to make that bed again.

Taryn sat alone in the darkness, anxiety weighing
heavy on her shoulders. She'd called twice, leaving a
message both times, but Romeo wasn't answering. She
had seen him hurt before, but never had she witnessed
pain in his eyes like she'd seen tonight.

Twisting an empty wineglass between her manicured fingers, she struggled with what to do, and how to
do it. Romeo's father was gone, leaving the man brokenhearted. It had barely been twenty-four hours since
Piano Man had revealed his connection to the son he
professed to love, and now he was gone from him, disappearing as abruptly as he'd come. Although none of
them had said the word, it had been a dying man's con-
fession that he'd spilled out of his heart that last night
the two men had shared. And now Romeo was left to
pick up the pieces.

Glancing quickly at his wristwatch, Romeo hurried
to his car. Aleta was waiting for him, having demanded
his audience, and he didn't want to be late. He was
eager to see what it was she had been holding for him

all these years. She had said the answers to all his questions could be found in the old chest she had kept since he'd been born.

Aleta stood patiently in the doorway as he pulled his automobile into the driveway. Walking down the short flight of steps, she opened the car door and hugged him tightly as he stepped out.

"I was afraid you weren't coming," she said anxiously, clutching his hand tightly.

Romeo laughed, an uneasy spray of noise that caught in his throat. "You know I wouldn't miss this for anything."

Aleta gestured for him to go inside.

"How are you doing?" Romeo asked, settling himself in a large brown wing chair in the living room.

Aleta's head continued bobbing. "I'm just fine. I'm doing really well. What about you?"

"I don't know," Romeo said. "I guess I'm doing as well as can be expected."

She poured him a cup of dark coffee before moving to sit on the sofa across from him. She sipped from her own cup of cream-drenched drink, and then said, "There's a large brown trunk on the floor in my bedroom. You go bring it here for me."

"Yes, ma'am."

Romeo rose from his seat and headed toward the back bedroom. Pausing, he inhaled deeply, suddenly nervous. He could feel Aleta's eyes on his back, watching him, and he turned to meet her gaze. She smiled, a warm turning of her lips that calmed him. Lifting her small hand, she waved him on, placing her coffee cup on the table before her.

Opening the bedroom door, Romeo spotted the old chest standing in the center of the floor, greeting him with its glistening shine, the wood-grained finish polished to a high gleam. Bending at the knees, Romeo lifted the chest into his arms and returned to the living room. He set it down on the floor at Aleta's feet.

"Sit here," she commanded, patting the sofa beside her. "Sit yourself right down here."

Romeo lowered himself next to her, feeling his insides clench in tension. Aleta ran her small hand along his thigh, the gesture comforting. She reached to lift the chest's lid, passing the gold-framed photo on top to Romeo.

"This was taken the summer of fifty-seven, right before your father disappeared the first time. The three of us had gone over to the carnival in Elliston. They sure made a nice-looking couple, didn't they?"

Romeo pulled the photo toward him, brushing his fingers over the glass cover. His mother's smile was as he remembered it, full and warm. Piano Man clutched her tightly, his own toothy grin broad and inviting. There was a glow in his mother's eyes that he only remembered seeing a few times, when she'd not known that he'd been watching her. A glow that had shone in shades of love and giving. Aleta stood out of place in the background, the smile on her face painfully distant. Romeo gazed toward her.

Aleta nodded her head, reading his thoughts. "I was always the third wheel with your mama and daddy, but neither one of them ever seemed to mind. They both always made me feel welcome, no matter what." She sighed a deep sigh, the warm exhale of breath mixing with the air.

Romeo laid the photo on top of the table and reached into the chest. Three piles of letters lay neatly bundled, some of the postmarks dating back to the 1940s. Aleta brushed her hand against Romeo's.

"Piano Man wrote all those letters. These here he

sent to your mother. Most of them haven't even been
opened. She used to read them all the time, but after
you were born she refused to even open them. Those
there he wrote to me about your mother and you. Wrote
them from his heart, he did. I tried to share them with
your mama, but she didn't want any part of them. That
last pile there are all the letters he wrote to you. He
started writing when you were about a year old and he
never stopped. Even after he found out your mama
wasn't going to open them or read them to you, he still
kept writing."

Tears misted in Romeo's eyes as he fingered the
faded stack of correspondence. Pulling one of the letters from the pile, he ripped the envelope open and
pulled the aged paper out. As he unfolded it, a five-
dollar bill fell onto his lap. He glanced at Aleta, who
sat cautiously watching him. She smiled faintly as he
began reading out loud.

> *"Dear Son,*
> *"You may never get this letter if your mama*
> *is still mad at me, but I wanted to write and*
> *tell you that I love you. I am sorry I cannot be*
> *there, but you deserve more than I can give you*
> *right now. Just know that your daddy is thinking*
> *about you and knows that your mama is doing*
> *the very best that she can for you. I am sending*
> *you five dollars and I want you to go buy*
> *yourself something really nice. I love you, son.*
>
> *"Always, your daddy, James Burdett"*

The tears slipped over Romeo's cheeks as he lifted
the five-dollar bill between his fingers, pressing it to
his chest. Aleta wrapped her arms about his broad

shoulders and hugged him tightly. Kissing his cheek, she wiped her own eyes, brushing the moisture against the back of her hand.

Romeo pulled a second letter from the other stack, ripped it open, and again read it out loud.

> *"My Beloved Irene,*
>
> *"I pray that you will read this letter and have been able to forgive me. I know that you don't want me to be bothering to write you, but I will not stop until I know that the cold in your heart toward me has warmed up at least a little. I am sure that it must not be easy for you to raise our boy by yourself and I am sorry that I can't be there with you. I cannot help being the man that I am and I know that you would not want me around our son if I cannot change my ways. I know you say he ain't my son, but I also know you don't want me to be hurting him like I hurt you. I am sorry I hurt you, Irene, because I love you so very much. I am sending you some money to help you out a bit. It's not much but it's something. I love you.*
>
> > *"Always, James Burdett"*

Reaching inside the envelope, Romeo pulled out five twenty-dollar bills, wrapped neatly in white lined paper. He shook his head in disbelief.

"Aleta, why didn't my mother . . ." he started.

Aleta shrugged her shoulders. "Your mama was just stubborn. Once she got something in her head, there was no changing her mind." Aleta stood up, walking over to the window before continuing. "When your daddy left the first time, your mama didn't know she could hurt so much. They'd been through so much together and things weren't right between them, no matter how much they tried to make it. Your mama's heart was broken as though someone had reached inside her chest and snapped it in two.

"Piano Man used to write her and tell her about what was going on with him and where he was playing, and for a long while she used to write back. She stopped when she heard that he had gone and married some girl he met in Detroit or Philadelphia somewhere." Aleta paused. "Anyway, it was a few years later when Piano Man came back home here. He wasn't a young boy anymore. He was a real man and you had to be blind not to see that there was still something between him and your mama. Didn't take long either before the two of them were back together like they should have been. That's when your mother got pregnant with you. She didn't want to tell him because he had this offer to go play for some big band. James begged Irene to go with him, but she wouldn't. All she wanted was to make a nice home for you."

Aleta paused, ancient memories flooding her thoughts.

"I remember when I told James about you being here. That was the first time I think I had ever seen fear in his face. It was like he didn't know what he should do, or where he should turn, and he didn't know how to ask anyone for help."

Romeo sat listening, nodding his head slowly. He chewed nervously on his bottom lip, the letters pulled close to his chest.

"Your mama seemed to understand his fear more than anybody, and I think that's when she decided to let him go for good. She told him that you weren't his and that he should just stay with that band he was touring around with. I think there was a part of her that was hoping that he would come back and stay, and when he didn't, that probably hurt her the most. He wrote me not long after that and told me that he knew she was lying. He knew you were his child, but there was just something in him that couldn't let him stay in one place for any time. He kept saying that he didn't know how to be nobody's daddy. I think he worked real hard to convince himself of that.

"After that, Irene didn't want to hear anything about James. Nothing. She'd toss his letters in the trash and I'd pull 'em out. I'd try to read them to her, but she didn't want to hear any of it. It was strange because I knew how much she still loved him. She never stopped loving him. I think that maybe she needed to cut him out of her life completely, just so she could still love him. I think she was afraid that if she didn't, that she might start hating him."

Romeo sat absorbed in his own thoughts, not sure whether or not he wanted to cry. There was still so much he didn't understand. "Aleta, why didn't he tell me he wrote me? When he and I last talked he made it sound like he had never ever tried to do right by me, but this"—Romeo said, lifting the stack of letters in front of him—"this proves he tried. Aunt Aleta, he was sending money to me, and to my mother. He was writing to us. He was trying. . . ." Exasperation raced across Romeo's brow as he tried to assimilate all the information just thrown at him.

Aleta smiled at him weakly. "Piano Man never knew anyone had saved all these letters. He must have thought that they'd been destroyed without ever being opened. I don't think he wanted to say anything bad against your mama, especially since he didn't have any proof of it."

"What could she have been thinking?"

"She was thinking that she had a boy who needed her protection more than anything else in life. She honestly believed that Piano Man couldn't do right by you so it was better that he didn't do anything at all. She never meant to hurt you, Romeo, but sometimes when we're making choices, we do so with a narrow view of the consequences. I think Irene half expected that Piano Man was going to show up dead at some point, so there was no reason to set you up for the hurt. I also think there was a part of her that was so angry with Piano Man that she decided not to share you— it was her only way of getting back at him. Whatever it was, though, it's done and over. And like your daddy would say, we can't do anything about it."

Romeo leaned forward on his elbows, wiping at his eyes with his fingertips. The letters spilled over his lap onto the floor. He stared at them briefly, before reaching down to pick them up, fingering them between his hands. Aleta reached over to take them from him, dropping them back into the wooden chest.

"There's a lot of memories inside here," she said, closing the top. "Your mama and daddy's entire history is captured here in some way or another. I'd started saving this stuff for your mama believing that she'd change her mind about wanting it. Then I decided to keep it for Piano Man, hoping that he'd want to give it to you one day and tell you the truth. After he came back the last time I knew that it was meant for you to have." She gave his shoulder a light squeeze. "Take it home with you. Do whatever you need to do with it. It all belongs to you."

Romeo smiled up at her, a weak bending of his lips before nodding his consent. Standing, he wrapped his arms about Aleta's shoulders. "Thank you," he whispered over the top of her head. "Thank you."

Reaching toward the table, he lifted up the gold-framed photo and pressed it into Aleta's hands. "Do you want to keep this?"

Aleta stared at it momentarily, then handed it back to him. "No," she said, shaking her head. "I don't need it anymore."

Romeo nodded his understanding. Securing the lock on the old chest, he lifted it up in his arms and headed for the door.

As Aleta twisted the knob and pushed open the screen door for him, she laughed warmly. "Romeo, I need you to do me a favor."

"Anything. You know that."

Aleta nodded. "I need to find me an owner for Amber House. I think it's time I retired."

Romeo paused, resting the chest atop his upper legs, leaning his weight against the door frame. "Are you sure?"

"Positive. In fact, what I would most like to do is give Amber House to you."

Romeo placed the chest onto the floor. "Why me?"

"Because you will see when you start going through all that stuff in that box that half of Amber House was owned by your daddy. He meant for you to have it one day, and I think now is as good a time as any."

Romeo shook his head, further stunned. "I don't know what to say."

"Don't say anything. We'll discuss it in detail as soon as you're ready. Okay?"

Romeo stared at Aleta in disbelief. "Okay, I guess."

Aleta smiled broadly. "You are so much your daddy's boy it's scary. Now, get out of here. I've got to go get ready for work. Can't have the family business going under now."

Romeo smiled back, kissing her cheek one last time. Then lifting the trunk back up into his arms, he headed for his car and home. Inside the doorway, Aleta stood watching him until he'd ridden out of sight, the faint glow of his taillights disappearing down the road. She stood there for a good while, inhaling the warming air as the gentlest of breezes blew through the trees, sweeping soft gusts around her body. As she turned to head back inside, she reached into the pocket of her jacket and pulled out her own blue letter. She reread the words one more time.

Dear Aleta, I do love you. Always, Piano Man.

Seventeen

Romeo replaced the cap on the half-empty bottle of scotch, tucking the amber-colored container back into its hiding place by the side of his chair. Across the room, Taryn's voice called out to him from the answering machine, but he couldn't will one muscle to move his body to answer her call. The message she left would sit with all the others she'd left, he thought, ignored, soon to be forgotten.

He'd grown comfortable wallowing in the self-pity that had consumed him since his meeting with Aleta. After getting the large trunk home, he'd settled himself in his bedroom, then began reading. It had taken him just over eight hours to read twenty-plus years of letters and postcards written by Piano Man. To be exact, eight hours, twenty-three minutes, and almost twenty thousand dollars in tens and twenties, to comprehend history rewritten in the man's scraggly handwriting. In the span of an average man's workday, everything Romeo had known and believed in had been turned upside down and twisted inside out.

With the last letter, his rage had been refueled, bitter and nasty, and now Romeo sat stewing in the filth of it.

He hated that his mother's anger had brought him to
this point, and since he could not level his own rage at
her dead body, he had turned on Taryn. He had trusted
his mother. He had believed that she would never do
anything to cause him harm, and now he had to accept
that she had not been totally truthful with him. She had
lied about Piano Man, as if his having the man for a
father would have cost him more hurt than not having
a father at all.

If his mother could do him wrong, then how could
he put his faith in any other female? How could he trust
the truth from Taryn and not have it come back to slap
him in the face? And so he turned, thrusting the worst
of himself at the one woman who stood in his path pro-
fessing to love him. Heaving a heavy sigh, Romeo
reached back to the floor for his bottle and the comfort
of bitter fluid that had become the only companion
he wanted.

Taryn didn't know him anymore, she thought as she
hung up the telephone. And she fully understood that
he didn't know himself either. There was something
about the hurt that floundered within Romeo that had
hardened his spirit, and after the drama had settled
down, he had allowed his anger to keep him from acting
right.

The last time they'd been together his touch had
been less than loving. He had lain above her almost
hostile, rage pounding against her thighs. When she
had pushed him away, he'd rolled to the edge of the bed
and had cried, tears falling onto the pillow like the
cascading flood of a waterfall.

Taryn's eyes brimmed with moisture as she recalled
the moment. Remembering how she'd reached out a

hand to comfort him, only to have him ask her to leave, caused the rush of salty moisture to spill down over her cheeks. She had left, catching the first flight crossing the Atlantic, and now she wondered if leaving him had been the right thing to do.

There is something that happens to a woman when a man is evil in spirit and he snatches her words before they're even spoken, or her thoughts before they're completely formed, or her emotions before she's had opportunity to feel them. Something happens when he snatches her peace from her and dashes it all beneath the weight of his foot. It leaves her wounded, the essence of her spirit broken, and Taryn now wallowed in the aftermath of such hurt. Romeo had snatched her peace, grinding it under the weight of his foot like trash, and now its heaviness bore down on her as if the man himself had slammed her full force to the floor.

Romeo's body ached. Pain was beating a drum line behind his eyes and across his brow. It thumped deep inside his eardrums, peaking to a full crescendo toward the back of his skull. Romeo winced from the hurt of it as he rolled against the mattress, rolling until his body fell off the side of the bed onto the floor.

He landed with a jarring thump against the hard wood. Every muscle vibrated from the shock, each sinewy fiber quivering with hurt. He lay flat on his back, lost in a semidrunken stupor. He yearned for a few minutes of uninterrupted sleep, but the nightmares refused to leave him in peace.

He forced his eyes open, staring up toward the ceiling. His vision was clouded, his eyes opening and closing on their own accord. He suddenly thought about toothpicks and chuckled loudly at the thought of propping both his eyelids open with a pair of little wooden spikes.

His mouth was dry, his tongue feeling too large to fit comfortably in the arid cavity of the orifice. Even his lips felt swollen and awkward against his face. As he rolled his tongue slowly across his top lip and then his bottom, he imagined that only a shot of alcohol could relieve the chapped tightness, moisture in liquid medicine. Romeo grinned stupidly.

He reached a hand out, watching it as it moved slowly up to his eyes. He counted his fingers, finding twice as many on the one hand as he knew should have been there, and this made him laugh even harder. The sound was harsh and jarring but he was content with it, grateful that there was something for him to laugh at.

His physical ailments were nothing when he compared them to the demonic hurt that had crippled his heart. The profusion of sheer misery had a tight hold on his senses, the viselike grip tightening with each passing day. *Brokenhearted* didn't seem adequate enough to describe the hurt he was feeling.

Shifting up and onto his knees, Romeo rested his palms against the top of the ottoman and pushed himself straight and tall onto his feet. He stood like that for just a brief second before staggering forward. He caught himself from falling back down, then slowly maneuvered his way to the stairs and down into the kitchen.

Empty bottles littered the marble countertop and the breakfast table. Dirty dishes overflowed the sink, garbage spilling to the floor and scattered across the room. Romeo squinted, skewing his nose at the filth he'd allowed to accumulate. He heaved a deep sigh and shook his head from side to side.

Searching frantically through the pantry, he pulled

an unopened bottle from an upper shelf, grinning widely as he held it up in front of him. The amber-colored fluid shimmered beneath the glow of light, seeming to call his name. Closing his eyes, he pulled the bottle to his chest, relishing the sensation of the cool glass resting next to his bare skin. He would feel better, he thought as he grabbed an empty glass from the counter. In a matter of minutes he wouldn't feel anything at all.

The doorbell rang incessantly, the loud chimes resounding through Romeo's mind. Hauling himself up off the floor, he pulled a large hand across his mouth, wiping at the film of saliva that had dried against his face. His long fingers rubbed at his eyes, wiping away the sleep that had held him prisoner just minutes before. Staggering down the steps toward the front foyer, he peered out the window to see who was leaning on his doorbell. Malcolm stood on the other side peeking back at him.

"What?" Romeo said, his voice heavy, the thick of his tongue filling the dry cavity of his mouth. "What do you want?"

Malcolm's hands fell onto his hips. "Looks like you could use a friend."

Romeo flipped his hand toward the man. "I don't need nobody."

"We all need somebody," Malcolm responded, closing the door behind him. "I'd ask how you're feeling but I think I can guess."

Romeo shrugged, heaving his shoulders up and down. "What time is it?"

"Just after twelve. You got any coffee in this house?"

"Don't need no coffee."

"Yes, you do. And you need a bath too." Malcom fanned a hand in front of his face.

"Why are you here?" Romeo asked, turning his back to the man as he stumbled over his own feet.

Malcolm grabbed at Romeo's elbow as the man staggered toward the kitchen. "We figured I was the only one who could handle you if you tried to throw me out."

"Who's 'we'?"

"Me, Taryn, Odetta, Aleta. Everybody's worried about you."

"Why? My father's gone. Aren't I allowed to mourn?"

Malcolm shook his head. "Your father left you almost two months ago. But he's far from being dead, so it's time you stopped mourning and started picking the pieces up so you can move on."

"Two months? What day is it?"

"It's Tuesday, the fifteenth."

"What month?"

"October."

Romeo gasped. "October?"

Malcolm nodded yes. "Don't remember much, do you?"

Romeo shrugged again.

The other man continued. "Booze'll do that to you. Steals the time away just like that. Man, you done gone through some alcohol. Done cussed me, cussed Taryn and everybody else who's been trying to check up on you."

"What about the club?"

"Club's fine. Aleta's been helping me managing things, and together we've all kept it going. People are asking about you though."

"I need a drink."

"No. You need a shower, a good cup of coffee, and some food. Then you need to talk about it."

"I don't want to talk."

"Well, we're going to talk anyway. So, do you need me to help your ass get in the shower or can you handle it yourself?"

"Go to hell."

"Been there. Didn't like it and ain't got no plans to go back any time soon."

Romeo laughed, wrapping his hands around his head.

Malcolm smiled. "That's more like it." He reached to rub his own palm against Romeo's shoulder. "Everything's going to be okay, Rome. I know you're tired of drinking, and you're tired of being angry. I figured you'd be ready to let it all go right about now. That's why I didn't come sooner. But I'm here now and we're going to make sure everything's going to be okay."

Romeo looked at his friend, who stood smiling at him. He winced, then asked, "Did I really cuss Taryn?"

"And Odetta and Aleta too. You know you got an ass-whooping coming. They are all hot with you," Malcolm replied.

Romeo headed toward the stairs. "Then I'm definitely going to need that drink."

An hour later, Romeo made his way back downstairs. Back in his bedroom, Malcolm had stripped his bed of the dirty sheets and had picked up the wealth of money scattered around the room, laying the bills neatly against the mattress top. Romeo's open bottle of scotch had disappeared, and the man had even removed the flask he kept hidden in the dresser drawer. In the kitchen, the noise of the dishwasher filled the air, the dirty dishes retrieved from around the house tucked neatly inside. Malcolm was scrambling eggs. He looked up as Romeo dropped his body down against the stool in front of the marble counter.

"I picked up a little, but we need to get that service over here to give this house a good cleaning," Malcolm said to him as he poured coffee into an empty cup.

"They stopped coming," Romeo answered.

"You cussed the cleaning woman, too."

Romeo shook his head as he sipped at the dark fluid. "I've made a mess of things, haven't I?"

Shaking salt and pepper into the eggs on top of the stove, Malcolm replied, "Yes, you have, but I don't think you've done anything that can't be undone. Set your mind to it and you can make it all right."

"It hurts, Malcolm. My mama lied to me, my father's gone, probably dead, and now it just all hurts so much."

Malcolm pushed eggs onto a plate and set it down in front of Romeo. "People make mistakes, Rome. I don't think your mama wanted to hurt you or that she purposely lied to you. She just made a mistake."

Water misted Romeo's eyes as he tried to focus on the food Malcolm had set before him. Nausea floated at the edge of his stomach, bile swelling in the back of his throat. Romeo inhaled deeply, trying to still the quiver in his midsection. He pushed the plate away from him. He dropped his head into the palm of his hands, clutching at the growth of hair that badly needed to be cut.

"My poor Taryn. What in the world have I done to my baby?" he suddenly cried aloud.

"Now, that will probably be your hardest fix," Malcolm said, pushing the plate of eggs back toward Romeo. "You messed up good there. It's probably going to take a lot of begging and groveling before you're able to repair that damage."

Romeo sighed as he pulled a forkful of eggs to his mouth. "What did I do?"

Malcolm sat down on the stool beside him. "You don't remember?"

"The last thing I remember is throwing her out."

"She came back, twice. The last time you were dead drunk. Threw a fit. Called her some pretty foul names, and then you punched a hole in the wall," Malcolm said, pointing at the tear of paint and drywall in the hallway. "She thought you were going to hit her. It scared her bad. Real bad. She's never seen that side of you before. Matter of fact, none of us has."

Romeo looked at him aghast. "I would never hit Taryn. Never," he said emphatically.

"Probably not. But then alcohol will make a man do a lot of things he wouldn't ever think about doing if he was sober."

The pools of water fell from Romeo's eyes to his cheeks. He brushed at the fall of moisture, turning his head away from Malcolm.

"Let me tell you a story, Rome. My wife and I divorced because I was an alcoholic. And I could be a pretty nasty drunk. I wasn't a good husband and she wasn't a great wife, but then we were so young I don't think either of us knew any better. She had her own addiction issues and she used to run around a lot. The more I drank, the more she used, the more she used, the more she ran. One day I found out she was messing with one of my best friends. I went crazy. Tried to kill him and her. Spent nine months in prison for assault and that sobered me up good. Haven't had a drink since. I think about it now and I know that if I'd been dry then, she and I probably could have made things work, or at least we would have been more willing to try. I've always blamed her because I figured if she hadn't been cheating, then I wouldn't have had any reason to drink. But I know if I hadn't been drinking, she wouldn't have felt like she needed to run around. I know now that I was as much at fault, if not more.

"In prison, I didn't care about much. But I had two girls I had to think about, and I figured how they saw me was just as important as how I saw myself. I loved my daughters, and I knew they loved me, but that I would never have their respect. That I had to earn and I couldn't earn it drinking. I made my mistakes. We all do. People who love us learn how to forgive us. Taryn will learn how to forgive you."

Romeo swallowed the last of the eggs, choking down dry toast and a short glass of orange juice behind it. "I don't know what got into me, Malcolm. I was just so angry."

Malcolm shrugged. "The alcohol is what got into you. It'll mess a man up every time. You found your daddy, then he leaves you. You didn't agree with the way your mother handled her life and yours, and you didn't know how to cope. You had every right to be angry. What you did not have the right to do was take it out on the people who love you. But you let the booze tell you how to handle things. You stopped thinking for yourself. That was your mistake. Now you'll get over it and so will we."

"I guess," Romeo responded, looking at Malcolm with acute uncertainty.

"Grab your coat," Malcolm said, tapping his palm against the counter as he rose to his feet. "We've got to make time."

Romeo looked at him, confusion etched on his face.

"I'm taking you to one of my AA meetings. I think you need it."

Romeo looked him in the eye, his stare piercing. "Look, Malcolm, I don't think—" he started.

Malcolm returned the gaze with one of his own, holding up his hand to interrupt Romeo's thoughts. "Twelve steps, Romeo. But you have to be willing to take the first one, and that's admitting you have a problem. Alcoholics Anonymous is a necessary step for a man who can't remember throwing his fist at a woman who loves him. Don't you think?"

Following behind the man, Romeo hung his head, badly wishing he could take just one last sip of strength to get him through whatever lay ahead of him.

Eighteen

Eight weeks and twice as many meetings had kept Romeo from picking up a bottle. The temptation still lingered against the back of his throat, an irritating itch a shot of scotch could have easily scratched, but Romeo sipped water instead. When the desire became overwhelming he turned to Malcolm, who had volunteered to sponsor him. Malcolm's blunt reminders that he had to take it one day at a time helped ease Romeo's anxiety. In this program of abstinence, he knew he had to take it minute by minute, one craving for a drink at a time. Strangely, he found this easier to do at the club, when there were other people around him, than when he was home, alone.

As Romeo lined the new shipment of alcohol against the wooden shelves, he noted to the minute the anniversary of his last drink. He'd fallen into a comfortable routine of work, work, and more work, adding an occasional night of sleep in between. Malcolm kept a watchful eye over him, being as supportive as Romeo would allow him to be. At first, Odetta and Sharon had walked on eggshells around him, afraid to set him back on his destructive path, and it had only been in the last few days that he could feel that old level of comfort returning between them. Taryn had not returned his calls. He sighed deeply as he placed the last bottle in its place.

He didn't want to miss Taryn anymore. He didn't want to deal with the uncertainty, the unspoken hurt that lay between them. He'd messed up, badly, and he knew that eventually he would have to at least face the truth of what he'd done before he could attempt to make amends for it. Taryn deserved that from him and more.

Aleta entered the room as he stood staring out into space, his gaze lifted upward in silent prayer. She watched him, studying the features that were so much like his father's features, and the hurt of missing Piano Man shot through her, sharp and raw. Closing her eyes tightly, she took a deep breath, inhaling oxygen as if there would be none left if she didn't. Romeo turned to stare in her direction, the two meeting each other's gaze with mournful eyes, and barely a stretch of a smile.

"Hey, Aunt Aleta," Romeo said, extending his arms toward her as he stepped in her direction.

"How are you, darling?" Aleta asked, returning the warmth of his hug as he wrapped his arms around her.

"I'm doing okay. Taking it a step at a time."

"I'm glad to hear that. And I'm glad to see that you're doing better. You had us all worried there."

"I still owe you an apology," Romeo said as he pulled a chair up for her to sit on. "I really am so sorry for how I behaved. I just wasn't myself. I was so lost and just couldn't figure out how to find me."

Aleta smiled. "I can understand that. It was a lot

thrown at you at once. Besides, your daddy could get just as mean when he'd been drinking too. You got it honest."

Romeo's eyes darted from side to side as he took in that statement. "He told me once that I was an alcoholic. I didn't pay him much attention though. I guess knowing that about himself helped him to see it in me."

Aleta wrapped her hands around his. "So, how is everything else? How's that young lady of yours holding up? I haven't seen Taryn around at all."

Romeo's eyes dropped down to the floor. He shrugged his shoulders. "She still won't speak to me. I haven't been able to make her understand that I wasn't myself."

"That's not what you need to make her understand," Aleta said, chuckling softly. "Romeo, she knows you weren't yourself. What she doesn't know is what's in your heart now and what steps you plan to take to insure you never behave that way again. She thought she could count on you and you failed her. You broke her trust and now you're going to have to work to build that back up."

"How do I do that when she won't even talk to me? I've left a dozen messages for her and she's not bothered to call me back once."

"Why should she? You threw her out. You broke her heart. Why should she make it easy on you by calling you back? She doesn't owe you a thing. Nothing. Bottom line, if you want her, then you're going to have to go after her. You're going to have to fight a hard fight to get her back and it is not going to be about whether or not she's willing to pick up the phone to call you, but just how much you're willing to do for her."

Romeo clasped his hands in front of him, throwing

his head back against his shoulders. He looked up toward the ceiling, then back at Aleta. "I get it, Aunt Aleta. I guess I was just afraid that if I put myself out there and she rejected me . . ." His voice stalled, the prospect of his words knocking the breath from him.

Aleta rubbed her hands against his. "It took your daddy most of his life to stop running from things that he thought would be too hard for him to deal with. I think he figured out in the end that had he dealt with the tough stuff head on, from the get-go, then things could have been very different for all of you. Learn from his blunders, Romeo. Don't make the same mistakes he did. You have far too much to lose if you do." The woman rose to her feet.

"Call me if you need me," she said, heading toward the door. "You know I'm here for you."

"Thanks, Aunt Aleta. I love you."

Aleta smiled, turning about in the doorway. "I love you too, baby boy. Now, go. Straighten out your mess."

Nodding his head, Romeo lifted a hand and waved good-bye.

It had taken five well-timed telephone calls to the right people to access the information that had Romeo waiting patiently for the arrival of British Airways' last flight out of London. With the plane already twenty minutes overdue, Romeo paced the floors in anticipation of Taryn's arrival. Anxiety coursed throughout his bloodstream, feeding his system with exaggerated energy. Above his head, the illuminated flight board announced that British Airways flight number 276 had landed. His anxiety increased at the prospect of finally reconnecting with Taryn.

Within minutes of the plane's arrival, passengers streamed down the ramp way into the airport waiting areas. Families greeted kin excitedly, the ring of exuberant voices wafting through the air. As Taryn stepped out into the open area of bodies and black metal chairs, Romeo felt his heartbeat increase as he drank in her appearance. He held up the placard that had been resting at his side, the woman's name printed in bold, black writing. He smiled shyly.

Taryn stopped short, meeting his wistful gaze with her own curious stare. Her expression was less than pleased as she took in the fullness of him, reacquainting herself with his fine features. Resuming her stroll, she brushed past him, not bothering to utter a word as she made her way to the luggage claim area. Romeo winced, inhaled deeply, then turned to race behind her.

"Taryn, please."

"Go away."

"Baby, I've got to talk to you. I'm so sorry for what happened."

Taryn glanced at him from the corner of her eye, barely gracing his body with a full gaze. "Why are you here?" she hissed, still strolling in the direction of the arrival area.

"You needed a ride home and I needed to apologize. I figured I could kill two birds with one stone."

"You were wrong."

"Taryn, don't do this. Please."

Taryn turned toward him in anger, her eyes racing from his freshly cut head to the tips of his leather shoes. "Don't do what? Don't tell you where you can go? Don't tell you what I think about you? And what if I do? Then what? Will you take a swing at me? Will you try to beat me? Will you call me a whore? Sorry, but we've been there, done that, and worn the T-shirt, so don't you dare tell me what I can or cannot do."

Romeo's head dropped down against his chest and swayed slowly from side to side. He struggled with the rise of water over his eyes. "I was wrong. I know that. But I would never do anything to hurt you, Taryn. I love you."

Taryn raised her hand, pointing a finger in his direction, pain spilling out with the words rushing past her lips. "No. Don't you dare say that. You did hurt me. If you had loved me you would never have done what you did."

Romeo reached out to clasp Taryn around the shoulders, pulling her tightly against him. Her tears washed down over his chest, the onslaught of moisture spilling openly over her cheeks. "I'm so sorry, baby. God knows I would hurt myself before I'd ever think about hurting you. I love you, Taryn. I messed up, big time, and I know it. I know that I have a problem and I've been working on it. But I can't do it without you, Taryn. I need you. You're the only thing good in my life that I have left. It will kill me if I lose you. I love you, Taryn. I love you so much."

Around them, a small crowd was pretending not to watch the commotion between them. Others stared openly, some whispering words of encouragement or taunting heckles. Romeo held her close within his arms as she clutched at the front of his shirt, her face pressed into his chest.

He dropped his head to whisper against her lips. "Please, baby. I'm begging, girl. Let me make it up to you. Let me try. I have never loved anyone the way I love you. Please, Taryn, please love me back." He kissed her softly, lifting her chin in the cup of his hand to press his mouth against hers. "I love you, Taryn," he repeated.

Taryn inhaled deeply, breathing in the scent of him. She shook herself out of his arms, fighting to regain her composure. Turning to the rotating belt lined with leather and canvas luggage, she reached for her bag and pulled it off the conveyor. "Does this mean the car service isn't coming for me?" she asked, turning back to look up into his face.

Romeo nodded sheepishly. "I'm it," he replied.

Taryn stood there still staring at him, neither one of them saying another word. Around them people were still stealing glances in their direction. Pushing her bag into his hands, the woman nodded her consent, then turned to follow him out of the airport toward the parking garage.

As they made their way to his car, Romeo could tell by her body language that he may have won a small battle, but the war had just begun. Taryn was not going to be moved so easily. Her lean figure was cautious, tension gripping her limbs. Her expression was painted with confusion and annoyance, her eyes purposely avoiding his as he placed her luggage into the trunk of his vehicle and then moved to open the passenger side door.

As she moved to get inside, Romeo stepped in toward her. His hand shook ever so slightly as he pressed his palm to the side of her face, gently stroking the soft flesh. When she lifted her gaze to meet his, the stare she gave him was challenging at best, but with the nearness of her invading his senses, Romeo felt more committed than ever to take himself to task.

He smiled, allowing the warmth of it to wash easily over her. And then he spoke. "I will do whatever it takes to prove myself to you, Taryn. I don't care how long it takes or what I have to do, but I plan to fight for us, for you. You're in my heart and I love you with everything in me."

He paused as he let his words settle around them both, the comfort of his proclamation wrapping around her shoulders like a much needed blanket. Taryn's stare was still locked with his, but she'd not responded at all. Romeo lowered his lips to hers and kissed her again. The gesture was slow and easy and his mouth skated gently against hers. Taryn moved as if to kiss him back, then broke the connection, stepping back out of his reach. She shook her head, waving it from side to side. Sliding into her seat, she finally responded. "Take me home, Romeo."

He chuckled under his breath as he glided to the driver's side of the car and got inside. His broad smile was like an exclamation point punctuating his emotions.

"I mean it," Taryn repeated. "Take me home. Now."

Romeo slipped his key into the ignition and started the car. "No. Not yet," he said, determination coating his words. "Not until we talk." He pulled the car out of the parking space and headed for the airport exit.

"We really don't have anything to talk about," the woman said, her voice rising ever so slightly.

Romeo shrugged. "I beg to differ. I have a lot to talk about. You can just listen if that's what you want."

Taryn glared, cutting an eye in his direction. "What I want is to go home."

Romeo sighed. "You will. Soon. But right now I need you to trust me. Please."

A pregnant paused filled the space between them,

swelling new and full with anticipation. "So, where are we going?" she finally asked, breaking the silence.

Romeo smiled again. "To find my absolution," he said softly.

Taryn rolled her eyes skyward, but she said nothing, settling back against the leather seat as he made his way toward the highway and the center of town. She watched him out of the corner of her eye as he reached to turn on the CD player, pushing gently against a CD that protruded out of the slot. The rich voice of blues songstress Gaye Adegbalola suddenly filled the space. It was her CD, one Romeo had gifted to her months earlier. They'd played it over and over again, memorizing the words and singing along as they'd traveled from place to place. Taryn had never once thought of taking it with her, feeling that it fit the space they shared as much as she had fit into Romeo's space and he into hers. She tossed him another quick look, noting how his head bobbed in time with the music.

When Gaye began her rendition of "*You've Really Got a Hold on Me*," Taryn reached her palm out without thinking about it and pressed it against Romeo's arm. She squeezed the flesh lightly, then shifted her hand back into her lap and her gaze out the passenger window. The warmth of the gesture flooded Romeo's spirit and he could feel the tears threatening to spill from his eyes. He heaved a deep sigh, the duo still not saying anything to each other.

Minutes later Romeo pulled off Oberlin Road into the parking lot of the First Presbyterian Church. The large stone structure was well lit from inside, light flowing from the stained glass windows to the outside. There were a number of cars in the parking lot and a number of people heading inside. Taryn looked at him curiously as he made his way to open the door for her, pulling her along by the hand. They hurried into the building, taking a flight of steps to the basement level of the building.

Inside, Malcolm stood waiting patiently for them. He grinned as he saw them approaching, reaching to wrap Taryn in a warm embrace. "Glad you could come, Taryn," he said.

She tossed Romeo a quick look. "I still don't know what's going on," she stated.

Malcolm nodded as he gripped her elbow and guided her toward one of many folding chairs that adorned the space, Romeo following close on their heels. "You'll understand in a minute," he said as he gestured to a bone-thin white man who'd taken the podium at the front of the room.

"Good evening," the man said, a smile blessing his face.

"Good evening," everyone responded.

The man introduced himself, and as understanding flooded Taryn's body, she turned to stare at Romeo, who was watching her as intently.

When the man in front asked if anyone wanted to speak, Romeo was the first to raise his hand and come to his feet. Taryn watched as he made his way to the front of the room, a rush of heat coloring his warm complexion. She shifted to the edge of her seat as he began to speak, Malcolm's broad hand gently patting her against the back.

"My name's Lawrence and I'm an alcoholic," Romeo started.

"Hello, Lawrence," the room chimed.

Romeo's gaze met Taryn's as he continued. "I've been sober for one hundred days now."

Everyone in the room clapped and Romeo smiled shyly as he pressed on. "I've always known I had a problem with my drinking, but I refused to admit to myself just how bad that problem actually was. I realized I hit rock bottom when I threw a punch at the woman I love. I thank God that I was so drunk that I missed, but I hate that I allowed myself to get so intoxicated that I would even think to hurt her that way." Romeo swiped the back of his hand across his brow as he paused. "When I sobered up I had to take a long hard look at myself and I made a decision about the type of man I wanted to be. I knew that I didn't want the woman I loved or the children I hope she and I will have together to ever see me like that." Romeo's gaze drifted around the room, moving quickly from one face to another before settling back on Taryn. "It's not easy. I live this one day at a time. But love can be a powerful motivator for change. I stopped drinking because not only do I love my woman and the future I know we can have together, but I also love myself as well."

As Romeo moved back to his chair, the room clapped again. When he took his seat, Malcolm shook his hand and nodded his approval, a wide smile gleaming across his face. Taryn reached for his hand and held it, her fingers pressed tightly against his.

Romeo pulled his car into Taryn's driveway. Glancing in the mirror on the visor, he checked his appearance, pulling a moist finger across his eyebrows. Taking a deep breath, he stepped from the car and padded his way to the front door. Behind the wooden structure, he could hear Taryn calling out to him, telling him to come on inside.

"I'm in my office," she announced as he stepped inside the marble foyer, calling out hello.

"Hi," Romeo greeted, leaning to press his lips to hers as he kissed her hello.

"Hello," Taryn responded, rising from the leather seat in front of her large oak desk. "You're early."

Romeo shook his head. "Sorry. Just anxious."

"That's okay. I was just putting stamps on these letters. Figured we could drop them into the mailbox on our way out." She gestured with the stack of legal-sized envelopes in her hand.

Romeo twitched nervously in place, his eyes darting back and forth around the room. "You switched out your artwork," he noted, his gaze resting on a new painting behind her desk.

Taryn's gaze followed his. "I was tired of looking at the other stuff. I needed a change. Are you ready to go?"

Romeo inhaled deeply. He nodded his head slowly, reaching to wrap his arms around Taryn's shoulders. "I'm nervous."

"Why?"

He shrugged, not bothering to respond.

"You don't have to do this, Romeo," she said, looking at him intently.

He stared back at her. "Yes," he responded, "I do. I have to do this. I have to do it for myself and I have to do it for us."

Returning his hug, Taryn held him tightly. Pulling away from him, she squeezed his hand, her eyes caressing the lines of his face. Then she led him out of the room, down the hall, and to his car.

Counseling had not been anything that Romeo had seen coming. He and Taryn had braved and weathered many a storm since making the decision to speak to a licensed professional about their problems. For the past eight weeks, the issues that had risen between them had not been what either had expected, but the resulting answers and final resolutions had been welcomed.

Dr. Margaret Bailey glanced from one to the other as they sat side by side on her office sofa. Taryn twisted a damp tissue tightly between her fingers as Romeo sat anxiously tapping his foot, his knee bobbing up and down against the edge of the couch.

"How does what you just heard make you feel, Romeo?" the woman asked, staring directly at the man.

Glancing up, Romeo looked first at Dr. Bailey, then at Taryn, before allowing his gaze to fall back on the doctor. The woman's shoulder-length dreadlocks swayed easily against her full face, accentuating her umber-toned complexion. He cleared his throat nervously, the beat of his tapping foot and bobbing knee increasing.

"It scares me," he started, his eyes dropping down into his lap. "It makes me wonder. . . . If I could do something like that, then what else am I capable of doing? I have to question what kind of monster I could be."

The two women sat silent as they allowed him to continue to speak. Romeo seemed to struggle with his thoughts as he searched for the words to express his emotions.

"I could never imagine doing anything that would hurt Taryn. Never. But knowing that I actually threw a punch at her kills me. It literally rips at my heart whenever I think about it."

"Do you understand why Taryn is scared?"

He nodded. "I do. I'm scared. But I can't take what

I did back. I want to make amends for it, though. I love Taryn. She's my life."

The doctor nodded. "Taryn, do you understand that Romeo has an illness? And that it's a condition he will have to battle for the rest of his life?"

"I do. I realize that when he drinks, the alcohol affects his behavior, and that he's not in control of himself. But I also know that he has the power to decide whether he's going to let that control go or not. What I have been struggling with is trusting that he won't make the wrong decision if things ever get rough again."

Romeo turned toward Taryn. "No one will ever understand what it feels like to lose control and have no memory of it unless they've been through it themselves. Knowing that I almost put my hands on you, and that I was verbally abusive to you, and that I can't remember it, tears me up. It does, Taryn. It literally makes me sick to my stomach to think that I could do something so foul and hurt you like that. But knowing that I did gives me the motivation to do anything I have to, whatever it takes, to make sure it never happens again. Anything."

"Would you give up the bar? You have to face that temptation every day. That can't be easy." As Taryn asked the question, she could see the answer in his eyes.

Romeo paused, tossing her question around in his mind. Reaching out for her hand, he pulled it toward him. "If you wanted me to give up the club, I would. But being at the bar just reinforces my commitment to stay sober. I don't crave the drink. It's not like I see scotch and I want scotch. With me, the scotch eased the hurt of things that were bothering me. I thought it made crap tolerable when things got rough. It was like a necessary bandage. I understand now that the scotch isn't what I need. What I need is to face my problems head on and deal with them. I need to talk things out and not let them well up inside."

The doctor let them both mull over Romeo's comments before she interjected. "Taryn," she asked, "would you ask Romeo to give up his club?"

Looking him in the eye, Taryn smiled faintly, then shook her head. "No. This is about trusting him to do right. If I trust him, then I trust that no matter where he is, he's not going to drink because he knows what can happen to him if he does. I trust that he will make the right decisions, not only for himself, but for me as well." She reached out her palm and gently stroked the top of Romeo's hand. "I love him," she concluded, "and I trust him."

Romeo smiled, then leaned to kiss Taryn's face. He pressed the black of his complexion next to hers, resting the round of his cheek against her skin.

Dr. Bailey smiled at the two of them as she reached for her desk calendar. "I would like to schedule our next session in four weeks. I don't think the two of you need to meet with me weekly anymore unless you would feel better doing so. Let's get together in a month, see how things are progressing, and then take it from there."

Taryn nodded in the woman's direction. "Thank you, Dr. Bailey."

The doctor directed her next comment at Romeo. "You should continue attending your AA meetings on a regular basis. They're a great support system and it would seem that your sponsor is serving you well."

"He's great," Romeo said, speaking warmly about Malcolm. "I couldn't have asked for a better friend."

Dr. Bailey looked down at her watch. "Well, you two take care, and if you need me before next month, please don't hesitate to call."

"Thank you, Doctor," Romeo and Taryn chimed in unison, before heading out the door hand in hand.

Nineteen

Taryn rang the doorbell and waited patiently for Romeo to let her inside.

Pulling open the door, he smiled widely. "Hey, you! Why didn't you use your key?"

Taryn kissed him on the cheek and eased past him. "Hi. I didn't want to just let myself in. That would have been rude."

Romeo closed the door, then hugged her. "This is your home too. You know I don't have any problems with you just letting yourself in whenever you want."

As he held her close, Taryn's body trembled at the memory of his body covering hers. She felt the familiar tingle dancing through her midsection. "So, what were you doing?" she asked, shaking the wave of emotion as she pulled away from him.

"I was upstairs, reading."

Taryn nodded her head. "Anything good?"

"Just a *Sports Illustrated* magazine. Nothing heavy."

The duo stood anxiously in the foyer. "Why don't we go on in," Romeo started, heading for the back of the house.

"No. Not yet," Taryn answered, her gaze dropping

to the marble floor as she dug an imaginary hole with the toe of her ballet shoe.

"What's the matter, Taryn?" Romeo asked, moving back to her side. "You seem nervous."

Taryn stared up at him, taking a deep breath before she spoke. "I quit my job," she said, blowing her words and a gust of air out quickly.

Romeo raised his eyebrows in surprise. "Quit? Why?"

Taryn took another deep breath. "I decided I didn't want to travel anymore. I just want . . ." She hesitated, the words catching in her throat. "I just want to be home. I want to be home with you."

"Are you sure?"

"Romeo, I love you. I want to be a part of whatever you're a part of. With you running both the Playground and Amber House, you're going to need help. I want to be that help." Taryn laughed nervously. "I also put my house on the market," she said. "I'm going to need a place to live."

Romeo pulled Taryn's hands into his, drawing her closer to him. He kissed her, his hands snaking back to curve possessively around her. "I love you so much," he gushed. "Marry me, Taryn. I asked you once, and you said yes. Then I screwed up. I want that behind us. So, I'm asking you again. Please, baby. Will you marry me?"

The man dropped down onto one knee, pressing his lips into the palm of her hand. He looked up, his eyes pleading as he waited for her to answer. Taryn laughed, then nodded her head yes, tears welling in her eyes.

Rising back to his feet, Romeo pulled her close, kissing her passionately. Sheer joy burst through both of them and Taryn pulled away, breathless.

"We can sell this house too, if you want," Romeo

said. "Buy something else together. Whatever you want
to do."

Taryn shook her head. "No. I love this house. I want
to raise our children in this house. This is our home."

Romeo kissed her again, his hands racing up the
length of her body. "I love you, Taryn," he whispered,
his lips murmuring sounds of want against her skin. "I
love you so much. And, baby, I want you so bad. I've
missed making love to you, Taryn."

Taryn smiled coyly, then reaching for his hand, she
pulled him along behind her, heading up the stairs to
the master bedroom. Inside, she turned around to face
him, easing just a hint of distance between them. Her
gaze was locked with his and he could feel himself
falling into the depths of it. Heat coursed through every
nerve ending of his body as he watched her, her body
moving seductively to the lull of music that played on
the sound system in the distance. She slowly undid the
row of buttons that ran the length of her silk blouse,
pausing after each one. The lines of a yellow satin bra
peeked from behind the fabric as she slowly began to
reveal soft brown skin that seemed to beg to be touched.
Romeo gasped loudly, clenching his fists at his side.
Blood surged like a tidal wave below his waist, carving
the muscles of his manhood into solid stone. As she
stepped out of her clothes, standing seductively before
him, his eyes drifted over her naked form, recalling the
curves and angles that he had been hungering for. The
heat between them was consuming, sending a shiver of
energy up his spine as he stripped quickly out of his
own clothes.

Taryn looked at him hungrily, standing naked before
him as he gazed at her with deep appreciation. She inhaled deeply, closing her eyes as he moved against her,
brushing the back of his fingers against the flat of her

stomach. A smile played over his lips as his fingertips danced against her skin. Taryn melted under his touch, falling back against the mattress top as he eased his own body on top of hers. From the speakers in the wall, an alto saxophone blew a ballad around the room as Romeo loved her slowly, as if it were their very first time.

Taryn had been the first to notice the roses budding on the bushes that lined the rear yard. She'd headed eagerly into the gardens, wanting to explore the explosion of new plant life the spring winds had ushered in. Ivy crept up and over foundations of rock and the trunks of some fallen trees. The multitude of tulip and daffodil bulbs she had planted in the fall were springing to life, the rise of flora painting color against the landscape. She had carved gardens out of the raw land, laying lines of growing color like a painter on a blank canvas. Romeo had marveled at how easily she'd seeded life into the shades of green that now blanketed the landscape, adding color to a backdrop of dry dirt and blue sky. He considered it a blessing beneath their feet as they sometimes walked the land around the property.

From the rear window, Romeo stood staring at her. Dressed in a pair of torn denim jeans and one of his oversized T-shirts, she meandered comfortably through the yard. The cotton fabric swallowed her body whole, hiding her figure beneath the thin folds. He smiled as he watched her pull weeds from the new flower beds. When she brushed a gloved hand through her hair, he noted the mark of dark earth that remained against her forehead.

Reaching for the telephone, he remained fixated on

watching her, not wanting to miss anything. As if she could sense his gaze upon her, Taryn shifted her attention in his direction, smiled, and then waved at him excitedly. He waved back as the telephone rang in his ear.

"Thank you for calling Giovanni's. How may I help you?" The woman who answered had a pleasant voice, a soft lilt with a faint Italian accent.

"Yes, I'd like to make a dinner reservation."

"For when, sir?"

"Tonight, around seven, if that's possible."

He could sense the woman hesitating as she scanned her reservation book. She cleared her throat before responding. "We're pretty well booked for this evening, sir. May I ask how many of you will be dining?"

"There will only be two of us."

Romeo could feel her nodding her head into the receiver. "Would eight be too late for you?"

"No. Not at all."

"Wonderful. May I have your name?"

"Marshall. Romeo Marshall."

The woman gasped. "Romeo, how are you? This is Mrs. Donato, Angelo's mother," the woman said warmly, referring to her oldest child and Romeo's former classmate. The two had played football together in high school.

"Oh, my goodness, Mrs. Donato. What a surprise! I'm doing well, thank you. How are you?"

"My son works me too hard. You'd think he'd let his old mother retire."

"Business must be good then."

"Exceptional. You know Angelo has four restaurants now," she said proudly.

"Yes, ma'am. That's wonderful."

"He'll be so excited when I tell him you called. He's working this evening so you'll be able to see him."

Romeo smiled. "I look forward to it."

"You come any time. We will have a table ready for you. Okay?"

"Thank you, Mrs. Donato. I appreciate that. We should be there between seven-thirty and eight."

"Wonderful. We'll see you then."

As Romeo placed the receiver back onto the hook, Taryn came in from outside, dropping her gardening gloves and utensils to the counter. She leaned up to kiss the spot beneath his chin.

"Who were you talking to?"

"I made dinner reservations for us. I thought we'd eat at Giovanni's tonight."

"Giovanni's? You were able to get reservations?" she said, asking about the exclusive five-star restaurant with its upscale clientele and extensive waiting list.

"I know the management," he said smugly, reaching out a palm and gently caressing the side of her face. He glanced at the watch on his wrist. "We should probably go get ready," he said. "I told Mrs. Donato we'd be there sometime after seven-thirty."

Taryn nodded. "Very nice. I hope I have something in your closet to wear. Otherwise we may have to run by my house so I can get dressed."

Romeo shook his head. "Not a problem. In fact, I've already taken care of it."

Taryn looked at him curiously. Before she could ask, he chuckled softly. "I bought you something," he said, gesturing up the stairs with his eyes. "It's on the bed."

Taryn smiled excitedly, a wide grin spreading across her face. "What did you do?" she asked, grabbing his hand and pulling him along behind her. As they traversed the stairway, Romeo shrugged, playfully ignoring her question. Entering the bedroom, he smiled, delighted at Taryn's excited expression when she caught sight of the large white box with the big red bow that lay against the mattress top.

She jumped excitedly on top of the bed, shrieking with glee. Taryn loved surprises and gifts, and never held her enthusiasm back. Her genuine expressions of gratitude and excitement were one of those things Romeo loved about her. She loved presents and enjoyed receiving them with a youthful exuberance that made the presenter feel good about the gesture, no matter how small. He also loved that she relished giving presents with the same fervor, her enthusiasm infectious.

Taryn pulled the bow from around the cardboard container and lifted the lid. As she tore at the folds of tissue paper inside, Romeo could not help but laugh. Glancing up at him, Taryn laughed with him, as she continued to unfold the inner contents. She stopped short when the silk dress was exposed. Lifting it up from the box, she gasped loudly.

"Romeo, it's beautiful," she said, holding the garment against her chest. The Nicole Miller cocktail dress was an off-the-shoulder design in deep green shantung silk. As he'd anticipated, the color was incredible against her complexion and Romeo found himself as excited at the prospect of seeing it on her as she was about wearing it. Her appreciation exploded across her face as she pressed herself into his arms.

"Thank you," she said, her voice dropping to a whisper.

He hugged her tightly. "No," he responded. "Thank you."

Taryn leaned her head against his chest. "What are you thanking me for?"

"You gave me a second chance. You believed in me and you entrusted me with your heart. I'll never be able to tell you how much that means to me. But I'll spend the rest of our lives trying to show you."

Their eyes locked as Taryn stared up at him. He held her close, his large hands tracing a path against her back, his fingers pressing lightly into her flesh. She reveled in his touch, the warmth of his body filling hers. When he leaned to press his mouth against hers, Taryn could feel her rising desire coursing through her bloodstream.

Letting her go, Romeo held her at arm's length, studying her with reverent intensity. "When I feel empty, Taryn, I think about you. I think about loving you, and laughing with you, and being with you, and suddenly I am so full that my heart feels like it's about to burst. It's an amazing sensation."

Pulling her close again, Romeo held her, not wanting to let go, and when they finally found their way to the restaurant, eight o'clock had come and gone.

Romeo and Taryn's daily strolls around the subdivision had become routine. As they made their way hand in hand, they'd occasionally stop to speak to one of the neighbors or to admire the richness of the landscape around them. Romeo had come to relish the moments he and Taryn shared walking as if they had nothing else to do. Sometimes they walked in the early morning, enjoying the warmth of a rising sun. At other times, they'd walk just as the rise of dusk was coming into its own, kissing the fullness of the day good-bye. It was a time of reflection for them both and they felt blessed to be able to focus on nothing but the quiet that existed between them.

As they rounded the last curve, the lines of their home coming into view, Taryn cleared her throat. She pressed Romeo's fingers between her own, squeezing tightly onto his hand.

"I need you, Romeo," she said softly, the words falling like an easy breeze past her lips. "I need you." The simplicity of her statement held more merit than any lengthy dissertation. The emotion behind her enunciation had weight, falling squarely against his broad shoulders, and he accepted its potential willingly.

Taryn continued, staring out into the distance as she spoke. "I have financial security. I'm a strong, independent woman. I've had an amazing career. There's no challenge that I haven't been able to meet, and meet successfully. And there is nothing that I couldn't do for myself if I needed to. But, I need you. I need you just as much as I want you." She sighed as she squeezed his hand again, raising her other arm to wrap her fingers around his bicep.

Romeo pulled the back of her hand to his lips, kissing the flesh gently. He said nothing as they continued to walk, making their way to the end of the driveway. The words caught in his throat, his response expressed with the tears that dripped past his lashes.

Out of the blue, Taryn had insisted they pack their bags for a three-day excursion to Transylvania County. Romeo welcomed the experience, turning the responsibilities of the bar over to Malcolm and Aleta. The drive, though long, had passed quickly as they chatted back and forth, talking about everything and about nothing. Romeo laughed as Taryn shared stories of her hotel experiences during business trips, at one point moving him to wipe the tears from his eyes so that he could see the road.

"You're kidding, right?" he asked, stealing a glance in her direction.

"I swear," she laughed. "But it gets even better. They know the woman is doing business out of the room, but without a complaint there's nothing they can do. One of her last nights there we counted nine men coming and going from her room."

"The hotel manager couldn't do anything?"

"She was paying over nine hundred dollars per night for that room. He wasn't about to run her off."

Romeo shook his head as Taryn continued.

"So now, to add insult to injury, they never tell you, but in Europe, if someone dies in their hotel room, you don't let the coroner declare them dead. You do everything you can to get the body moved out. They can declare them dead in the parking lot, but if they're declared dead in the room, then the hotel's not allowed to rent the space out for three days, sometimes more. Well, that would be unheard of—to have a room vacant for three days—so when her last john had a heart attack, they told her he was suffering from indigestion and the built up gas had caused him to pass out. Then they told her he'd complained about the service and she had to go."

Romeo chuckled as he pulled off the highway into the city of Brevard. He drove until he reached Lake Toxaway and the Greystone Inn, a magnificent six-level Swiss mansion. Taryn had reserved a suite and the resort welcomed them warmly, its quiet ambiance reflecting the couple's mood.

The following day they lay side by side, face down on two massage tables as the spa staff worked the tightness out of their muscles. At one point, Romeo turned to look at Taryn, a smile rising to his face as she lay in bliss before him, the masseur's hands dancing up the length of the woman's torso. It was in that moment he knew what he wanted to do most.

Two hours later, refreshed and invigorated, Romeo had tracked down a local minister to marry them. An elderly couple visiting the inn for the week stood up as witnesses, the gray-haired duo as excited about the ceremony as he and Taryn.

In casual khakis and a navy blue polo shirt, Reverend Eric Wideman smiled politely as he held a large, black Bible in his hands. "I understand you want to say your own vows?" he questioned.

Both Taryn and Romeo grinned, nodding their heads excitedly.

Romeo started, pulling Taryn's hands between his own. "Taryn, without you, I am only a shell of myself. You complete me. You make me whole. With you in my life, I am a better man. I have loved no one as much as I love you, and every day I love you more and more. If I make only one promise to you from this point forward, it would be that you will always have my love. I will protect you. I will cherish you. My heart will belong only to you."

Taryn smiled up into his eyes, her gaze a gentle caress across his spirit. "There aren't words to express just how much I value you in my life. You have become my hopes, my dreams, and everything I aspire to be and to have. I trust you with my heart and give it to you willingly. I will be your partner, your lover, your confidant, and your friend. I will be mother to your children. I will respect you as king in our home, knowing that I sit on your side as queen. I pledge myself to you and only you. I will be proud to be your wife."

The old woman wiped a tear from her eye as the

minister pronounced Taryn and Romeo man and wife, blessing the union between them. As they all stood gathered on the natural rocks of the North Carolina mountain range, the rush of the Toxaway waterfalls rippled downward in excitement, shimmering under the warmth of the afternoon sun.

Laughter rang through the small room as Romeo and Taryn celebrated their news with their friends over large plates of fried chicken, potato salad, collard greens, and more southern foods that Odetta and Sharon had prepared in their honor. From where they sat at the head of the small kitchen table, Romeo and Taryn brimmed with delight.

"Let's play some bid whist when we get done with the food," Odetta said, swallowing a mouthful to speak. "We ain't played no whist in a good jump."

"I'm in," Malcolm exclaimed, licking the flavor from his fingertips. He smacked his lips. "This was good. You two outdid yourselves."

Both women beamed.

"Wait until you see the cake Sharon made," Odetta said, nodding toward the countertop. "She did a nice job on the decorations."

Sharon blushed. "It wasn't anything really."

Odetta rolled her eyes as Aleta chuckled. "What we gon' do with her?" Odetta said with a wide grin.

"You all have been so sweet," Taryn said, wiping her own fingers against a white paper napkin. "This has been better than any reception we could have ever planned."

"Ya'll didn't need to go running off to have no wedding," Odetta chimed. "We could have had a nice ceremony down at the club."

Romeo shook his head. "This is just as good, Odetta, girl. Having you all here to celebrate with us is ceremony enough."

"So what's next for you two?" Malcolm asked, shifting his gaze from one face to another.

"Babies," Aleta answered before either of the couple could. "I hope they're planning on having babies."

The newlyweds laughed. "Let us be married for a few days first," Romeo said with a deep chuckle.

"Please," Taryn said firmly, nodding her agreement. "One step at a time, thank you very much."

Aleta rolled her eyes, tossing a look toward Malcolm and the other two women. "That's what you say now. We'll see."

Romeo leaned to kiss Taryn's face. "Whenever my baby is ready," he said. "That subject is Taryn's call."

"I love babies," Sharon said with a giggle. "I'd babysit anytime."

"Me too," Odessa chimed.

"Me three," said Malcolm.

Aleta smiled. "Well, that's settled. You two need to hurry up. We need some babies running around getting in our way. We need to keep this family going."

As he pondered her comment, Romeo smiled at each of them. They were indeed family.

Aleta's excitement spilled over her face. She reached for the tea kettle of boiling water, filling the three mugs on the counter, before placing them into a tray and the tray onto the kitchen table. The afternoon had been long and the trio was glad for the quiet.

"If I didn't say it enough earlier, I hope you know how happy I am for you both," she said, turning her attention to Romeo and Taryn, who sat comfortably in the wooden chairs. "You two belong together."

"Thank you, Aleta," Taryn said with a wide smile, reaching out to press her palm against Romeo's hand. "I am so glad we didn't wait to have a big wedding. This was so perfect for both of us."

Aleta took a seat beside them. She smiled over at Romeo. "Your father would have been very happy for you. He thought you two were perfect for one another."

"I wish he could have been here," he said, his mind falling away from the conversation.

Aleta's thoughts also drifted off to memories of Piano Man. She shook the daze from her spirit. "So, how are you doing with the drinking?"

Romeo grinned. "Really well. I take it minute by minute. I'm not letting this demon get the best of me." He pressed his fingers between Taryn's, the warmth of her hand instilling energy into his spirit.

Aleta nodded approvingly, not needing to say another word. "So, any decisions yet about the club and what I suggested?" she asked, changing the subject.

Romeo shrugged. Taryn focused her gaze upon the man's face. "I don't know, Aunt Aleta. It wouldn't be the same," he said finally.

"It would be good business," Aleta said. "And Piano Man would have approved. You know how much he loved his music. He would have wanted you to do this."

Romeo stared at Taryn, searching her eyes for answers. "What do you think?" he asked her. "Do you think we should hire a new piano player?"

"I think Aleta's right," she said. "You should do this. It's good business, and it would be a wonderful tribute to your father. You can't deny the man's talent. So don't let what Piano Man built fall by the wayside. He and

Sharon had something really special going. You need to continue that."

Taking it all in, Romeo pondered what this could possibly mean for them all. As they sat quietly, chatting easily around the table, he knew the decision had already been made, but he still wasn't sure he could handle the inevitability of it.

Twenty

As Romeo sat pouring over a pile of invoices, he couldn't help thinking that time had an uncanny way of getting away from a body, rushing past with a mind of its own. Turning the page of his desk calendar, he realized that he and Taryn would soon be celebrating two years of marriage and much good fortune. He'd also been sober for just as long. Although many things had changed for him, most aspects of his life had remained the same. Business was still doing well as Malcolm and the girls continued to hold dominion, keeping him in check. Aleta and he had fostered a profitable partnership and Taryn rounded out their management team. Together they were all family, and he couldn't have asked for any greater blessing than the love they all shared for one another.

The commotion on the other side of the door pulled his attention. By the time Malcolm knocked, Romeo had already risen from his seat to see what was going on.

"What's up?" he asked as he pulled open the office door. "What's all the noise about?" Behind Malcolm, Odetta and Sharon were grinning broadly.

A floral arrangement sat perched in the palms of Malcolm's hands. "These were just delivered for you," Malcolm said, pushing the large display toward him.

Romeo stared at the bouquet, then at Malcolm, his gaze racing from one face to another. His arms hung down at his sides, his mind not being able to will them to take the flowers from his friend. His concentration was lost on the message he read on the balloons attached to the distinct container.

Malcolm held the porcelain rocking horse gently, his head bobbing up and down excitedly. From the horse's back, miniature yellow roses spilled over the sides. And two helium-filled balloons were tied around the horse's neck, both printed in bright pastel colors that read *Welcome, New Baby*.

"Well, read the card," Odetta exclaimed. "Don't just stand there looking foolish!"

Malcolm reached up to pull the card from the container, extending it toward Romeo.

"You look scared to death," Sharon said, causing the other two to laugh aloud.

Romeo smiled, nervous energy gracing his face. As he pulled the small white note card from the envelope, tears sprang to his eyes.

From the front doorway, Taryn's voice rang through the room. "The card says '*Happy Father's Day, Daddy. With love, your new baby and his mommy.*'"

Their friends stepped aside as Taryn made her way toward her husband. Her hand lay pressed against her abdomen. "Congratulations, you," she said as she reached his side. "We're going to have a baby." Wrapping her arms around him, she hugged him tightly. "I love you," Taryn said softly, lifting her face toward his. "I love you so much."

Romeo pressed his lips against hers. Tears ran down his cheeks as he began to laugh with excitement. "We're going to have a baby," he chimed, looking over Taryn's shoulders at his friends. "We're going to have a baby!"

As Taryn stood off in the corner, smoothing the fabric of her maternity dress over her bulging belly, Romeo smiled at her warmly. She smiled back, conscious of the heavy weight of her protruding midsection. The baby wasn't due for another two weeks, but Odetta had predicted Taryn would drop her load at any minute. "Look how low she's carrying that child," Odetta had exclaimed. "Dem doctor's don't know what they talking 'bout. That baby gon' come here when he's ready and I can tell he's ready."

Romeo watched as Taryn eased herself onto a bar stool, brushing her hand across her brow. Wiping the last table, he sauntered over to stand beside her. Encircling his arms about her, he kissed the top of her head lightly, resting the palms of his large hands atop her pregnant midsection.

"You look tired."

She nodded. "Your child won't stop moving. He's dancing like a madman inside here," she said, gesturing toward her belly.

"Why don't you let me take you home so you can rest?"

"Not yet. If it gets too bad I'll go lie down in the office. Besides, Sharon says she's got a surprise for me tonight. She wrote a new song just for me and my little guy here. I can't miss that."

Romeo kissed her again, brushing his tongue lightly

against hers. "I love you," he whispered, pulling the palm of her hand to his lips.

She smiled up at him as he pulled her close, pressing her face against his chest. "I love you too," she responded, just as Malcolm called out to him.

"Hey, Romeo, you got a minute?" Malcolm repeated from the other room.

"What's up?" Romeo answered as he headed into the stockroom.

Malcolm stood leaning against the back wall, a large manila folder laid open between his hands. "I found this down between these old file boxes. I thought you might want to keep it somewhere else," he said, handing the pile of papers to Romeo.

Opening the file, Romeo smiled lightly as an aged press release of Piano Man's debut performance stared up at him. As he flipped through each article, note, and photo that captured a momentary public facet of Piano Man's life, his eyes misted over lightly. Closing the folder, he smiled at Malcolm broadly, and said, "I'd forgotten this was in here. Thank you."

Malcolm nodded. "So, how's that lady of yours doing? She looked like she was about to explode a few minutes ago."

"It won't be too much longer now. Taryn's been ready for this baby to get here. She says she wants her body back."

Malcolm laughed. "What about you? You ready for some little bugger to be calling you Daddy?"

Sighing heavily, Romeo eased himself onto an old wooden chair, laying the folder he was holding onto his lap. "Man, I don't think I will ever be ready for this. I'll be honest, Malcolm. I'm scared. I was never big on responsibility like this if I didn't have to be, and now I have to take on the biggest responsibility a man can."

Malcolm's head bobbed eagerly in agreement. "I know how you feel. I remember when Claudia and Cleo were born. I was ready to turn tail and run. I no more wanted to be a father than the man in the moon. But when they placed those two babies in my arms and I got to really take a good look at them, there was no other place I wanted to be than right there taking care of those two angels. They were my baby girls, mine, and suddenly that was the most important thing to me. When them two girls call me Daddy I feel more important than I ever thought I'd ever be able to feel."

"Piano Man and I were talking once about how hard it is to raise kids now. I just worry that I won't teach my children all they'll need to know to survive these days. It's not like when we were growing up. It's harder. There's just too damn much that can get a hold of a kid today and pull him away from you."

"You've got to trust that you will do the best that you can possibly do. If your child knows he is loved and that you have faith in him, then you did okay."

Romeo nodded. "I know you're right, but I also know that if I mess up, Taryn is going to kick my butt royally."

They both laughed. "Well, it's time to get to work," Romeo said, rising as he tucked the folder beneath his arm. "Do you need help with anything back here?"

"No, I'm finished. We just needed to refill the gin stock and I did that already."

Romeo nodded. "I'm going to need you to close up for me tonight. As soon as things slow down a bit, I'm going to make Taryn go home and get some rest. She's being bullheaded at the moment, but she's not going to last much longer."

"No problem. You know I got your back whenever you need me."

Romeo slapped Malcolm warmly across the back as they entered the main room. The crowd had started filtering in and Taryn had gone to stand behind the bar, beginning to fill drink orders. As Malcolm took the bottle of Seagram's Gin from her small hands, he kissed her on her cheek, then pushed her gently out of his way. Romeo gestured at her to sit down and she complied meekly, not wanting to give in to the heaviness fighting to consume her. When she was settled into a chair, a tall glass of orange juice before her, Romeo nodded approvingly, then sauntered toward the door to greet the first of his guests.

The space was soon crowded, bodies filling the room with loud bantering, hushed whispers, and a meandering of strong perfumes and colognes. From his usual position, Romeo greeted the regular clientele, pausing every so often to introduce himself to a new face who'd discovered the secret that lay behind the large doors of the Playground.

As a melody sprang from the piano, Romeo looked over to where the band sat. Walter "Lightning" Louis, the Playground's new piano player, was doing a soft-shoe across the keys, building himself up for a long evening. A cigarette dangled unconsciously from the right side of his mouth, faint wisps of smoke dancing in the young man's face. He was a tall, thin boy with skin like melted caramel. Jet black hair curled smoothly atop his head, which to Romeo appeared awkward on his thin shoulders, but the women loved him and he had helped bring in another, younger crowd. Business had been better than usual since Romeo had replaced Piano Man's empty bench, an audition process that had taken well over six months to accomplish. Romeo sighed lightly as the boy's long fingers dashed back and forth across the piano keys.

Odetta tapped him heavily on his arm. "That baby ready to come here right now. That fool wife of yours sitting up there scared to death to admit that it's time for her to go have that child, but I can see from the expression on her face that her pains coming real hard now." Odetta pointed in Taryn's direction as she continued. "You best get her to the hospital before she be having that boy on the bar over there. Lord knows that won't be no pretty sight. Shoot. Would sho' 'nuff scare the people off tonight, and I needs my tips."

Romeo squeezed Odetta's elbow as he pushed his way past her. As he strolled toward Taryn, he could see that the brown in her face had drained to a faint yellow and that she clutched heavily onto the edge of the wooden counter.

"Hey, you? Something else we should be doing right now?" he asked sarcastically.

"I guess it's starting to get obvious, huh?" Taryn answered, panting lightly.

"Woman, what the hell are you waiting for? Why didn't you say something?"

Taryn shrugged, tears welling up in her eyes. "I didn't think it was anything serious. I thought maybe I was just having some cramps and they'd go away. It's really starting to hurt right now though," she gasped as she gripped the edge of the bar once more.

Romeo shook his head, signaling for Malcolm. "You guys are on your own tonight, my friend. Looks like we're going to have a baby," he shouted over the roar of the crowd as he lifted Taryn onto her feet and guided her out the door.

In the car, he raced toward Rex Hospital, which seemed a long ten miles away from the club. Taryn's breathing came in heavy gasps as she struggled to maintain her calm. Shaking, she reached out for Romeo's arm, clutching him tightly.

"Ouch," she sputtered. "That one really hurt."

Romeo accelerated the vehicle, spinning the tires through an intersection, the light above just turning crimson. "We're here, Mrs. Marshall. Won't be much longer now," he said, racing toward the emergency room entrance to find some assistance.

As a nursing attendant pushed the wheelchair toward the maternity ward, making light conversation with Taryn as she did, Romeo noted the stark whiteness of the hospital, the walls graced sporadically with pictures of Catholic saints and crucifixes. In an examining room, the nurse pushed a green hospital gown into his hands as the doctor lifted Taryn's legs into the stirrups to examine her. Romeo winced slightly as he saw the man's hands disappear between his wife's legs.

"Look's like you made it just in time," the rotund man with his balding crown said. Turning toward Romeo, he continued. "You better suit up. She's already dilated nine centimeters. Once she hits ten we're going to deliver this baby."

Taryn smiled weakly as another contraction ripped through her midsection. Gasping for air, she gripped the side of the bed, perspiration beading up on her forehead. Romeo pried the crisp white sheet from her clutched fist, entwining her fingers between his.

"You're doing just fine," he cooed lightly.

"Sure I am," Taryn said, sarcasm edging her words. "This mess hurts. No one told me it was going to hurt like this."

"Dr. Brandt, can she have something for the pain?" Romeo asked.

The doctor smiled passively at Romeo, then directed his attention back to Taryn. "Taryn, you are doing really well. I really don't want to give you anything if I don't have to, especially with you dilated as much as you are. Just concentrate on your breathing. Try to focus on relaxing and this will go by real quick."

Taryn nodded. "I'll live," she said loudly as another contraction hit her broadside. "Then again, maybe I won't," she gasped anxiously.

Romeo squeezed her hand. "You know I'd do this for you if I could, don't you?"

"Please. You couldn't take this pain, as big of a baby as you are. Who are you trying to fool?"

Romeo laughed. "I thought I'd give it a try. I thought I sounded pretty convincing."

"Damn," Taryn cursed loudly, squeezing his fingers tightly. "Doc, I really need to push here. I can't take this any longer."

Examining her again, the doctor settled himself comfortably between her knees. "You're ready to go, Taryn. The baby's head has started to crown."

As the doctor shouted instructions, first to the nurse, then to Taryn, Romeo watched the crown of silky black hair ease slowly past Taryn's labia. With each push, Taryn clamped down tightly on his hand, tears streaming down her face. As Romeo struggled to support her, he watched as the doctor nonchalantly pulled the screaming brown mass from her womb. "It's a boy," he announced, laying the small figure atop her stomach.

Romeo's son peered up, struggling to focus, his small body shivering. Taryn laughed and cried excitedly, cradling the small baby with her arm.

"Hey there, baby," she whispered, beaming up at Romeo, who sat numbed, a wide grin fixed on his face. "Say hello to your daddy."

As Romeo peered down at the child's small, wrinkled body, he could feel the pride swelling within his chest, spreading throughout his body. His eyes followed the nurse's every move as she took the baby from Taryn so that the infant could be cleaned and examined.

"Congratulations, Mr. Marshall. You have a son," Taryn said, beaming up at him, her face glistening slightly from perspiration.

"You did good, Mrs. Marshall, real good," Romeo said as he leaned down to kiss her cheek. "Thank you," he whispered lightly into her ear. "Thank you."

Taryn stroked his face lightly, her hand shaking slightly. "So, what are we going to name this boy of ours?"

Romeo responded without hesitation. "James Burdett Marshall, after Piano Man. What do you think?"

Taryn nodded. "I like that. I like that a lot."

Romeo smiled brightly. "I figured we could call him JB for short."

"JB Marshall. Sounds quite distinguished if I say so myself."

Beaming, Romeo silently thanked God for the blessing bestowed upon them.

Hours later, as Taryn and the baby slept comfortably, the infant's small body curled warmly against his mother's, Romeo returned to the Playground. As he made his way to the bar, Odetta and Sharon rushed to his side to greet him.

"We been waiting all night for you to call us," Odetta cried, gripping his arm. "What she have? It was a boy, wasn't it?"

Romeo nodded yes. "Congratulate me, people. Taryn and I are the proud parents of a beautiful baby boy. James Burdett Marshall was born at ten thirty-two PM and weighed in at nine pounds, eight ounces." Romeo laughed as Malcolm pumped his hand up and down vigorously.

"Told you people that baby was a boy," Odetta said, laughing. "A good size one too."

"How's Taryn?" Sharon asked.

"She's doing really well. Tired of course, but she says she feels great," Romeo said, looking tired but exuberant himself. "Malcolm, break out that case of champagne," he commanded, as Sharon made her way to the stage.

Taking the mike, she gestured for the room to quiet down. "Ladies and gentlemen, if I can have your attention for a minute, please." Sharon was radiant as she smiled out toward the crowd, her newfound confidence projecting from every pore. "The Playground is very excited tonight to welcome a new member into our family. Our illustrious owners, Mr. Romeo Marshall and his lovely wife, Taryn, have just become the proud parents of a beautiful baby boy. Please join me and the rest of the staff here at the Playground in welcoming Master James Burdett Marshall into this world. I know you all will join me in wishing the entire Marshall family much love and happiness."

As the crowd broke into applause, Romeo raised his own glass of apple cider in appreciation.

"Champagne's on the house," he called out over the cheers as Odetta and the new waitress, Carol, began to pass glasses among the patrons, filling them to the brim with bubbly fluid.

Odetta reached over to hug him warmly. "A baby boy. I told you so, didn't I?" she cooed for a second time, wiping a moist tear from her eye. "I bet he gon' be a handsome sight too, just like his daddy," she beamed as Sharon came back to join them.

"Damn right," Romeo gushed, raising his glass to

his lips. "That's one good-looking boy I have there."
Then boasting, "Shoot, he makes his daddy look ugly."

They all laughed as Malcolm interjected. "That's
good, then we can be sure he must take after his mama."

Sharon reached out to squeeze Romeo's hand. "I
like the name too. Piano Man would have liked that."

Romeo nodded, gazing off toward the piano.
"Yeah . . ."

His thoughts of Piano Man were interrupted by a
brisk slap on the shoulder. "Congratulations, my man,"
Jenkins shouted, patting him on the back. "That's real
good. A man needs a son. I gots me three, you know."

"Three hoodlums you mean," Odetta said, wrapping
her arm around Jenkins's waist.

Jenkins grinned. "Did good, didn't I, woman? They
took right after they daddy."

"Lord, let's hope not," Odetta said, grinning. "I
don't think this world could handle three more like
you."

"Thanks, Sam," Romeo nodded, as Jenkins made
his way back to his table, a newly filled glass in his
hand.

By the end of the night, Romeo felt as if he'd said
"thank you" a billion times. The crowd had been wild,
reveling in his good fortune, and though he was appreciative, he was also tired and he wanted to go back to
the hospital to be with Taryn and the baby.

He gestured for Odetta, who scampered over anxiously to do his bidding.

"Everything okay, boss?"

Romeo nodded. "Yeah, just watch the bar for a
minute. I need to talk to Malcolm before I take off."

Odetta nodded. "No problem. I'll send him into the
office for you."

Romeo nodded his thanks, squeezing her arm lightly,

then turned toward his office. Closing the door behind him, he suddenly welcomed the silence. The music had begun to wear on his nerves.

Seconds later, Malcolm knocked, then entered. "You look busted," he said, closing the door behind him, a cup of hot coffee in hand.

Taking a quick sip of the hot fluid passed to him, Romeo nodded, then rested his head in the palms of his hands. "I am and I want to go back to the hospital."

"Well, don't worry about a thing here. I'll close up for you. In fact, I'll probably just stay the night if you don't mind my sleeping on your couch?"

"Not at all, and I appreciate your help."

"Hey, I told you I always got your back. You can count on me."

"I know," Romeo responded, smiling slightly. He paused, inhaling deeply, as Malcolm made himself comfortable in the seat in front of him. "I can't get over it, man," Romeo said, shaking his head. "Everything's different now. One minute it was just me and Taryn, and suddenly . . ." Romeo gasped loudly.

Malcolm nodded his head. "Ain't it something? It's like I told you, they put that bundle in your arms and the whole world looks different to you," he exclaimed excitedly. "I can remember thinking that if miracles like bringing a baby into the world can happen, then anything is possible. Babies help you see hope when you think it's lost to you."

Tears swelled suddenly in Romeo's eyes. Biting his lower lip, he fought to keep the briny solution from falling onto his cheeks. "Malcolm, I'm scared, man. I have never been so scared in all my life. What if I don't do right by him? What if I fail him like I thought my father failed me when I was younger? I don't know how to be a good father. I never had anyone to show me." He rose to go stare out the window.

Malcolm stared at him intently. "That's not true," he responded softly. "I think your mama showed you how to be a good parent if nobody else did. You just have to show him how much you love him. Piano Man not only showed you how not to be, but he also showed you how you can be your best.

"Romeo, it's about being there when he least expects it, no matter what. It's about teaching him right from wrong by your actions and your words, and having enough faith in him and in yourself to know that he'll make the right decisions when the time comes. It's about laughing with him and crying with him and showing him just how special he is. It's letting him know that he has worth and that he's here for a purpose and that he's the best part of you that you could ever let go of. It may not be easy going all the time, but if it means anything to you"—Malcolm paused, shrugging his shoulders—"then it will be well worth all the effort you put behind it."

Nodding, Romeo closed his eyes, then dropped his chin onto his chest. Exhaling, he hugged his arms about his shoulders. "I know you're right, but I'm still scared as hell."

Malcolm laughed. "Don't worry. You never get over it. You'll be old and gray and still worrying about whether or not you raised him right. But by then you and Taryn will have at least five more to be worrying about too."

Romeo laughed at the thought. "I don't think so. One, maybe two more, but I know Taryn will never go for having six kids. But hell, here I am just getting started with the first crumb crusher and you're wishing five more on me." He wiped his eyes.

Malcolm rose to his feet. "Let me get back. Odetta's probably given half the bar away by now." As he reached for the doorknob, he turned back toward Romeo. "Don't sweat it, my friend. You'll do just fine," he said as he turned and walked out of the room. "Yes, sir, you will do just fine."

Romeo sat alone for a few minutes more. As he stood to leave, the phone in his pocket vibrated for his attention. Retrieving the device and looking at it, he didn't recognize the number. He depressed the answer button and said hello.

"Yes, sir, I'm trying to reach Mr. Lawrence Marshall."

"This is him."

"Mr. Marshall, I'm calling from UNC Hospital in Chapel Hill. Mr. James Burdett has listed you as his next of kin."

Romeo felt himself holding his breath. "James Burdett?"

"Yes, sir. He's had a stroke and was admitted this evening. We found your contact information in his pocket."

Epilogue

Taryn slept heavily, her worn body desperate for rest. Romeo had wrapped the floral comforter tightly around her sleeping frame before he'd lifted JB from his cradle and walked him downstairs. As the baby cooed at him from his baby seat, Romeo tested the temperature on the bottle he had just warmed, then settled them both down in the large rocker.

As his small jaw pulled anxiously at the rubber nipple, JB stared up into Romeo's face, his expression seriously pensive. Romeo smile down at him. It had been sixteen weeks since they'd brought him home from the hospital, and Romeo now felt as if JB had always been with them. In fact, he could not remember when the child had not been around. He and Taryn had settled easily into parenthood and Romeo relished these early morning feedings when he would come home from the club and could cuddle JB close to his chest as Taryn rested upstairs. This was their time, and Romeo would converse with him as if he could respond.

The child's tiny legs kicked out from beneath the long gown he wore, his small feet lost beneath the fuzzy yellow socks Taryn had covered them with. His small hands curled into tight fists, one grasping tightly onto Romeo's large finger. Romeo had never imagined that so small a figure could have such power and control over the essence of his very being, but JB did. Every hope and dream Romeo had for himself was now manifested in his child and would be accomplished for his son, if for no one else.

Romeo dwelled on his son's fine features, marveling at his perfection. God could not have created any other child more beautiful. His skin was like soft cotton and as he was beginning to put on weight Romeo likened his body to that of cinnamon-colored dough. His coloring was all Taryn's, the warm red undertones peeking from beneath the brown, but it was his father's dark eyes that peered back at you. Silky black hair adorned his small crown, the fine strands swirling in intricate patterns.

As Romeo lifted the child to his shoulder, gently patting his upper back to help him release the bubbles of air he'd sucked in while nursing, he pressed his nose gently into the folds of satiny flesh about the baby's neck. Romeo loved the smell of new baby, the heavy scent of talcum powder and Taryn's clean, fresh aroma clinging to JB's skin. He brushed his face gently against JB's, kissing him on his forehead and his cheeks.

"So, how was your day yesterday, little man?" Romeo whispered, cradling the cooing baby in the crook of his arm. "You don't say! My, my, my, you and your mommy are just having so much fun, huh?"

JB kicked his legs excitedly, pulling a clenched fist into his mouth.

Romeo opened his mouth wide into an exaggerated

gasp, then laughed warmly as JB's eyes widened in curiosity and bewilderment.

"Yeah, dad had a pretty good day too." Romeo's mind drifted momentarily before he continued.

The baby gurgled.

Romeo pretended to be serious, his tone deeper, the intonation sterner. "No, I don't spoil you. I'm the parent who wears the pants around here, don't you forget that."

Thin, milky drool eased down JB's chin. He fidgeted slightly as Romeo wiped his mouth gently with the white cloth diaper draped over his left shoulder.

"Okay, so maybe I spoil you a little." Romeo smiled.

JB put his fist into his mouth, sucking hungrily on the appendage.

"Okay, okay. What do you want to talk about today? Huh? What's on your mind, boy?"

The baby chortled gleefully, his little legs kicking a mile a minute.

"Boy, you've got to slow down. We've got plenty of time, you and I." Romeo studied his son lovingly before he continued. "Your Aunt Sharon sang a special song by The Manhattans last night. She dedicated it to your grandpa," he stated, his thoughts intense. The crystal lyrics, which had bounced off the walls of the Playground, were haunting. *"There's no house without a home . . . no child without a dream. . . . There's no me without you. . . ."* Romeo sighed heavily.

"When I was younger I used to imagine what it would be like to be a father and have a son. I imagined us playing ball and riding bikes and doing all the stuff I wished Piano Man had been there to do with me. I remember thinking that my son would join me and already be twelve years old and every day would be a party for just the two of us. I knew that my son would be able to look over his shoulder and always see me standing right there to support whatever he was trying to do no matter how great the obstacles. I imagined that being someone's daddy was going to be the easiest thing in this world for me to do."

Romeo inhaled deeply. "I've got my work cut out for me though, don't I? I don't want to mess up, JB. I want you to be proud of me, so if I start screwing up, baby boy, you'd better tell me, okay? It's a deal then."

The baby wiggled comfortable into Romeo's chest, wiping his sleepy eyes with his tiny fists.

"Somebody's sleepy, huh?" Romeo rocked slightly, gently stroking the baby's arm with his fingers. "It's okay. Daddy understands. I can be boring sometimes. Your mama tells me on a regular basis, so it's okay if you do too." Romeo smiled as JB's eyes closed easily, fluttering slightly as he slipped into the warmth of his own nocturnal movie. "I love you, James. No matter what, your daddy will always love you."

As Romeo rocked easily, slipping off to sleep with his son, Piano Man played in the distance, his hands two-stepping atop the ivories, his shoulders swaying with the ebony keys. He sat tall and regal, his muscular frame a solid foundation of history and belonging. The music ran races beneath his fingertips, and he spun a tune of hope and promises, wrapped in dreams yet to be fulfilled, then watched with a hopeful smile as the silvery melody danced into his son's heart.

Hours later, Romeo made his way into the nursing home at Treyburn. The staff greeted him warmly, hands waving as he made his way down the short length of corridor to Piano Man's room. His son was cuddled close to his chest and a spray of flowers was in his hands. He moved into the room and greeted the patriarch warmly.

"Hey, old man. How are you doing?"

Piano Man lay with his frail body propped against a backdrop of pillows. His one good hand shook from side to side in greeting.

Romeo smiled brightly. "JB and I thought we'd come watch the ball game with you," he said, nodding his head.

The stroke had devastated Piano Man's body, but his mind was still sharp and his eyes even more vibrant. He gestured again with his hand, pointing at the baby.

Easing the child from the carrier straps wrapped around his chest, Romeo laid the infant against his father's lap. Excitement gleamed from the patriarch's dark eyes. He gently trailed the pad of his index finger over the little boy's profile.

Romeo's eyes misted lightly with moisture, but he did not cry. Instead, he shifted JB up closer to Piano Man's chest, brushing his lips alongside the baby's delicate skin. He sat down against the side of the bed and smiled.

"I tried to sneak you a shot of scotch, but Taryn and Aleta weren't having it. Those women are keeping a tight rein on the two of us." He paused again. "Things are really good, man! My woman loves me as much as I love her and we love this little boy with everything in us. And we miss you down at the Playground. Everybody really misses you a lot, Piano Man."

He smiled down at the child, watching as his little arms and legs quivered with excitement. Piano Man's hand tapped the baby gently.

As he sat watching the two together, Romeo found

the silence that had once filled his heart subsiding, the emptiness replaced with a new energy. It was an easy vibrancy he had not felt for some time, and he was pleased.

He whispered into the warm air, his words blowing skyward on the faintest twinkle of music playing in the distance. "I love you too, Daddy."

Don't miss Deborah Fletcher Mello's

Playing for Keeps

On sale in November 2015 at your local bookstore!

One

The employees at the Glenwood Avenue Starbucks greeted Malcolm Cobb by name. It was just past five-thirty in the morning and their cheery demeanors always amazed the man. He had finished his morning run ahead of schedule and was one of the first in line to get his coffee to kick off his day.

"Will you be having your usual today?" a young woman named Allison questioned.

Malcolm nodded. "I will, Allie."

The girl gave him a bright smile. "One venti caramel macchiato, skim milk and extra caramel coming right up!"

Malcolm nodded. "Thank you."

"We had a great time at your nightclub this past Saturday," another Starbucks employee chimed as he blended coffee and cream into an oversized container. "I took my girl and her sister. They're still talking about it!"

"I appreciate that," Malcolm said as he moved from the order lane to the pickup counter. While he waited he made conversation with the staff and the man in line behind him. The morning chatter was casual and easy as they caught up on their weekend endeavors and mused over the news headlines.

Malcolm looked across the room as the bell chimed over the entrance door, announcing a customer's arrival. His eyes widened as he caught sight of the woman coming through the door. He knew beyond any doubt that the full-figured beauty was a woman who garnered a lot of attention when she came into a room because she definitely had his. She had an air of sophistication and glamour that few other women he knew possessed. She was dressed in a form-fitting dress that showcased her voluptuous curves, four-inch pumps, and she carried a high-end leather bag across her arm. Her hair was abundant, a healthy mass of natural curls that cascaded past her shoulders. Her makeup was meticulous and flattering to her biracial brown complexion. She actually took his breath away, and it was only when the Starbucks employee called for his attention that he realized he was staring.

"Mr. Cobb, is there anything else we can get for you?"

Malcolm's head snapped as he pulled his attention back to the young employee looking at him, a bright smile across her face. He nodded. "Yes, there is something you can do," he said as he leaned over the counter, his voice dropping to a whisper. "Charge my credit card for that woman's order. Whatever she wants."

Allison looked toward the end of the line. "The woman in the blue print dress?" she asked.

Malcolm nodded. "Yes."

The girl smiled. "Not a problem, sir."

Moving out of the line, Malcolm took his macchiato and a cinnamon Danish to a corner table. Settling down in his seat, he watched as the woman placed her order. As she reached into her handbag for her wallet, Allison pointed in his direction. He smiled and waved a slight hand.

Cilla Jameson had noticed the man when she'd entered, the handsome stranger catching the eye of a few women in the room. She'd barely given him a quick glance though, as her mind had been elsewhere, too many thoughts racing through her head. Foremost was whether or not she had paid her credit card bill and if her card would be accepted when they swiped it to pay for her morning coffee. She was desperate for a good cup of coffee. His generosity was a welcomed blessing.

She studied him curiously. She recognized him from somewhere but was having a hard time remembering where. It wasn't often that she couldn't remember a handsome face when she saw one, and the man was definitely handsome. He was tall and dark, his beautiful complexion smooth and clear like black ice. He had a slim build but he was fit, and from his running shoes, shorts, and sweat-stained shirt she reasoned he'd either just left the gym or had finished a long run. His jet black curls were cropped low and close to his head, the precision cut and meticulously lined edges flattering to his face. There was an abundance of attitude shimmering in his dark eyes and a bad boy aura that surrounded him. If a stranger picked up the tab for her morning meal she was thankful he was a good-looking stranger.

Picking up her order, she crossed over to where he sat, a bright smile across her face. "Thank you. That was very kind of you," she said, nodding her head in appreciation.

Malcolm smiled back as he gestured to the empty seat on the other side of the table. "Do you have a minute to join me?"

Cilla hesitated for a brief second before she said, "I think I have a minute." She placed her beverage against the tabletop. She was only slightly surprised when he stood up and moved behind her, pulling out her chair. She tossed him a quick look over her shoulder. "Thank you."

He nodded as he sat back down. "My name's Malcolm. Malcolm Cobb."

"It's a pleasure to meet you, Malcolm. I'm Priscilla Jameson, but everyone calls me Cilla."

"Cilla . . . that's a beautiful name."

She smiled. "I keep thinking that I know you from someplace but I can't figure out where."

"Did you go to school here in Raleigh?"

"I was born and raised in Charlotte. I graduated from UNC–Chapel Hill."

"I went to school here. I did my undergrad at Shaw University and my graduate work at NC State. I studied industrial design and engineering."

"I majored in prelaw but I'm working in pharmaceuticals at the moment."

Malcolm smiled. "I'm not sure how to take that," he said, the hint of laughter in his tone.

"I don't deal drugs if that's what you're implying," Cilla said with a slight roll of her eyes. "I'm a health care administrator for a biotech company in Research Park."

"Well, I own a nightclub downtown."

Cilla snapped her fingers. "That's where I know you from. You and your business partner were featured in the *News and Observer*."

Malcolm smiled. Since its grand opening, the nightclub had been featured in the local newspaper a number of times. Most recently, word of their success had reached a national level, the Playground being named a must-stop on things to do in Raleigh. Co-owned with

Romeo Marshall, his best friend and fraternity brother, their nightspot was now the place to be and both of them the men to know. The success of the Playground had propelled them right into the spotlight. "It wasn't a good picture," he said. "They didn't get my best side."

Cilla laughed. "Which is your best side?"

"The one they didn't show."

There was a moment of pause as the two sat grinning foolishly at each other.

"So, your club is a jazz and blues bar, right?" Cilla questioned.

"It is, with a hint of R&B and soul." He reached into his pocket for his wallet and pulled a business card from inside. "If you have some time maybe you can stop by," he said as he passed it to her.

She studied it momentarily. "The Playground . . . sounds like it would be a good time."

"It will be," he said. "I'll be there."

She smiled. "You don't know when I'm coming."

He shrugged. "I'm always there, so you can't miss me."

Cilla took a quick glance down to her wristwatch. She took one last sip of her morning brew. "Thank you again for the coffee. I really appreciate it."

He stood up with her. "I'm here every morning, same time," he said. "In case you're interested in another cup."

Cilla laughed, the soft lilt of it stirring a wave of heat through Malcolm's spirit. "Always here, always at the club—doesn't sound like you have any time for much else," she said.

Malcolm's mouth pulled into a seductive grin. "I would make time for you, Cilla Jameson."

* * *

"I said now!" Claudette Cobb shouted, her deep alto voice vibrating through the home. "And I mean it!" the matriarch concluded.

Malcolm Cobb laughed as he moved from his downstairs office into the home's foyer. He leaned to kiss his mother's cheek.

"Where have you been?" she exclaimed, pressing a hand to her chest. "You scared me!"

"Sorry about that, but I snuck in through the back door. I went for a run and then grabbed a cup of coffee from Starbucks. I thought I'd get some paperwork done before I lie down for a nap."

"I don't know why you waste good money when we have that coffeepot sitting right there in that kitchen."

"I like Starbucks. It helps to clear my head after a long night."

"Hmph!" his mother grunted, her expression strained.

"But good morning to you!" Malcolm exclaimed, changing the subject.

"It was a good morning until them girls decided to work my one good nerve," she said, her smile brightening her face.

Malcolm chuckled warmly. "Math test today. Neither one wants to go to school."

Claudette shook her head from side to side. "I don't know why. They both always do well. They whine that they're going to fail and then they always pass with flying colors."

Her son shrugged his broad shoulders. "I don't know what to tell you." He leaned against the banister and called upward. "Cleo, Claudia, if you're late for school, you will both be grounded for the weekend and I mean what I say. Get a move on it."

Seconds later his daughters both shuffled across the

hardwood floors and down the stairs. Malcolm eyed one and then the other. Identical, the two girls were making it their mission to express their individuality in their attire. Claudia, the eldest by three minutes, was going for a Little House on the Prairie look, with a ruffled maxiskirt, a blouse buttoned up to her neck, and low-heeled boots. Cleo, the youngest, was hoping for more of a video vixen look.

He shook his head and pointed skyward. "Change, Cleo. Now!" he snapped, his brusque tone voicing his displeasure.

"What's wrong with what I'm wearing?" the girl snapped back, defiance billowing across her face.

"You don't have on any clothes," her grandmother quipped.

Malcolm moved quickly in the child's direction, her eyes widening as her father took the first four steps in one swift leap. He stood eye to eye with her, everything about his expression declaring there would be no discussion.

"I'm changing," the girl muttered as she turned abruptly and raced back to her room.

Her sister stood laughing. Malcolm shifted his gaze, eyeing her with a narrowed stare. "Your lunch is on the counter. Grab a Pop-Tart or a banana for breakfast and get your tail to the bus stop."

"Yes, sir," Claudia responded, moving quickly toward the kitchen.

Minutes later Cleo returned, her skirt more modest and her blouse appropriate. She eased her way past her father, not bothering to comment as he repeated the same instructions to her. As the two girls headed out the front door, he kissed both their cheeks and slipped a five-dollar bill into each child's pocket.

"Bye, Daddy," Claudia said as she kissed him back.

"Love you, Daddy," Cleo whispered.

He nodded. "I love you too, baby girl. And you and I will talk when you get home this afternoon."

"We're going to Mommy's this afternoon," the girl responded, reminding him of their weekday visitation with his ex-wife.

"Then we'll talk when you get back," he said.

"Do we have to go?" Cleo questioned. She met the look her father was giving her.

Interrupting, their grandmother pushed her way between them. "You're going to be late and if you miss the bus I'm going to have to take you to school. Let's go, and I'll pick you up when school gets out so we can meet your mother on time. You know how she gets if you're late."

Malcolm watched as the girls hurried to the corner, their grandmother standing at the end of the driveway to see them get on the bus. Both had thrown him one last look and he wished he could have told them no, that they didn't have to visit with their mother if they didn't want to. But that wasn't an option for either of them, his divorce decree dictating their mother's visitation rights. One weekend per month, one month each summer, and every other Monday the girls had to spend time with their other parent whether any of them liked it or not. And none of them liked it.

Malcolm blew a deep sigh. He knew he'd eventually have to take it back to court and allow the girls to express their own wishes, but he wasn't ready for the drama that would ensue. Dealing with his ex-wife had always come with much drama. So much so that he'd purposely avoided pursuing any serious relationship since they'd split. He'd been burned, badly, and hadn't been willing to put his heart on the line since.

He suddenly thought about the beautiful woman who'd taken his number. Cilla had him intrigued and, although she'd captured his attention, he didn't know if he could see it going but so far. As he reflected on their morning exchange he couldn't help but wonder just how far that might be.